FLINX & PIP

"Look, kid, if there's no available credit, you can pay us in goods. I saw plenty of valuable stuff when we came in." He shrugged indifferently. "Or we can shoot you, take what we want, and if anyone investigates, claim that you attacked us when I tried to reclaim my property."

In response to Flinx's rising level of upset and concern, Pip began to dart back and forth against the roof like a giant moth, the equivalent of pacing nervously in midair. Curious, the player-owner looked up in her direction.

"What is that thing, anyway?"

"That," Flinx murmured, enlightening both the speaker and his two accomplices, "is an Alaspinian minidrag. You don't want to make her any madder than she already is now."

"Why not?" The owner smiled. "Is it going to bite me?" The muzzle of his pistol came up.

"No," Flinx told him. "She doesn't have to."

The owner nodded. Turning to the man on his left, he uttered a single brusque command.

"Kill it."

—From "Sideshow"

By Alan Dean Foster
Published by The Random House Publishing Group:

THE BLACK HOLE
CACHALOT
DARK STAR
THE METROGNOME and Other Stories
MIDWORLD
NOR CRYSTAL TEARS
SENTENCED TO PRISM
SPLINTER OF THE MIND'S EYE
STAR TREK® LOGS ONE-TEN
VOYAGE TO THE CITY OF THE DEAD
... WHO NEEDS ENEMIES?
WITH FRIENDS LIKE THESE ...
MAD AMOS
THE HOWLING STONES
PARALLELITIES
IMPOSSIBLE PLACES
DROWNING WORLD
THE CHRONICLES OF RIDDICK
LOST AND FOUND

The Icerigger Trilogy
  ICERIGGER
  MISSION TO MOULOKIN
  THE DELUGE DRIVERS

The Adventures of Flinx of the Commonwealth
  FOR LOVE OF MOTHER-NOT
  THE TAR-AIYM-KRANG
  ORPHAN STAR
  THE END OF THE MATTER
  BLOODHYPE
  FLINX IN FLUX
  MID-FLINX
  REUNION
  FLINX'S FOLLY
  SLIDING SCALES

The Damned
  Book One: A CALL TO ARMS
  Book Two: THE FALSE MIRROR
  Book Three: THE SPOILS OF WAR

The Founding of the Commonwealth
  PHYLOGENESIS
  DIRGE
  DIUTURNITY'S DAWN

IMPOSSIBLE PLACES

ALAN DEAN FOSTER

THE RANDOM HOUSE PUBLISHING GROUP • NEW YORK

This book contains an excerpt from the forthcoming edition of *Drowning World* by Alan Dean Foster. This excerpt has been set for this edition only and may not reflect the final content of the forthcoming edition.

A Del Rey® Book
Published by The Random House Publishing Group
Copyright © 2002 by Thranx, Inc.
Excerpt from *Drowning World* by Alan Dean Foster copyright © 2002 by Thranx, Inc.

All rights reserved under International and Pan-American Copyright Conventions. Published in the United States by The Random House Publishing Group, a division of Random House, Inc., New York, and simultaneously in Canada by Random House of Canada Limited, Toronto.

"Introduction," copyright © 2002 by Thranx, Inc.; appears for the first time in this volume.
"Lay Your Head on My Pilose," copyright © 1992 by Thranx, Inc.; first appeared in *Futurecrimes*.
"Diesel Dream," copyright © 1991 by Thranx, Inc.; first appeared in *Solved*.
"Lethal Perspective," copyright © 1992 by Thranx, Inc.; first appeared in *Dragon Fantastic*.
"Laying Veneer," copyright © 1992 by Thranx, Inc.; first appeared in *Journeys to the Twilight Zone*.
"Betcha Can't Eat Just One," copyright © 1993 by Thranx, Inc.; first appeared in *Betcha Can't Eat Just One*.
"Fitting Time," copyright © 1993 by Thranx, Inc.; first appeared in *The King Is Dead*.
"We Three Kings," copyright © 1993 by Thranx, Inc.; first appeared in *Christmas Forever*.
"NASA Sending Addicts to Mars!" copyright © 1994 by Thranx, Inc.; first appeared in *Alien Pregnant by Elvis*.
"Empowered," copyright © 1994 by Thranx, Inc.; first appeared in *Superheroes*.
"The Kiss," copyright © 1995 by Thranx, Inc.; first appeared in *The Book of Kings*.
"The Impossible Place," copyright © 1996 by Thranx, Inc.; first appeared in *Space Opera*.
"The Boy Who Was a Sea," copyright © 1997 by Thranx, Inc.; first appeared in *Destination Unknown*.
"Undying Iron," copyright © 1997 by Thranx, Inc.; first appeared in *Absolute Magnitude*.
"The Question," copyright © 1998 by Thranx, Inc.; first appeared in *Absolute Magnitude*.
"The Kindness of Strangers," copyright © 1998 by Thranx, Inc.; first appeared in *The UFO Files*.
"Pein bek Longpela Telimpon," copyright © 1999 by Thranx, Inc.; first appeared in *Future Crime*.
"Suzy Q," copyright © 1999 by Thranx, Inc.; first appeared in *Alien Abductions*.
"The Little Bits That Count," copyright © 1999 by Thranx, Inc.; first appeared in *Moonshots*.
"Sideshow," copyright © 2002 by Thranx, Inc.; appears for the first time in this volume.

Del Rey is a registered trademark and the Del Rey colophon is a trademark of Random House, Inc.

www.delreydigital.com

ISBN 0-345-45041-8

Manufactured in the United States of America

First Edition: September 2002

OPM   10   9   8   7   6   5   4   3   2

To the memory of Raphael A. Lafferty,
The elf from Oklahoma,
Who could do things with words
that most writers can only do with dreams.
May he rest in comfort.

CONTENTS

INTRODUCTION

Every professional needs a workout. Basketball players shoot free throws and jump shots. Golfers retire to the driving range to practice their swing. Lawyers argue in front of mirrors; actors perform in summer stock; artists work with pencil and pastel in sketchbooks. Landscapers fill flowerpots; swimmers do lap after lap; gem cutters try different cuts with flawed stones.

Writers write short stories.

Except—sometimes the longest drive comes not on the course, but on the driving range. Occasionally the finest piece of art leaps out not from the finished oil on canvas, but from the sketchbook. Now and then, the most expansive, the most beautiful flower blossoms are not in the elaborate garden, but in the simple pot.

Writers write short stories.

There are all kinds of freedom attendant to composing shorts. Most obviously, a good deal less time is involved. For professionals, that's more than a little important. Then too, the creative freedom that is inherent in and so important to the writing of fantasy and science fiction is magnified in reverse. The shorter the story, the greater the freedom. It's easier for artists to let themselves go in an afternoon than over a period lasting four or five or six months, or a year or two. Doesn't matter if you're writing, or painting, or composing music. Time is precious to us all.

So we can let ourselves relax, and have fun in ways that we can't with a novel. We can play, and spout, and polemicize, and gibber, and even make funny faces if we want to. Because no editor is going to ask for thousands of words of revision, and if the tale doesn't sell, no one in the family is likely to starve as a consequence of it. In the '30s and '40s and '50s it was different. But today the novel reigns supreme. Tomorrow it may be the on-line interactive story, or the video game.

No matter, though; there will always be a place for story. Especially for the fast-paced tale, the quick yet brilliant idea, the build-up to a belly laugh. The literary bonbon that is also a bon mot. That's why I wrote the stories contained in this collection, which only go to prove a favorite aphorism.

Eat dessert first.

Alan Dean Foster
Prescott, Arizona

LAY YOUR HEAD ON MY PILOSE

The deep Amazon is a wondrous and fearful place. I'm not talking about Iquitos or Manaus—big cities that tourists fly into and out of in less than a week. I'm talking about the rain forest primeval, where every step looks the same as the next, where giant lianas and buttress roots and fallen trees rise out of the leaf litter to trip you up at every step and where the sweat pours off your body in tiny rivers even if you stand still and don't move a muscle.

Those whose visits to such places are restricted to watching National Geographic or the Discovery Channel might be forgiven for thinking that in such jungles it's the big predators who rule; the jaguars and harpy eagles and anacondas. Don't you believe it. It's the insects who are the kings of the green domain. The insects, the arthropods, and the even smaller parasites.

It's the small creatures with the many legs and the sucking mouthparts who rule the rain forest, and it's they of whom visitors should most properly be terrified . . .

From the moment his tired survey of the town was interrupted by the glory of her passage, Carlos knew he had to have her. Not with haste and indifference, as was

3

usual with his women, but for all time. For thirty years
he had resisted any thought of a permanent liaison with a
member of the opposite sex. His relationships hitherto
had consisted of intense moments of courtship and con-
summation that flared hot as burning magnesium before
expiring in the chill wash of boredom.

No longer. He had seen the mooring to which he intended to anchor his vessel. He could only hope that she
was mortal.

There were those in Puerto Maldonado who knew her.
Her name was Nina. She was six feet tall, a sultry genetic
frisson of Spanish and Indian. The storekeeper said she
was by nature quiet and reserved, but Carlos knew better. Nothing that looked like that, no woman with a face
of supernal beauty and a body that cruised the cracked
sidewalks like quicksilver, was by nature "quiet and reserved." Repressed, perhaps.

Their love would be monumental; a wild, hysterical
paean to the hot selva. He would devote himself to her
and she to him. Bards would speak of their love for generations. That she was presently unaware of his existence
was a trifle easily remedied. She would not be able to resist him, nor would she want to. What woman could?

There was only one possible problem. Awkward, but
not insoluble.

His name was Max, and he was her husband.

Carlos loved South America. One could sample all the
delights a country had to offer and move on, working
one's way around the continent at leisure, always keeping a comfortable step ahead of the local police. So long
as depredations were kept modest, the attentions of Interpol could be avoided. They were the only ones who
concerned Carlos. The local cops he treated with dis-
dain, knowing he could always cross the next border if

he was unlucky enough to draw their attention. This happened but rarely, as he was careful enough to keep his illegalities modest. Carlos firmly believed that the world only owed him a living, not a fortune.

As for the people he hurt: the shopkeepers he stole from and the women and girls whose emotions he toyed with, well, sheep existed to be fleeced. He saw himself as an instructor, touring the continent, imparting valuable lessons at minimal cost. The merchants would eventually make up their modest losses; the women he left sadder but wiser would find lovers foolish enough to commit their lives to them. But none would forget him.

He'd had a few narrow escapes, but he was careful and calculating and had spent hardly any time in jail.

Now for the first time he was lost, because he had seen Nina.

Nina. Too small a name for so much woman. She deserved a title, a crown: poetical discourse. *La Vista de la Señora hermosa de la montana y la mar y la selva quemara.* The vision of the beautiful lady of the mountains and the sea and the burning jungle. My lady, he corrected himself. Too beautiful by far for a fat, hirsute old geezer like Max who probably couldn't even get it up on a regular basis. He was overweight, and despite the fact that he was smooth on top, the hairiest man Carlos had ever seen. Lying with him must be like making love to an ape. How could she stand such a thing? She was desperately in need of a rescue, whether she knew it or not, and he was the man to execute it.

They ran a small lodge, a way station really, up the Alta Madre de Dios, catering to the occasional parties of tourists and scientists and photographers who came to gaze with snooty self-importance at the jungle. Gringos and Europeans, mostly. Carlos could but shake his head at their antics. Only fools would *pay* for the dubious privilege of standing in the midday heat while looking for bugs and lizards and the creatures that stumbled through the trees. Such things were to be avoided. Or killed, or skinned, or sold.

They also grew food to sell to the expeditions. And a little tea, more by way of experiment than profit. But it could not be denied that the foreigners came and went and left behind dollars and deutsche marks and pounds. Real money, not the debased currencies of America Sur. Max saved, and made small improvements to the lodge, and saved still more.

Nina would have been enough. That there might also be money to be had up the Alta Madre de Dios helped to push Carlos over the edge.

Like a good general scouting the plain of battle he began tentatively, hesitantly. He adopted one of his many postures; that of the simple, servile, God-fearing hard worker, needful only of a dry place to sleep and an honest job to put his hands to. Suspicious but over-worked Max, always sweating and puffing and mopping at his balding head, analyzed this uninvited supplicant before bestowing upon him a reluctant benediction in the form of a month's trial. It was always hard to find good workers for the station because it lay several days' travel by boat from town, and strong young men quickly grew tired of the isolation. Not only did this stranger both speak and write, he knew some English as well. That was most useful for dealing with visitors.

Max watched him carefully, as Carlos suspected he would. So he threw himself into his work, objecting to nothing, not even the cleaning and treating of the cess-pool or the scraping of the bottom of the three boats that the lodge used for transportation, accepting all assignments with alacrity and a grateful smile. The only others who worked for Max were Indians from the small village across the river. Carlos ignored them and they him, each perfectly content with their lot.

For weeks he was careful to avoid even looking in Nina's direction, lest Max might catch him. He was friendly, and helpful, and drew praise from the foreigners who came to stay their night or two at the lodge. Max was pleased. His contentment made room for gradual relaxation and, eventually, for a certain amount of trust. Three months after Carlos had been hired, Max tested him by giving him the task of depositing money in the bank at Puerto Maldonado. Carlos guarded the cash as though it were his own.

A month later, Max appointed him foreman.

Even then he averted his eyes at Nina's passing, especially when they were alone together. He knew she was curious about him, perhaps even intrigued, but he was careful. This was a great undertaking, and he was a patient man.

Once, he bumped up against her in the kitchen. Apologizing profusely, he retreated while averting his gaze, stumbling clumsily into hanging pots and the back counter. She smiled at his confusion. It was good that she could not see his eyes, because the contact had inflamed him beyond measure, and he knew that if he lifted his gaze to her face it would burn right through her.

Each week, each day, he let himself edge closer to her. A tiny slip here, a slight accidental touch there. He trembled when he suspected she might be responding.

There came a night filled with rain like nails and a suffocating blackness. The lodge was empty of tourists and scientists. Max's progress back from town would be slowed. The Indians were all across the river, sheltering in their village.

It began with inconsequential conversation intended to pass the time and ended with them making love on the big bed in the back building, after they shook the loose hair off the sheets. It was more than he could have hoped for, all he had been dreaming of during the endless months of screaming anticipation. She exploded atop him, her screams rising even above the hammering rain, her long legs threatening to break his ribs.

When it was over, they talked.

She had been born of noble blood and poverty. Max was older than she would have chosen, but she had enjoyed little say in the matter. As a husband he was kind but boring, pleasant but inattentive.

He would not take her with him to town because someone had to remain behind to oversee the lodge or the Indians would steal everything. Nor did he trust anyone to do business for him in Maldonado. He had discovered her in Lima, had made arrangements with her parents, and had brought her back with him. Ever since, she had been slowly going mad in the jungle, here at the foothills of the Andes. She had no future and no hope.

Carlos knew better.

He did not hesitate, and the enormity of his intent at first frightened her despite her anguish. Gradually he won her over.

They would have to be careful. No one, not even the Indians, could be allowed to suspect. They would have to wait for the right day, the right moment. Afterward, they would be free. They would sell the lodge, take the savings, and he would show her places she had hardly dreamed of. Rio, Buenos Aires, Caracas—the great and bright cities of the southern continent.

They had to content themselves with sly teasing and furtive meetings upon Max's return. They touched and caressed and made love behind his back. Trusting, he did not see, nor did he hear the laughter. Not only was he a cuckold, he was deaf and blind. Carlos's resolve stiffened. The man was pathetic. He would be better off out of his misery.

"I think he suspects," Nina confided to him one afternoon out among the tea leaves. They were supposed to be inspecting the bushes, and Carlos had insisted on inspecting something else instead. Nina had agreed readily to the change of itinerary, laughing and giggling. Only afterward did she express concern.

"You are crazy, love. He sees nothing."

She shook her head dubiously. "He *says* nothing. That does not mean he does not see. I can tell."

"Has he said anything?"

"No," she admitted. "But he is different."

"He hasn't said anything to me."

"He wouldn't. That is not his way. But I can feel a difference."

He touched her, and she closed her eyes and inhaled sensuously. "When you do that I cannot concentrate. I am worried, my darling."

"I will help you forget your worries."

It was growing harder to restrain himself, to act sensibly and carefully as he always had. But he managed. Somehow he managed. Then, when accumulated frustration threatened to explode inside him, Providence intervened.

It was to be a routine trip downriver. The rain had been continuous for days, as it usually was at that time of year. Though there were few travelers to accommodate, the lodge still needed certain supplies. Max had tried to choose a day when the weather looked as though it might break temporarily to begin the journey to Maldonado, but the rain was insistent.

The two Indians who usually accompanied them were off hunting, and no one knew when they might return. In a fit of irritability, Max announced that he and Carlos would go alone, the Indians be damned. Carlos could barely contain himself.

It would be so easy. He'd been so worried, so concerned, and it was going to be so easy. He waited until they were well downriver from the lodge and village, far from any possible human sight or understanding. Then he turned slowly from his seat in the front of the long dugout.

Through the steady downpour he saw Max. The older man's hand rested on the tiller of the outboard, its waspish drone the only sound that rose above the steady splatter of rain on dugout and river. His gaze dropped to the tiny pistol Carlos held in his fingers, the pistol Carlos had bought long ago in Quito and had kept hidden in his pack ever since.

Max was strangely calm. "I didn't know you had a gun. I hadn't thought of that."

Carlos was angry that he was trembling slightly. "You don't know anything, old man. Not that it matters."

"No. I guess it doesn't. I don't suppose it would change your mind if I just told you to take Nina and go?"

Carlos hesitated. He did not want to talk, but he couldn't help himself. "You know?"

"I didn't for certain. Not until this moment. Now I do. Take her and go."

Carlos steadied his hands. "The money."

Max's eyebrows lifted slightly beneath the gray rain slicker. Then he slumped. "You know everything, don't you? Tell me: did she resist for very long?"

Carlos's lips split in a feral smile. "Not even a little." He enjoyed the expression this produced on the dead man's face.

"I see," Max said tightly. "I've suspected the two of you for some time. Stupid of me to hope it was otherwise."

"Yes, it was."

"I mean it. You can take her, and the money."

"I do not trust you."

For the first time Max looked him straight in the eyes. "You're not the type to trust anyone, are you, Carlos?"

The gunman shook his head slowly. "I've lived too long."

"Yes, you have." Whereupon Max lunged at him, letting the tiller swing free.

The unguided prop swung wildly with the current, sending the dugout careening to port. It surprised Carlos and sent him flying sideways. He was half over the gunwale with Max almost atop him before he had a chance to react. The old man was much faster than Carlos had given him credit for, too quick, a devil. Carlos fired wildly, unable to aim, unable to point the little gun.

Max stopped, his powerful fat fingers inches from Carlos's throat. He straightened slowly, the rain pouring off him in tiny cascades, and stared downriver, searching perhaps for the destination he would not reach. A red bubble appeared in the center of his forehead. It burst on his brow, spilling off his nose and lips, thickened and slowed by the dense hair that protruded from beneath the shirt collar where he was forced to stop his daily shaving, diluted by the ceaseless rain.

He toppled slowly over the side.

Breathing hard and fast, Carlos scrambled to a kneeling position and watched the body recede astern. Spitting out rain, he worked his way to the back of the boat and took control of the tiller. The dugout swung around, pounded back upstream. There was a boiling in the water that did not arise from a submerged stone. The blood had drawn piranhas, as Carlos had known it would.

He circled the spot until the river relaxed. There was nothing to be seen. It was quiet save for the yammer of the engine and the ceaseless rain. He tossed the little pistol into the deep water, then headed for shore. When he was within easy swimming distance he rocked the boat until it overturned, then let it go. From shore he watched it splinter against the first rocks. Exhilarated, he turned and started into the jungle, heading back the way he'd come.

Almost, he had been surprised. Almost. Now it was finished. Nina was his, and he Nina's. Max was a harmless memory in the bellies of many fish. Carlos thought of the hot, smooth body awaiting him, and of the money, more than he'd ever dreamed of having. Both now his to play with. Together they would flee this horrible place, take a boat across the border into Bolivia, thence fly to Santiago. He harbored no regrets over what he had done. To gain Paradise a man must be willing to make concessions.

She was waiting for him, tense, sitting on the couch in the greeting room of the little lodge. Her eyes implored him as she rose.

He grinned, a drenched wolf entering its den. "It's over. Done."

She came to him, still unable to believe. "The truth now, beloved. There was no trouble?"

"The ape is dead. Nothing remains but bones, and the river will grind them between its rocks. By the time the Madre de Dios merges with the Inambari there will be nothing left of him. We will speak of it as we planned; that the boat hit a rock and went over. I swam to shore, I waited; he did not surface. There is nothing for anyone to question. Everything is ours!" He swept her into his arms and fastened his mouth to hers. She responded ferociously.

They were alone in the lodge, the buildings empty around them, thunder echoing their passion as she led him toward the back building. There she flung back the thin blanket and put a knee onto the bed, her eyes beckoning, her breasts visible behind the neck of her thin blouse. He leaned forward, only to pause with a grimace.

"Dirty, as always." He bent and began brushing at the sheets. She nodded and did likewise. Only when the last of the brown, curly hairs had been swept to the floor did he join with her in the middle.

They spent all that night there and all the following morning. Then he crossed the river and paid one of the Indians to carry downstream the message announcing the unfortunate death of Max Ventura.

They ate, and made a pretext of tidying the lodge lest the swollen river carry any unannounced tourists to their doorstep. Then they showered, soaping each other, luxuriating in their freedom and the cleanliness of one another, and walked out through the rain toward the back building.

Once again Carlos was first to the bedside, and once again he was compelled to hesitate. "I thought we cleaned out the last of him yesterday." He indicated the sheets.

Nina too saw the curving brown hairs, then shrugged and swept them onto the floor with a hand. "There was always hair everywhere from him. Not just in the bed. In my own hair, in the clothes, on the furniture, everywhere. It was disgusting."

"I know. No more of that." He brushed hard until he was sure his own side was spotless, then joined her.

No police came the next day, or the next. It would take three or four days by motorized dugout to reach Maldonado, a day again to come upstream to the lodge.

Carlos wasn't worried. The jungle was dangerous, the river unforgiving, and he, Carlos, had been made foreman of this place. Why would he kill his beloved employer? Indeed, hadn't he risked his own life to try to save him, battling the dangerous current and threatening whirlpools before exhaustion had forced him to shore? It was a sad time. Nina cried manfully for the Indians who came to offer their sympathies, while Carlos hid his smile.

In the bed that night they found the hair again.

"I don't understand." She was uncertain as she regarded the sheets. "I swept and dusted the whole building. We brushed these out."

Clearly she was in no mood for lovemaking. Not while memories of *him* still lingered in this place and in her thoughts. Angrily he wrenched the sheets from the bed, wadded them into a white ball, and tossed them across the room. Hairs spilled to the floor.

"Get fresh sheets. I'll wash these myself. No." Carlos smiled. "I'll burn them. We should have done that days ago."

She nodded, and her own smile returned. With the bed freshly remade they made love on the new sheets, but there was a curious reluctance about her he had not noticed before. He finished satisfied, saw she had not. Well, it would not be a problem tomorrow.

He burned the old sheets in the incinerator in the maintenance shed, the damp stink of the cremation hanging pall-like over the grounds for hours. By nightfall the rain had cleansed the air.

That night he made a point of carrying her to the bed. Though it was woman's work he had cooked supper. His concern touched her. She relaxed enough to talk of all they were going to do as soon as it was decorous enough to sell the lodge and leave. By bedtime her languid self-assurance had returned.

He tossed her naked form onto the sheets, watched her bounce slightly, and was about to join her when she screamed and scrambled to the floor.

He lay on the bed, gazing at her in confusion. "My love, what's wrong?"

She was staring, her black hair framing her face, and pointing at her side of the bed. Her face was curiously cold.

"L-look."

He turned, puzzled, and saw the hair. Not just one or two that might have floated in from a corner of the room left undusted, but as much as ever, brown ringlets and curlicues of keratin lying stark against the white sheets.

"Damn!" Rising, he swept sheets and blanket off the bed, went to the cupboard and removed new ones, made the bed afresh. But it was no good. She could not relax, could not make love, and they spent an uneasy night. Once she woke him, moaning, and he listened in the dark until she finally quieted enough to sleep.

The next morning she was curiously listless, her gaze vacant, and his anger turned to alarm. Her forehead seemed hot to the touch. She tried to tell him not to call the doctor, saying that it would cost too much money, money better spent in Rio or Caracas, but he was truly worried now and refused to listen.

He paid the village chief an exorbitant sum to send two men downstream in the lodge's best remaining boat, to go even at night and return with the doctor from Maldonado. He was in an agony waiting for their return.

Meanwhile Nina grew steadily worse, unable to walk, lying in bed and sweating profusely from more than the heat. She threw up what little food he tried to feed her. When he spoke to her she hardly reacted at all.

Not knowing what else to do, he applied cold wet compresses to her forehead and did his best to make her comfortable. By the fourth day he was feeling feverish himself, and by the sixth he was having difficulty keeping his balance. But he was damned if having won everything he would give up now. He had fought too hard, had committed what remained of his soul. Where was the goddamn doctor? He tried to cross the river but was unable to start the remaining outboard.

That afternoon a couple of Indians approached the bank on which the lodge was built, but when they saw him they turned and paddled furiously back the way they'd come. He yelled at them, screamed and threatened, but they paid both threats and imprecations no heed.

Her fever grew steadily worse (there was no longer any doubt it was a fever). He tried to feed her medicine from the lodge's tiny pharmacy, but by this time she could keep nothing down. Her once supple, voluptuous form had grown emaciated with shocking speed, until he had to force himself to look at the skeletal frame beneath the sheet when he cleaned her from where she had dirtied herself.

Nor did he prove immune to whatever calamity it was that had struck so suddenly. He found himself losing his way within the lodge, having to fumble for the sink and for dishes and clean towels. By the eighth day he alternated between crawling and stumbling, stunned at his own weight loss and weakness.

He staggered toward the back building, spilling half the pitcher of cold water he was carrying to her. He dropped the clean washrag but was too dizzy and tired to go back for it. Shoving the door aside, he nearly fell twice as he stumbled over to the bed.

"Nina." His voice was a dry croak, a rasping echo of what once had been. His swarthy machismo had evaporated along with his strength.

He tried to pour a glass of water, but his hand was shaking so badly he couldn't control it. The icy liquid shocked his hand and wrist. Frustration provided enough strength for him to heave the glass against the far wall, where it shattered melodiously. Exhausted by the effort he sank to his knees next to the bed, his forehead falling against his forearms as he sobbed helplessly. He lifted his eyes, hardly able to gaze upon her shrunken face anymore.

Emotions colder than the water rushed through his veins. For an instant he was fully alive, wholly aware. His vision was sharp, his perception precise.

There was hair in the bed. Always hair in the bed, no matter how much they'd swept, how hard they'd brushed and dusted, no matter how many times they changed the sheets. Brown, curly hair. His hair. It was there now.

One of the hairs was crawling out of her nose.

He knelt there, the bed supporting him, unable to move, unable to turn away from the horror. As his eyes grew wide a second hair followed the first, twisting and curling as if seeking the sunlight. He began to twitch, his skin crawling, the bile in his stomach thickening.

A hair appeared at the corner of her beautiful right eye, twisting and bending, working its way out. Two more slid out of her left ear and fell to the bed, lying motionless for a long moment before they too began to curl and crawl searchingly, imbued with a horrid life of their own.

With an inarticulate cry he stumbled away from the bed, away from the disintegrating form. More hairs joined the others, emerging from the openings of her

body, from nostrils and ears, from between her once perfect lips, falling to the sheets, brown and curling and
twisting. He reached up to rub at his disbelieving eyes, to
grind away the nightmare with his own knuckles, and
happened to glance at his hands. There were at least half
a dozen hairs on the back of the right one, moist and
throbbing.

Screaming, he stumbled backwards, frantically wiping
his hands against his dirty pants. Staggering out of the
room, he stumbled back toward the lodge. After weeks
of unending rain the sun had finally emerged. Steam rose
around him as accumulated moisture was sucked skyward. The mist impeded his vision.

Thin lines crisscrossed his line of sight. The lines were
moving.

Crying, babbling, he flailed at his own eyes, delighting
in the pain, digging at the hair, the omnipresent hair, the
memories of *him* and what had been done. He felt the
crawling now, no more than a slight tickle, but everywhere. On the surfaces of his eyes, in his ears, his nose,
pain in his urethra and anus, tickling and scratching and
burning, burning. He fell to his knees, then onto his side,
curling into a fetal position as he dug and scratched and
screamed at himself, at his wonderful body which was
betraying him without reason, without explanation.

The doctor's assistant gagged when he saw the body in
the garden, and the Indians muttered to themselves and
drew back. The doctor, who was an old man, thin and
toughened from forty years of practicing medicine in
that part of the jungle known as the Infierno Verde,
forced himself to bend over and do his job. There wasn't
much left to examine.

The smell led them to the rear building. This time the

Indians wouldn't enter at all, and the doctor had to use all the strength in his elderly frame to drag his reluctant assistant with him. Up till now the young man had made good on his internship. Eventually he would return to a fine hospital in Lima where he would issue papers and prescribe pills at excessive fees for wealthy *Limineros*, while the doctor would remain in his sweltering office in Maldonado, treating insulting ungrateful tourists for diarrhea and locals for promised payment that the government sometimes sent and sometimes didn't.

The corpse on the bed had been that of a woman. If possible (and until he had actually seen it the doctor would not have thought it was), it was in a state of even more advanced desiccation than the one on the grass outside. He examined it closely, careful not to touch any of the small, squirming shapes that were burrowing through what remained of what had once been a human form.

"Here, give me a hand."

"What for?" The intern held a handkerchief over his face, protection against the odor.

"I want to look at the back."

They used towels to protect their hands. Turning the body was a simple matter. Having been consumed from the inside out, it weighed next to nothing. The sight thus revealed forced even the old doctor to jump back involuntarily.

Beneath where the body had been lying, the entire bed was a seething mass of millions of tiny, twitching brown shapes.

"Nematodes," the doctor announced with a grunt, though if he was worth anything at all, his youthful companion had already reached the same conclusion on his own. "Without question the worst Secernentea infestation I have ever seen." He leaned fearlessly over the boiling mass. "Here, see? The mattress is stuffed with horsehair. That would provide sufficient protein for them to propagate within. These unfortunate people were infected through the bed." He extended a hand. "My case."

The intern barely had enough presence of mind remaining to hand over the doctor's kit. The old man rummaged inside and removed a small stoppered tube and a tweezer. Carefully he extracted one of the millions of swarming worms from the mattress, slipped it into the glass container, where it coiled and twisted frantically, feeling for meat.

"This would appear to be a particularly virulent species. The selva is full of thousands of such loathsome parasites, many of them still unclassified. See how they seek the darkness inside the bed? I would venture to guess that this variety feeds nocturnally and is dormant during the day, which might explain how an infection could be overlooked until it was too late. Treatable at a hospital, I should think, but in the advanced stage such as we see here, immune to simple over-the-counter remedies." His eyes narrowed sorrowfully as he regarded the sack of skin and bones crumpled on the bed.

"Once infected, they were doomed. You would have thought that, living here, they would know about this particular parasite and would have taken proper precautions to keep it out of their living quarters. It always astonishes me how little interest some people have in their immediate surroundings." He raised the specimen. "Observe."

The intern reluctantly took the glass tube, twirling it back and forth between his fingers as he studied its single wiry, voracious occupant. "It doesn't look like much, just one of them."

"No," agreed the doctor. "Not just one." He stared at the heaving, pulsating mattress, tapped the glass tube. "Notice how much it resembles nothing so innocuous as a human hair?"

DIESEL DREAM

When the big rig passes you on the road, do you ever pause to wonder what the driver of that monster of an amalgam of rubber and steel and petroleum products is thinking? Do you think he's just looking out for you and your fellow drivers? What image do you have of him (or her)? Chances are it's wrong. He doesn't look the way you think he probably looks, and he doesn't think the way you probably think he does.

Truckers are just folk, more independent than most. Seamen of the highway, sailing narrow concrete seas, always impatient to make the next port of call and then as equally impatient to leave it. They get places most of us never think about, dream dreams the rest of us don't have the time for.

Sometimes, rarely, ports and journeys and dreams all come together in the oddest ways and places . . .

Whatthehell. I mean, I know I was wired. Too many white crosses, too long on the road. But a guy's gotta make a living, and everybody else does it. Everybody who runs alone, anyway. You got a partner, you don't have to rely on stimulants. You half a married team, that's even better. But you own, operate, and drive your own rig, you gotta compete somehow. That means al-

22

ways making sure you finish your run on time, especially
if you're hauling perishables. Oh sure, they bring their
own problems with 'em, but I'd rather run cucumbers
than cordite any day.

Elaine (that's my missus), she worries about me all the
time. No more so than any trucker's wife, I guess. Goes
with the territory. I try to hide the pills from her, but she
knows I pop the stuff. I make good money, though. Better'n most independents. Least I'm not stuck in some
stuffy little office listening to some scrawny bald-headed
dude chew my ass day after day for misfiling some damn
piece of paper.

Elaine and I had a burning ceremony two years ago.
Mortgage officer from the bank brought over the paper
personal and stayed for the burgers and beer. Now
there's a bank that understands. Holds the paper on our
house, too. One of these days we'll have another ceremony and burn that sucker, too.

So I own my rig free and clear now. Worked plenty
hard for it. I'm sure as hell not ready to retire. Not so
long as I can work for myself. Besides which I got two
kids in college and a third thinking about it. Yep, me.
The big guy with the green baseball cap and the beard
you keep seein' in your rearview mirrors. Sometimes I
can't believe it myself.

So what if I use the crosses sometimes to keep going?
So what if my eyesight's not twenty-twenty every hour of
every day? Sure my safety record's not perfect, but it's a
damnsight better than that of most of these young hon-
chos who think they can drive San Diego–Miami nonstop. Half their trucks end up as scrap, and so do half
of them.

I know when I'm getting shaky, when it's time to lay
off the little white mothers.

Anyway, like I was gonna tell you, I don't usually stop

in Lee Vining. It's just a flyspot on the atlas, not even a real truck stop there. Too far north of Mammoth to be fashionable and too far south of Tahoe to be worth a sidetrip for the gamblers. A bunch of overinsulated mobile homes not much bigger than the woodpiles stacked outside 'em. Some log homes, some rock. Six gas stations, five restaurants, and one little mountain grocery. Imagine: a market with a porch and chairs. Lee Vining just kind of clings to the east slope of the Sierra Nevada. Wouldn't surprise anyone if the whole shebang up and slid into Mono Lake some hard winter. The whole town. The market sells more salmon eggs than salmon. Damn fine trout country, though, and a great place to take kids hiking.

Friendly, too. Small-town mountain people always are, no matter what part of the country you're haulin' through. They live nearer nature than the rest of us, and it keeps 'em respectful of their humanity. The bigger the country, the bigger the hearts. Smarter than you'd think, too.

Like I was saying, I don't usually stop there. Bridgeport's cheaper for diesel. But I'd just driven nonstop up from L.A. with a quick load of lettuce, tomatoes, and other produce for the casinos at Reno, and I was running on empty. Not Slewfoot: she was near full. I topped off her tanks in Bishop. Slewfoot's my rig, lest you think I was cheatin' on Elaine. I don't go in for that, no matter what you see in those cheap Hollywood films. Most truckers ain't that good-lookin', and neither are the gals you meet along the highway. Most of them are married, anyway.

Since diesel got so expensive I'm pretty careful about where I fill up. Slewfoot's a big Peterbilt, black with yellow-and-red striping, and she can get mighty thirsty.

So I was the one running on empty, and with all those

crosses floating around in my gut, not to mention my head, I needed about fourteen cups of coffee and something to eat. It was starting to get evening and I like to push the light, but after thirty years plus on the road I know when to stop. Eat now, let the crosses settle some, drive later. Live longer.

It was just after Thanksgiving. The tourists were long gone from the mountains. So were the fishermen, since the high-country lakes were already frozen. Ten feet of snow on the ground (yeah, feet), but I'd left nearly all the ski traffic back down near Mammoth. U.S. 395's easier when you don't have to dodge the idiots from L.A. who never see snow except when it comes time for 'em to drive through it.

The Department of Transportation had the road pretty clear and it hadn't snowed much in a couple of days, which is why I picked that day to make the fast run north. After Smokeys, weather's a trucker's major devilment. It was plenty cold outside; cold enough to freeze your BVDs to your crotch, but nothing like what it would be in another month or so. It was still early, and the real Sierra winter was just handing out its first calling cards.

Thanks to the crosses I kind of floated onto the front porch of a little place called the Prospector's Roost (almost as much gold left in these mountains as trout), 20 percent of the town's restaurant industry, and slumped gratefully into a booth lined with scored Naugahyde. The window behind me gave me something besides blacktop to focus on, and the sun's last rays were just sliding off old Mono Lake. Frigid pretty. The waitress gave me a big smile, which was nice. Soon she brought me a steak, hash browns, green beans, warm rolls with butter, and more coffee, which was better. I started to mellow as my stomach filled up, let my eyes wander as I ate.

It's tough to make a living at any one thing in a town the size of Lee Vining. If it don't take up too much floor space, some folks can generate an extra couple of bucks by operating a second business in the same building. So the north quarter of the Prospector's Roost had been given over to a little gift shop. The market carried trinkets and so did the gas stations, so it didn't surprise me to see the same kind of stuff in a restaurant. There were a couple racks of postcards, film, instant cameras, bare-necessity fishing supplies at outrageous prices, Minnetonka moccasins, rubber tomahawks for the kids, risk-kay joke gifts built around gags older than my Uncle Phil, Indian turquoise jewelry made in the Philippines. That sort of thing.

Plus the usual assortment of local handicrafts: rocks painted to look like owls, cheap ashtrays that screamed MONO LAKE or LEE VINING, GATEWAY TO YOSEMITE. T-shirts that said the same (no mediums left, plenty of extra large).

There was also a small selection of better-quality stuff. Some nice watercolors of the lake and its famous tufa formations, one or two little hand-chased bronzes you wouldn't be ashamed to set out on your coffee table, locally strung necklaces of turquoise and silver, and some wood carvings of Sierra animals. Small, but nicely turned. Looked like ironwood to me. Birds and fish mostly, but also one handsome little bobcat I considered picking up for Elaine. She'd crucify me if I did, though. Two kids in college, a third considering. And tomorrow Slewfoot would be thirsty again.

The tarnished gold bell over the gift shop entrance tinkled as somebody entered. The owner broke away from his kitchen and walked over to chat. He was a young fellow with a short beard, and he looked tired.

The woman who'd come in had a small box under one

arm that she set gently on the counter. She opened it and started taking out some more of those wood carvings. I reckoned she was the artist. She was dressed for the weather, and I figured she must be a local.

She left the scarf on her head when she slipped out of her heavy high-collared jacket. I tried to look a little closer. All those white crosses kept my eyes bopping, but I wasn't as sure about my brain. She was older than I was in any case, even if I'd been so inclined. Sure I looked. It was pitch black out now and starting to snow lightly. Elaine wouldn't have minded—much. Contented or not, a man's got to look once in while. It's just a—what'd they call it?—a biological imperative.

I guessed her to be in her mid fifties. She could've been older, but if anything she looked younger. I tried to get a good look at her eyes. The eyes always tell you the truth. Whatever her age, she was still a damn attractive woman. Besides the scarf and coat she wore jeans and a flannel shirt. That's like uniform in this kind of country. She wore 'em loose, but you could still see some spectacular countryside. Brown hair, though I thought it might be lighter at the roots. Not gray, either. Not yet.

I squeezed my eyes shut until they started to hurt and slugged down another swallow of coffee. A man must be beginnin' to lose it when he starts thinking that way about grandmotherly types.

Except that this woman wasn't near being what any man in his right mind would call grandmotherly, her actual age notwithstanding. Oh, she didn't do nothin' to enhance it, maybe even tried hiding it under all those clothes. But she couldn't quite do it. Even now I thought she was pretty enough to be on TV. Like Barbara Stanwyck, but younger and even prettier. Maybe it was all those white crosses makin' gumbo of my thoughts, but I couldn't take my eyes off her.

The only light outside now came from gas stations and storefronts. Not many of the latter stayed open after dark. A few tourists sped through town, fighting the urge to floor their accelerators. I could imagine 'em cursing small towns like this one that put speed limits in their way just to keep 'em from the crap tables at Reno a little longer.

I considered the snow. Drifting down easy at the moment, but that could change fast. No way did I need that tonight. I finished the last of my steak and paid up, leaving the usual good tip, and started out to warm up Slewfoot.

The woman was leaving at the same time, and we sort of ended up at the door together, accidental-like. Like fun we did.

"After you," she said to me.

Now, I was at least ten years younger than this lady, but when she spoke to me I just got real quivery all through my body, and it wasn't from the heavy-duty pharmaceuticals I'd been gulping, either. She'd whispered, but it wasn't whispering. I knew it was her normal speaking voice. I've had sexier things whispered to me than "After you," but none of 'em made me feel the way I did right then, not even those spoken on my fourth date with Elaine, which ended up in the back of my old pickup truck with her murmuring throatily to me, "Whatever you want, Dave."

Somebody has to be real special to make "After you" sound like "Whatever you want." My initial curiosity doubled up on me. It was none of my business, of course. Here I was a married man and all, two kids in college and a third thinkin', and I oughtn't to be having the kinds of thoughts I was having. But I was running half an hour ahead of my schedule, and the snow was staying manageable, and I thought, well hell, it don't hurt nothing to be friendly.

"You local?"

She smiled slightly, not looking up at me. It got darker fast when we stepped outside, and those damn crosses were making like a xylophone in my head. But damned if I didn't think she was so pretty she'd crack, despite the fine lines that had begun to meander their way across her face. She pushed her jacket up higher on her body and turned up the sheepskin collar.

"It's cold, and I've got to go," she muttered. Her words made me shiver slightly, and it wasn't from the snow. "Nothing personal. I just don't believe in talking to strangers."

What could I say? How could I reassure her? "Heck, I don't mean no harm, ma'am." I think maybe that got to her. Not many folks these days say *heck* and *ma'am*, especially truckers. She glanced up at me curiously. Suddenly I wasn't cold anymore.

"Where are you from?"

"I asked you first."

"All right. I live here, yes. You?"

"L.A. right now, but me and my wife are from Texas. West Texas. The back o' beyond." Funny how Elaine had slipped into the conversation. I hadn't intended her to. But I wasn't sorry.

"Nice of you to mention your wife." She'd picked up on that right away. "Most men don't. That's why I try to come into town around dark. You'd think an old lady like me wouldn't have that kind of trouble."

"No disrespect intended, ma'am, but I've never set eyes on an old lady looked like you do." I nodded toward the cafe/gift shop. "You do those wood carvings?"

"Yes. Do you like them?"

"I've seen a lot of that kind of stuff all over the

country, and I think yours stack up real well against the best. Real nice. Good enough to show in a big gallery somewhere."

"Willie's place is good enough for me." Her voice was honey and promise. "This is my home now. The people up here leave you alone and let you be what you want to be. I'm happy."

"You married?"

"No, but I have friends. It's enough that they like me for what I am. I've been married before, more than once. It never worked for me."

The snow was starting to come down harder.

"I'm sorry."

She must have seen the concern on my face. "Got far to go?"

"Reno and on to Tahoe. Groceries for them folks that are trying to make it the easy way. Can't let the high rollers go hungry." Her smile widened slightly. It made me feel like I'd just won a new rig or something.

"No, I guess you can't." She tossed her head slightly to her left, kind of bounced a little on her feet. "It's been nice talking to you. Really."

"My name's Dave."

"Good meeting you, Dave."

"You?"

She blinked away a snowflake. "Me what?"

"What's your name?"

"Jill," she said instantly. "Jill Kramer." It was a nice name, but I knew it was fake.

"Nice meeting you too, Jill. See you round, maybe."

"See you too, Dave."

That's what did it. She didn't so much say my name as sort of pucker her lips and let it ooze out, like a little hot cloud. She wore no lipstick. She didn't have to.

White crosses. White crosses and bennies and snow. Damn it all for a clear head for two lousy minutes!

I tried to think of something to say, knowing that I had to glue my eyes to the blacktop real soon or forget about driving any more at night altogether. I couldn't afford that. Nobody pays a bonus for brown lettuce and soft tomatoes.

"I thought you were dead," I finally blurted out. I said it easy, matter-of-fact, not wanting to startle her or me. Maybe the crosses made me do it; I don't know. She started to back away, but my country calm reassured her.

"I knew I shouldn't have talked to you this long. I try not to talk to anyone I don't know for very long. I thought by now . . ." She shrugged sadly. "I've done pretty well, hiding everything."

"Real well." I smiled reassuringly. "Hey, chill out. What you've done is no skin off my nose. Personally I think it's great. Let 'em all think you're dead. Serves 'em all right, you ask me. Bunch of phonies, the lot of 'em."

She still looked as if she wanted to run. Then she smiled afresh and nodded. "That's right. Bunch of phonies. They all just wanted one thing. I spent all my time torn up inside and confused, and nobody tried to help. Nobody cared as long as they were making money or getting what they wanted. I was just a machine to them, a thing. I didn't know what to do. I got in real deep with some bad people, and that's when I knew that one way or another, I had to get out, get away.

"Up here nobody cares where you come from or what you did before you got here. Nice people. And I like doing my carvings. I got out of it with a little money nobody could trace. I'm doing okay."

"Glad to hear it. I always did think you were it, you know."

"That wasn't me, Dave. That was never me. It was just

something that I made up. That was always the problem. I'm happy now, and that's what counts. If you live long enough, you come to know what's really important."

"That's what me and Elaine always say."

She glanced at the sky, and the light from the cafe fully illuminated her face. "You'd better get going."

"How'd you work it, anyway? How'd you fool everybody?"

"Like I said, I had some friends. True friends. Not many, but enough. They understood. They helped me get out. Once in a while they come up here and we laugh about how we fooled everyone. We go fishing. I always did like to fish. You'd better get moving."

"Reckon I'd better. You keep doing those carvings. I really liked your bobcat."

"Thanks. That one was a lot of work. Merry Christmas, Dave."

"Yeah. You too—Jill."

She turned away from me, knowing that I'd keep her secret. Hell, what did I have to gain from giving her away? I knew how she must feel, or thought I did. About the best thing you can do in this too often sad, mean world is not step on somebody else's happiness, and I wasn't about to step on hers. It's too damn hard to come by, and you might need somebody else to do you a similar favor sometime. It doesn't hurt to establish a line of credit with the Almighty.

I watched her walk away in the falling snow, all bundled up and hidden inside that big Western jacket, and I felt real good with myself. I'd still make Reno in plenty of time, then pop over to Tahoe, maybe get lucky and pick up a return load. My eyes followed her through the dark and white wet, and she seemed to wink in and out of my sight, dreamlike.

White crosses. Damn, I thought. Was she real or

wasn't she? Not that it really mattered. I still felt good. I sucked in the stinging, damp air and made ready to get back to business.

That's when she sort of hesitated, stopped, and glanced back at me. Or at least, whatever I saw there in the Sierra night glanced back at me. When she resumed her walk it wasn't the stiff, horsey stride she'd been using before but a rolling, rocking, impossibly fluid gait that would've blasted the top knob off a frozen thermometer. I think she did it just for me. Maybe it was because of the season, but I tell you, it was one helluva present.

Not knowing what else to do, I waved. I think she waved back as I called out, "Merry Christmas, Norma Jean." Whacking my chest with my crossed arms, I hurried across the street to the parking lot to fire up Slewfoot.

LETHAL PERSPECTIVE

Don't do the expected. What's the point? You'll be bored with it. Worse, so will the reader. There's a huge market called More of the Same, and sometimes we're all forced to sell to it. That's why short stories are so valuable.

Me, I like a challenge. Take the obvious and twist it, knot it, turn it upside down and inside out and see what the result looks like. It may turn out twisted, knotted, upside out and inside down, but even if it's not successful, at least it won't look like everybody else's.

Take dragons. Please. In today's fantasy market, if I had scales, I could retire to some tropical paradise on the royalties (come to think of it, there's a story there. But not the one I'm about to tell). You try hard to make the overly familiar a little different, maybe a little contemporary, a little unexpected, and sometimes it can gag in your throat.

In this case, that's a good thing.

They assembled in the Special Place. Though a considerable amount of time had passed, none forgot the date and none lost their way. It took more than several days for all to arrive, but they were very long-lived, and none took umbrage at another's delay.

34

It was the very end of the season, and a small team of climbers from France was exploring a new route up the south col of K5 when one happened to look up instead of down. He shouted as loud as he could, but the wind was blowing and it took a moment before he could get the attention of the woman directly ahead of him. By the time she tilted her head back to scan the sky, the apparition had vanished. She studied her climbing companion warily and then smiled. So did the others, when they were informed.

They put it down to momentary snow blindness, and the climber who'd looked up at the singular moment didn't press the point. He was a realist and knew he had no chance of convincing even the least skeptical of his friends. But to his dying day he would know in his heart that what he'd seen that frigid morning just east of Everest was not an accident of snow blindness, or a patrolling eagle, or a figment of his imagination.

The Special Place was filling up. Legendary nemesis of the subcontinent, Videprasa had the least distance to travel and arrived first. Old Kurenskaya the Terrible appeared next, making good time despite his age and the need to avoid the aging air-defense radar based in southern Kazakhstan.

O'mou'iroturotu showed up still damp from hours of flying through the biggest typhoon to hit the South China Sea in more than a decade, and Booloongatta the Night Stalker soon after. They were followed by Cracuti from central Europe, Al-Methzan ras-Shindar from out of the Empty Quarter, and Nhauantehotec from the green depths of Central America.

It grew crowded in the Special Place as more of the Kind arrived. They jostled for space, grumbling and rumbling until the vast ancient cavern resounded like the

Infinite Drum itself. Though solitary by nature, all gathered eagerly at this special predetermined time.

Despite the incredible altitude and the winter storm that had begun to rage outside, conditions within the Special Place remained comfortable. Creatures that are capable of spontaneous internal combustion do not suffer from the cold.

As the Elder Dominant, Old Kurenskaya performed the invocation. This was concluded with a binding, concerted blast of flame the largest napalm ordnance in the American armory could not have matched, resulting in a massive avalanche outside the Special Place as a great sheet of ice and snow was loosened from beneath. The French climbing team far to the west heard but did not witness it.

"It is the time," Kurenskaya announced. He was very old, and most of his back scales had faded from red to silver. But he could still ravage and destroy with the best of them. Only these days, like all the recent others, he was forced to be more circumspect in his doings.

He glanced around the crowded cavern, vertical yellow pupils narrowing. "I do not see As'ah'mi among us."

There was a moment of confusion until Nhauantehotec spoke up. "He will not be joining us."

Kurenskaya bared snaggle teeth. "Why not? What has happened?"

Nhauantehotec sighed, and black smoke crept from his nostrils. "He was not careful. As careful as we must all be these days. I think he forgot to soar in the stealthy manner and was picked up on U.S. Border Patrol radar. Not surprisingly, they mistook him for a drug runner's plane and shot him down. I heard him curse his forgetfulness as he fell, and altered my flight path to see if I could help, but by the time I arrived he was nothing but fully combusted brimstone and sulfur on the ground."

A smoky murmur filled the cavern. Old Kurenskaya raised both clawed forefeet for silence. "Such is the fate of those who let time master their minds. We sorrow for one of our own who forgot. But the rest are come, healthy and well." He gestured to the one next to him with a clawed foot the size of a steam-shovel bucket. "As first to arrive it falls to you, Videprasa, to regale us with tales of your accomplishments."

She nodded deferentially to the Elder Dominant and instinctively flexed vast, membranous wings. "I have since the last gathering kept myself properly hidden, emerging only to wreak appropriate havoc through the guises we have had to adopt since humans developed advanced technologies." Raising a forefoot and looking thoughtful, she began ticking off disasters on her thick, clawed fingers.

"Eleven years ago there was the train wreck north of New Delhi. The devastating avalanche in Bhutan was one I instigated twenty years ago. There was the plastics plant explosion in Uttar Pradesh and the sinking of the small freighter during the typhoon that struck Bangladesh only a few years past." She smiled, showing dentition that would have been the envy of a dozen crocodiles.

"I am particularly proud of the chemical plant damage in Bhopal that killed so many."

Al-Methzan ras-Shindar snorted fire. "That was very subtlely done. You are to be commended." He straightened proudly, thrusting out his scaly chest and glaring around the cavern. "You all know what I have been up to lately."

Quong the Magnificent flicked back the tendrils that lined his head and jaws. "You were fortunate to find yourself in so efficacious a situation."

Al-Methzan's head whipped around snakelike. "I do not deny it, but it required skill to take advantage." Eyes

capable of striking terror into the bravest man glittered
with the memory. "It was purest pleasure. I struck and
ripped and tore and was not noticed. The humans were
too busy amongst themselves. And around me, around me
every day, were those wonderful burning wells to dance
about and dart through and tickle my belly against." Al-
Methzan ras-Shindar stretched luxuriously, the tips of
his great wings scraping the ceiling.

"I haven't felt this scoured in centuries."

There was a concerted murmur of envious delight
from the others, and Old Kurenskaya nodded approv-
ingly. "You did well. How else have you fulfilled the
mandate?"

Al-Methzan ras-Shindar resumed the recitation of his
personal tales of mayhem and destruction. He was followed by Booloongatta the Night Stalker, and then the
rest of them. The hours and the days passed in pleasant
companionship, reminiscence, and safety as the storm
howled outside the gathering place. They were out of
harm's way here. The Roof of the World saw few humans
in the best of times, and in the winter was invariably little
visited.

There was more to the gathering than mere camaraderie, however. More to the boasting of accomplishments than a desire simply to impress others of one's
kind. For the gathering and the telling constituted also a
competition. For approval, surely, and for admiration,
truly. But there was more at stake than that.

There was the Chalice.

It hung round Old Kurenskaya's neck, suspended from
a rope thick as a man's arm woven of pure asbestos
fibers. It was large for a human drinking utensil, tiny by
the standards of the Kind. The great Berserker Jaggskrolm
had taken the prize from the human Gunnar Rakeiennen
in 1029, in a battle atop Mount Svodmaggen that had

lasted for four days and rent the air with fire and fury. When all had done and the killer Rakeiennen lay dead, his fortress razed, his golden hoard taken, his women ravished (the great Jaggskrolm having been ritually mindful of the traditions), practically nothing remained unburned save the jewel-studded, golden chalice with which the most beauteous of Rakeiennen's women had bought her freedom (not to mention saving herself from an exceedingly uncomfortable time).

Ever since, it had been a symbol of dominance, of the most effective and best-applied skills of the Kind. Old Kurenskaya had won it during the last Tatar invasion of his homeland and had kept it ever since, having last been awarded it by acclamation (the only way it could be awarded) for his work among the humans during the purges and famines of the 1920s and '30s. Admittedly, he'd had human help, but his fellows did not feel cheated. Such assistance was to be welcomed, and cleverly used. As Al-Methzan ras-Shindar had utilized recent events in the Middle East so effectively.

It seemed truly that because of his most recent accomplishments, ras-Shindar had the inside track on securing the Chalice. Nhauantehotec had been working particularly hard, and the devastating achievements of skillful Mad Sunabaya of the Deep impressed all the assembled with their breadth and thoroughness. Despite his years, Old Kurenskaya wasn't about to give up the Chalice without a fight, and it had to be admitted that his brief but critical presence at Chernobyl would go down as a hallmark accomplishment of the Kind in modern times.

When at last all had concluded their recitative, and waited content and with satisfaction for the vote of acclamation, Old Kurenskaya was pleased. It had been a gathering free of discord, unlike some in the past, and had demonstrated conclusively that the Kind could not only survive but prosper in their efforts despite the technical exploits of their old enemy, humankind. He was elated, and ready. All, in fact, were anxious for the choosing, so they could be on their way. Though all had enjoyed the gathering, they preferred to keep to themselves, and by now were growing irritable.

"If then each has stipulated and declaimed their deeds, and retold their tales, I will name names, and call for the choosing." He raised a clawed forefoot to begin.

Only to be interrupted.

"Wait, please! I have not spoken."

Dire reptilian heads swiveled in the direction of the voice. It was so slight as to be barely intelligible, and those of the Kind with smaller hearing organs than their more floridly eared brethren had to strain to make out individual words. But it was one of them, no doubt of that, for it spoke in the secret and ancient language known only to the Kind.

Something like a small, scaly hummingbird appeared in the air before Old Kurenskaya and hovered there almost noiselessly.

"What is this?" Videprasa emitted a smoky burst of flame and laughter. "A bird has slipped in among us, to find safety from the storm, no doubt!"

"No," Cracuti roared, the sharp spines of her back flexing with amusement, "this is not a bird, but a bug!"

The minuscule speaker whirled angrily. "I am Nomote, of the Kind." Laughter and smoke filled the gathering place. "I demand to be heard!"

Old Kurenskaya raised both clawed forefeet, and the ferocious, terrific laughter gradually died down. He scowled at the tiny visitor. "There are three recent-born among us. I did not know of a fourth."

"Who would admit to birthing this?" Videprasa

snorted, and another round of awesome laughter shook rock from the walls of the cavern.

Old Kurenskaya looked around reprovingly. "This Nomote is of the Kind, if . . . somewhat lesser than most of us. Give to him the deference he deserves, as befits the traditions." At this stern admonishment, an abashed silence settled over the gathering.

The Elder Dominant nodded to the hovering mite. "Speak to us then of your exploits." One of the assembled sniggered, but went quiet when Old Kurenskaya glared threateningly in his direction. "Tell of what you have done to fulfill the traditions of the Kind." He sat back on his hindquarters, his leathery, age-battered wings rumpled elegantly about him.

"I am young and have not the experience or strength of others who have accomplished so much." A few murmurs of grudging approval sounded among the assembled. "I have had to study our ancient adversaries and to learn. I have struggled to master the stealthy ways needed to carry out the work without being noticed by the humans and their clever new machines." It hesitated, wee wings beating furiously to keep it aloft in one place.

"Alas, I have had not the skill, nor the strength, nor the prowess to do as so many of you have done. I have done but one thing, and it, like myself, is small."

Nomote's humbleness and modesty had by now won for him some sympathy among the assembled, for who among them could not, save for the intervention of fortuitous fate, imagine himself in such a poignant condition.

"Tell us of what you have done and what you do," Old Kurenskaya said encouragingly. He glared warningly one more time, but by now the gathering was subdued. "None of the Kind will laugh, I promise it. Any offender will have to deal with me." At that moment Old Kurenskaya did not look so old.

Nomote blinked bright, tiny eyes. A small puff of dark smoke emerged from the tip of his snout. "I go invisibly among those humans who are ready and those who are reluctant; I breathe the addiction into their nostrils and their mouths; and then when they weaken and are finally susceptible, I light their cigarettes."

They gave him the Chalice, which was too large for him to carry, much less wear around his neck. But Nhauantehotec moved it to a convenient lair for him, and though he could not fly with it shining broadly against his chest as had his glorious predecessors, it made a most excellent bath in which to relax upon returning from a good day's work among the execrable humans.

LAYING VENEER

In 1989 my wife and I took a couple of weeks and drove from Brisbane, Australia, all the way up to Port Douglas, eventually getting as far north as the Bloomfield River. The euphemistically named Bruce "Highway" was in actuality a narrow two-lane road, rarely flanked by the comforting shoulders common to American roads. For long stretches you'd drive for kilometers without seeing another vehicle. Then a road-train, consisting of an enormous diesel truck fronted with roo bars (to ward off wayward kangaroos, lest by colliding with them they somehow damage these moving mountains of steel) and towing three or more trailers would come hurtling toward you, taking up more than its narrow lane and forcing you off the side of the road where you hoped the wheels of your vehicle would find enough purchase to get back on the pavement.

Ah, the pavement. Shimmering with heat, undulating like a mild stomach upset, receding into the distance among the dreaming gum trees and grass, ever in need of upkeep and repair. We passed many road repair crews; sometimes wiry, sometimes large, always muscular men clad in light-gray shorts and white undershirts and floppy-brimmed hats, leaning on shovels or picks or in the seats of downsized backhoes and graders, cigarettes dangling from their mouths or beers from their hands.

We rarely saw them working, and tut-tutted at their singular lack of energy.

Without wondering if there might be reasons for it beyond the obvious.

———————

"Take it easy, mate. Have a beer."

Harbison was not mollified. "National Highway, my ass! National disgrace is more like it."

The foreman was not insulted. "You won't get any argument from me. Maybe that's why they decided to try bringing in some people from the States." He proffered a cold can.

The engineer deliberately pushed it aside. "Frankly I'm not surprised. I've driven over a thousand miles this past week, and I didn't see one road crew that wasn't squatting on their butts guzzling that stuff. When they weren't drinking beer, they were swilling wine for lunch and hard liquor for dinner and after. No wonder your so-called National Highway is falling apart."

Kent glanced out the window. Moreton Bay was clear of clouds. That meant it would be calm out on the reef. Good fishing. With an effort he forced himself to turn back to the American engineer.

"Your first time Down Under, isn't it?"

"So?"

Kent sipped brew. "Despite what you've seen and what you may think, we can build roads, Mr. Harbison. Look around Sydney or Melbourne."

"I have. The roads there are fine. That's not why I was sent for." He stared unforgivingly at the foreman. "If you can build there, why not everyplace else?"

Kent looked away. "It's this country. You get out away from the cities, there's nothing. I mean, you're talking five million people scattered over empty territory the size of the continental U.S. The Outback isn't kind to men, machinery, or plans. It doesn't matter who you put on a job; pretty soon things start to slow down. Work gets sloppy. Machinery starts to act up, break down. So do men, if they're not careful. Why do you think most of our roads outside the cities are still dirt? Because we like it that way?"

"Because of lack of determination. Because somebody hasn't been doing their job."

"They do what they can," Kent argued. "You don't know what it's like out there, what you have to deal with. But you'll find out. The Outback gets to everyone. It'll get to you, too."

"Bullshit. I've built roads in the Amazon, in Africa, all over the world. There's nothing special about the terrain here. I know. I've just driven a thousand miles of it. All I found was lousy work and excuses." He smiled humorlessly. "That will change."

Kent shrugged. "That's what you've been hired for. Believe me, I wish you the best of luck. The best. I don't like driving that road in the condition it's in any more than you did. Neither does anyone else."

"Then why haven't you fixed it? Why go all the way to the States to find a supervisor?"

The foreman eyed him over his beer. "Mate, don't you think we've tried?"

It was hot, but it had been hotter in Brazil. Harbison felt a stabbing pain in his leg, slapped fast, and saw the March fly tumble to the ground. He jammed it into the earth with the heel of his boot, looked up through his sunshades.

They were twenty kilometers north of Rockhampton, working on the middle of the highway. Not far to the

east was the portion of the Pacific aptly named the Coral
Sea. To the west lay the mountains of the coast range and
beyond, nothing. Nothing all the way to the Indian
Ocean save sand and dry plains and gravel.

It was bad enough here. Scattered gum trees (euca-
lyptus back home), a few bushes, desultory grasses, all
bathed in sunlight that tinted everything beige.

Ahead the road stretched north to Townsville, the next
community of any real size and the beginnings of the true
tropics. Behind lay Rockhampton, an undistinguished,
extraordinarily humid community built on cattle and
commerce.

Harbison had three crews going: one south near Ca-
boolture, one working down from Cairns, and this one,
in the center. He'd chosen to spend most of his time here,
where it would be easiest to deal with all three crews and
any problems they might encounter. He watched the men
work; good-natured, broad-shouldered, muscular. As
competent as any road crew back home, but slow. It
puzzled him. They seemed capable enough, but there
was no enthusiasm, no desire. They shuffled through
their work; the asphalt spreaders, the men on the heavy
equipment, all of them.

The only time they showed any spirit was during their
regular breaks, which were inevitably accompanied by
the opening of coolers full of the ubiquitous, high-
alcohol beer. He'd remonstrated with them personally
about drinking so heavily on the job but to no avail. The
breaks, and the beer, were sacrosanct.

He'd tried putting his foot down with the northern
crew, only to have them go out on strike. When he
threatened to fire the lot of them, they simply smiled and
shrugged, as though it didn't matter if he did or not. Any
new men he hired would act exactly the same.

The road stretched northward, a black arrow piercing the baked landscape. The National Highway. He snorted. Back home it wouldn't pass muster as a farm road. Two narrow lanes full of potholes, with no shoulders, crumbling into dust at the edges. How eighteen-wheelers and cross-country buses managed to navigate the disintegrating course without smashing into one another was nothing short of a miracle. Back home the entire thousand miles would've stood a good chance of being condemned.

It made no sense. Sure the conditions were harsh, but no more so than in Arizona or Florida. He'd ordered repeated checks of the materials, had the bitumen exhaustively analyzed. Standard paving asphalt. The road base had been properly prepared, packed and leveled. It ought not to be crumbling this fast. After several months of work he was beginning to think there might be something in the ground rather than in the asphalt that was failing.

So he'd had the earth itself analyzed, to no avail. It was neither unusually acidic nor alkaline. It should be holding up far better than it was. Kent had shown him stretches that had been repaved only the year before. Already the edges were cracking, breaking off in big chunks, turning to gravel and dirt.

He removed his wide-brimmed hat and wiped sweat from his forehead. Someone in the crew, sitting in the shade with his mates, waved a beer in his direction. Irritably he shook his head and looked away. Kent had been right. The beer wasn't the problem. There was something else going on here, something he couldn't put a finger on. But he would. It was what he was getting paid to do.

He looked sharply to his right. There were several

aborigines on the road crew. They sat with their white mates, race relations having progressed farther out in the country than in the city. One of them was clapping a pair of sticks together, beating time to an ancient unknown rhythm. His companion was playing that long tube, what was it called? A didgeridoo. Except it wasn't an actual didgeridoo he was playing. He was cycle-breathing on a four-foot-long section of plastic PVC pipe. Remarkably, the sound was the same as that produced by the traditional wooden native instrument.

The music hung like a fog above and around the gum trees, as if some massive fantastical creature lay sleeping just beneath the surface. Sometimes Harbison found himself hearing it at night, which bothered him. It did not sound quite like anything else he'd ever heard. It tickled his brain.

When he'd asked Kent about it, the foreman had smiled and explained that some of the men on the road crews, isolated in the Outback, believed that the music of the didgeridoo kept away the quinka, the evil spirits of the land that snatched men's souls from the real world.

He stared. The white roadworkers seemed to be enjoying the music as much as their darker colleagues. It was the kind of camaraderie he'd rarely observed in the cities, where the only aborigines he'd encountered were aimless groups of drunken men and women who spent their time arguing in city centers or sprawled tiredly in public parks. Here, out in the country, on the fringes of civilization, it was different.

He'd seen that elsewhere. In rough country there was no time for such absurdities as racial prejudice. All of them were too dependent on one another, too busy trying to survive, to worry about inconsequentialities like the color of a neighbor's skin. You were much more interested in what kind of a mechanic he was.

The break stretched on. Several of the blonder workers had shed their shirts in defiance of the tropical sun. They wore shorts and shoes only. Their bodies, Harbison mused. If they wanted to burn, let them burn, so long as they kept working.

He drove himself hard. He was the first one on site in the morning and the last to leave. He meant the two-kilometer section north of Rockhampton to be an example, a demonstration of what could be achieved with American know-how and determination. It would be a real highway: four lanes with divider and paved shoulders both directions. A proper piece of interstate.

It took longer than he'd anticipated, but once the last asphalt had been laid and smoothed, he was able to content himself with the look of it. Beautiful it was, like reflective obsidian under the relentless sunshine, a straight dark path through the gum forest. Only a dead kangaroo, hit by a car the previous night after the new section had been opened to the public, marred the ebony perfection.

Even Kent was impressed. He stared at the roadway and nodded. "Well, I have to admit, you did it. Didn't think you could, but you did. She's a beaut, that's for sure."

"Three years." Harbison surveyed his work with satisfaction. "Three years and the whole highway from Brisbane to Mossman can look like this. All it needs is money and the right attitude."

"Maybe so," Kent agreed. He straightened. "Care for a beer?"

Harbison almost, but not quite, smiled. "I told you when I got here and I've been telling you all along, I don't drink. Especially not that stuff you call beer. Too strong."

"Suit yourself." The foreman turned toward his car. "Need a ride?"

"No. I want to run a final check here. Then I'm moving up to Cairns. They're still having trouble with their section up there."

"So I heard. They need you, Harbison." Kent smiled admiringly and climbed into his car.

Harbison lingered, not wanting to leave, enjoying the looks on the faces of motorists as they shot past him at a hundred kph plus. For a little while, for the first time in hundreds of kilometers, they could actually relax and enjoy driving.

The sun was going down. He slid behind the wheel of his big Holden, almost headed off down the right side of the road before remembering where he was and correcting. On the way south he passed the striping crew, knocking off early as usual. He shook his head. It was a wonder they ever finished anything. Without him driving them, they never would have.

The onset of evening brought with it only a slight break in the heat. The gum trees closed in tightly around him, separated only by the four-lane roadway. A brush fire burned unattended to the very edges of the road. It would be ignored, he knew, left to burn itself out. Valuable wood and forage left to burn, as though nobody cared. No doubt the members of the local fire department were already gathering at their favorite pub, he knew, and wouldn't wish to be disturbed. Social activity in every little Outback town centered around its pubs, or the bottle shops where liquor could be purchased for takeout.

Near the southernmost part of the new section he

slowed, pulling over onto the neat, wide-paved shoulder. Frowning as he climbed out, he walked around the front of the car and knelt by the side of the road. He pushed with a hand and stared as a section of asphalt the size of his fist broke free and crumbled into powder.

It was like that all along the shoulder, on both sides of the roadbed: big pieces breaking free, crumbling, the neatly laid edge already being taken over by eager grasses and weeds. It made no sense. This section was less than three months old. It should be solid, impervious, yet it was coming apart as though made of sand. The asphalt that had been used had been rigorously checked prior to application. The surface was designed to hold up without maintenance for a minimum of two years.

He straightened and stared into the forest. The gum trees stood silent, their pale slick bark peeling like his workers' skin. It was dead quiet; no birds, no insects whining in the brush. Only there; a cluster of roos, traveling noiselessly in great leaping bounds at the limits of his vision.

He blinked. There were no roos. Quinka? Didgeridoo music drifted through his brain, hypnotic and unsettling. Suddenly conscious of the age of the land around him, of his isolation, he found himself backing toward the car, his eyes trying to focus on suspected movement in the brush. He tried to think of something else, anything else, except the inescapable fact of his aloneness in a vast and inhospitable land.

It was hot, so very damn hot. The heat seemed to come not from the sun but out of the earth itself. Dust hung suspended in the air like talcum, making breathing difficult. The moan of the didgeridoo was a pounding in his temples.

A March fly landed on his arm, and he smashed it

before it could bite. It spiraled indifferently to the ground, as though its death didn't matter even to itself.

As he fumbled with the door handle of the car he stared wide-eyed at the road, brand new but crumbling, unable to resist something he could not fathom, could not analyze. It ran north through the fringes of the Outback, a feeble lifeline stretching from the cities of the south toward the hostile tropics. Stretched too thin?

Bad place for a road, he decided. The problem was simple enough. It wasn't wanted here. The country, the land, didn't want it. Yet as he was wont to do, man persisted in trying to defy the obvious, to bend to his will a part of nature too ancient to know it had no choice in the matter.

A growling sound made him whirl, but it was only a truck coming toward him. A dozen men rode in the open bed. As it slowed to pull over, several of them eyed him knowingly.

"Car trouble, mate?" one of them asked.

"No," Harbison replied slowly. He gestured. "There's something wrong with the road here. There shouldn't be."

Several of the crew exchanged glances. One of them smiled down at him. "Don't worry, mate. She'll be right. You worry too much, I think." He squinted at the silent, suggestive gum forest through the beige-tinted heat. "Can't worry too much out here. Gets to ya."

"Not a good place to be standin' about alone," the man next to him said. "Hang about too long and a bloke's liable to go troppo. Start seein' things, know what I mean? This ain't Bondi Beach." His tone was sympathetic, understanding. "Care to join us in a beer?"

A new image filled Harbison's brain, shoving aside the cloying, suffocating silence that pressed tight around the intruding road. A cool dark room surrounded by thick walls that shut out the oppressive heat, the dust and the flies. Shut out the hum of the didgeridoo and hallucinated roos. Kept the quinka at bay.

Better to drink than to think. Thinking was wasted in this place. Ambition was excess baggage. This country battled both, all the way. It always had. No wonder the aborigines had never developed much of a civilization like other primitive peoples.

Man had spread his highways, his parking lots, his civic centers and shopping malls across the face of the planet. Everywhere the land had accepted the insult in silence. Except here. Here the land fought back, fought every incursion, every attempt to domesticate it. Not with violence, but with ennui. It wore you out, just as it wore out the roads.

There was a reason why people here kept tight to their few cities, clung to the cool southern coasts. Up here, in the north, in the great center, the Dreamtime still held sway, still dictated the pace of life and decay, of people and of roads. It sucked the drive out of a man, and if one wasn't careful, the life.

He understood the drinking now, the intensity and the frequency of it. It held the land at bay, kept it out of a man's mind, kept him from thinking too much about the vast open empty spaces. Prevented them from invading one's spirit and taking over.

God, he was tired.

His shirt was soaked through. He pulled it over his head, threw it up into the truck.

"Yeah, sure," he mumbled, accepting a hand up. "I'd like a beer."

Someone could pick up the car later. It didn't matter. Nothing mattered now, except getting to the pub.

The truck drove off. Once more the shiny new section of road was silent and empty. A beetle struggled out from beneath a bush, to be snatched up by a silent, watching magpie. Already the black sheen of the newly laid asphalt was fading, turning to a tired gray.

A foot-long crack appeared in the southbound lanes. Soon it would widen.

BETCHA CAN'T EAT JUST ONE

When I was growing up, two of my favorite foods were Hostess Cupcakes and Twinkies. I'd put them in the fridge and eat them cold. That way, the chocolate on the cupcakes didn't melt so fast, and the cream centers had more of the flavor and consistency of ice cream. I never gave these gustatory affectations a second thought. After all, food was food, and if your body could digest it, then how bad could it be for you? Really.

It was only much later that I encountered the significant body of deprecation that hovers about these gooey concoctions like hard lumps of sarcasm orbiting a soft, chewy, defenseless center. I foreswore my childhood addiction and moved on to more healthful, nourishing victuals—like cappuccino mousse, super-premium ice creams, and 77 percent dark chocolate. There are times, though, when I look back fondly at lost childhood pleasures like Twinkies and Ho Hos. Innocent pleasures all.

Aren't they?

———

"Can I help you find something, sir?"

Moke glanced sharply at the checkout clerk. He was more nervous than usual these days, with the Study so near completion. Always having to watch his step. Never knew when they might be watching.

"You cannot. I can find everything by myself, when I want to. I simply choose to proceed at my own pace." He offered up a smug smile. "I've found a great deal already, and am in the process of finding more all the time."

She eyed him uncertainly. Lately, the majority of the people she found wandering in this aisle wanted to know the location of the new Adolescent Altered Killer Gerbil Cookies, the latest kid food and comic sensation. This customer was different. For one thing, he was bigger. And he seemed not so much lost as preoccupied.

That's when she noted the microcassette recorder he was carrying in lieu of a shopping bag. "You from the Health Department or sump'in? You want I should get the night manager?"

"No. If I was from the Health Department I'd already have shut down this unholy establishment—and every one like it, until they agreed to change their policies. I'm not in a position to do that—yet." The widening of his humorless grin failed to enlighten the baffled clerk. Or to reassure her.

It was one in the morning—near closing time for this particular market. A few amnesiatic shoppers remorselessly cruised the aisles, dumping toilet tissue, canned dog food, cereals and breads and optimistically dolphin-safe tuna into their carts. Their expressions were resigned, their postures lethargic. Except when they passed through this aisle. Then cheerful gossip freshened the air like verbal Muzak.

Everyone, absolutely everyone, bought something from Aisle Six, and luxuriated in the process.

The clerk was reluctant to abandon her morose, angular stray. "So if you don't mind my askin', mister— what's to shut down? We're as clean as anyplace in town, an' our inventory's just as fresh. We ain't violating no ordinances. We ain't guilty of nothin'."

"No?" Moke's sweeping gesture encompassed the entire aisle. "You're like everyone else. You don't see what's going on here. You really don't see it."

The clerk blinked at the shelves, seeking enlightenment and finding only cellophane and plastic.

"This, all this, is garbage, young lady. Offal, swill, chromatic slops: the insidious poisoning of a people who have forgotten the nature of real food."

Until now emotionally becalmed, the clerk straightened. "Our stock is checked and replaced every day, sir. Everything on our shelves is fresh. If you don't like it here, why don't you shop someplace else?"

"It wouldn't make any difference. It's the same everywhere," Moke informed her sorrowfully. "Do not think that in my ire I have singled out your place of work for especial condemnation. The entire supermarket industry in which you are but an insignificant if courteous cog is equally culpable. All participate eagerly in the general conspiracy." He peered intently at her.

"Are you aware that today's junk food contains more than a hundred times the volume and variety of chemical additives than the junk food of just twenty years ago? That the very companies that disgorge this mountain of hyena chow on an innocent unsuspecting public have little or no idea of how the human body will react to increased consumption of their products over a reasonable period of time?"

The checkout clerk relaxed. Everything was clear enough to her now for her even to forget that she'd been called an insignificant cog. She even managed a sly smile.

"I know—you're a health-food nut."

"And proud of it. Do you know that ever since I first unearthed the conspiracy and swore to expose it I haven't touched any of this stuff?" He indicated the marshaled ranks of sugar-stuffed cakes, of candy-coated marshmallow, of puffed imitation cheese and fried air. "And that since then I haven't been sick a day? Not a day! Not a cold, no flu: nothing. There *has* to be a connection. And I'm going to reveal it."

"Uh-huh." The clerk had begun to slowly back away.

Moke noticed the look in her eyes. "You're the one who should be afraid of these remasticated additives; not me. My system is clean, pure. I'm a trained scientist, young lady. My specialty is nutrition chemistry. I have devoted all of my adult life to this Study, and next week I shall at last begin to publish. What I will reveal will rock the American junk food industry to its grotesquely profitable core."

She halted, grinning insouciantly. "I ain't afraid of no potato chips."

"You should be, because I have discovered that they, in common with most other popular junk foods, contain hidden within their artificial flavorings and artificial colors and preservatives and pseudoingredients newly developed complex amino acids of extraordinary vitality and volatility. Either the food companies have been far ahead of the pharmaceutical and pesticide industries in genetic engineering or else we are witnessing sustained sequential organic mutation on an undreamt-of scale.

"To what nefarious end the food companies are striving I have yet to discover, but rest assured that I will. Some of the molecules I have isolated within Shoo-pie Bunny Cakes, for example, are positively Byzantine. Something sinister is taking place within our groceries, and whatever it is, it's finding its way into our children's lunch pails." He turned wistful.

"Thirty years ago I would've said it was all a Russian plot, but I think the poor Russians are likewise on the verge of succumbing to the same sort of global gut-busting infiltration."

"Right." She made a production of checking her watch. "Well, you'd better finish up your studies here fast, Professor. We close in thirty minutes."

"I need more time than that."

"Thirty minutes." She turned and headed north, in the direction of the checkout registers, and safety.

Idiots, Moke thought. Blind fools. He was going to save the country, save the world, in spite of its slavish ingrained genuflection to oversweetened dreck. Considering current dietary habits it was a wonder the species continued to survive at all.

Facts were undeniable. When his paper finally exploded on the world convenience food scene, specialists would rush to confirm his findings. Too late then for the bloated minions of a bilious multibillion-dollar industry to conceal the truth any longer from a hitherto thoroughly duped market-going public.

Emerging from beneath the concealing pile of uncrushed cartons, he climbed out of the compacter and surveyed the storage room at the rear of the market. It was dark and deserted. Refreshed from his nap, he had a couple of hours before the store reopened. It was all he would need.

Using his keychain flashlight, he returned to the aisle where he'd had the encounter with the young clerk. Going to save her too, he thought determinedly, before her body was unalterably poisoned. It was his crusade, and his alone. The big health-food groups didn't have a clue. Or his analytical expertise.

A few final notes and his research would be complete. Then to the computer, to integrate final thoughts with the rough manuscript. Polish and publish, then sit back to await the coming explosion.

This was the last store on his list, the final line of the last page of statistics in a study that had taken decades to compile and encompassed more than fifty cities and towns. All visited personally by him. He couldn't trust graduate students to carry out the fieldwork. They were all contaminated by the very products he was sworn to eradicate from the shelves of the world's supermarkets. He'd been forced to do all the research on his own.

It was the same wherever he went. Identical eccentric molecules and weird peptide chains in dozens of products, regardless of brand name. Clever they were, but Moke had stumbled on their secret. Soon he would expose the full nature of their callous perfidy to a shocked public.

Aisle Six stretched on ahead of him; shelves crammed full of brightly colored air-puffed victuals utterly devoid of nutritional value and inherently antithetical to the digestive system of the human body. They all but glowed behind their glistening, brightly colored wrappings; tantalizingly easy to consume, irresistibly crammed full of false flavor, quisling comestibles capable of rapidly weakening both mental and physical resolve. He knew them for what they were: opiates for the progressively brain-damaged.

Something quivered slightly on the shelf just behind his left shoulder.

He whirled, saw nothing. Chuckling uneasily to himself, he sauntered on. And froze.

They were moving. The packages on the shelves ahead. Twitching slightly, jerking against their containers and restraints. Huge bags of intimidating chips, densely packed containers of vacuum-restrained pretzels, stacks of creme-filled non-cakes. All gyrating and weaving and rustling invitingly. And he could hear the sound now—a low, insinuating moan. The tempting murmur of empty calories, of empires of gluttony built on mountains of salt and plains of refined white sugar.

"Eat us," the enticing susurration whispered coaxingly. "You have deprived yourself for too long, have put yourself outside pleasure for no reason. Devour, and delight in us."

He blinked, clapping his hands over his ears. The microcassette recorder slipped from his fingers to strike the unyielding, Hawaiian Punch–stained floor. Its cover popped open and the tape flew out. Pained, he knelt to recover it.

Something landed on his back.

Forgetting the recorder, he reached around wildly. Something soft and sticky squished between his fingers. The tactile sensation was oddly sensuous. Terrified, he found himself staring down at a handful of smashed, bloodred lunch-box cherry pie that contained no cherries and no pie. It oozed from between his fingers, the unctuous crimson gunk packing in beneath his fingernails.

"Eat me," the glutinous mass urged him. "Suck me up. You'll like it."

With a cry, he rose and flung the fragments of pseudo-pie as far as he could—but some of it stuck to his fingers anyway. Stumbling backward, he crashed into the nearest shelves. Flailing wildly, he brought down on top of himself piles of chips, stacks of Cheetos, heavy lumps of sponge cake and devil's food cake and white cake and lemon cake differentiated solely by the type of artificial coloring and flavoring they contained.

They were all over him now, moving, surging lugubriously to and fro; those strange molecules he'd discovered boldly asserting themselves. They wanted, cried out, demanded to be consumed. He struggled beneath their empty weight and tried to scream for help, but the eight-year-olds who could have rescued him were tucked snug in their beds far from the shuttered market.

Looking down, he saw bags of pretzels and honey-roasted Cornnuts splitting open; their overbaked, over-saturated, oversalted entrails spilling across his chest and legs. He kicked wildly, sending crumbs flying but unable to get to his feet. His arms and chest were slowly disap-pearing beneath thick cords of plaster-white creme and dark imitation fudge filling.

His eyes widened as he saw them humping sinuously toward his face; death reduced to spongy sweet bland-ness. They crammed themselves into his mouth, shoving his lips apart, forcing themselves down his throat. He continued to struggle, to fight, but it was useless. They overwhelmed him, relentless and unyielding in their de-sire to please, to slavishly gratify the basest of human desires.

The light began to fade from his eyes. He'd been care-less, he realized. Unwilling to envision what they were capable of. But who could have imagined? Did even the bioengineers who'd given impetus to such syrupy muta-tions imagine what the ultimate result of their work might be? He doubted it. Surely the lethal reality he was experiencing exceeded even their capacious greed.

He was going, going—but at least he wouldn't die hungry.

"Gawddamn! What a mess."

The officer wrinkled his nose at the sight and its at-tending smell. Forensics was finishing up, making way for the coroner. Their jobs were relatively straightforward.

It was the mortician he didn't envy.

The coroner's assistant was writing on a pad. The of-ficer nodded to him. They knew each other well.

"Kerwin."

"Hey, man." The assistant looked up. "Ever see anything like this before?"

The cop shook his head. "What do you think happened?"

The coroner glanced up the aisle. "Off what I'm used to seeing on the street, my first guess is that he swallowed a twelve-gauge shell that went off inside him, but there's no sign of powder or shell fragments. I'm beginning to think he just overbinged and self-destructed. Gastrointestinally speaking."

"The hell you say. Look at him."

"I'd rather not. At least, no more than I have to." The coroner's reluctance was understandable. Most of what had once reposed in the cavity between the dead man's sternum and crotch lay scattered across the supermarket floor and shelves, shockingly vivid amidst the frozen, undulating sea of partly digested cakes and cookies, snack foods and fruit chewies.

"As near as we've been able to figure, the guy went on a junk food binge to end all junk food binges. It was like he couldn't control himself. As if he had no resistance to the stuff, no resistance at all. Like the Polynesians who were suddenly exposed to European diseases to which they had no built-up immunity.

"You know how much air they cram into this junk. Ordinarily it doesn't give you anything except maybe a little gas now and then. But he was downing the stuff so fast it must've blocked his colon. Then he choked on it, and with no escape valve, as it were, the pent-up gas, well—he just blew up. Damnedest thing I ever saw."

"You ain't alone, ol' buddy. Wonder what made him do it?"

"Beats me." The coroner shrugged, finishing his notes. "He's got all the signs of someone who's been force-fed, except that he obviously did it to himself. Like a French goose on the pâté line. And I thought I knew every way a person could commit suicide." He shook his head ruefully. "This is one business where you don't get a kick out of learning something new." He put his pen to his lips. "What the hell am I going to list as 'reason for demise'?"

The cop looked thoughtful. "If it was up to me I'd put down 'Accidental' and leave it at that. It'll get you off the hook until something better turns up."

The assistant coroner looked resigned. Then the corners of his mouth turned up slightly. He scribbled on the pad, showed it to his friend.

"I can't turn it in this way, of course. The boss'd have my ass."

The officer looked down, smiling in spite of himself.

CAUSE: Death by Twinkie.

They shared a chuckle. The coroner pocketed his pad. As he turned to leave he noticed a slightly torn but otherwise undamaged package on the floor. Reaching down, he rescued a couple of orphaned creme-filled cupcakes with garish orange icing, passing one to his friend. With a wink the cop bit deeply into his own.

The sensation as the thick-cremed, sugar-saturated, calorie-rich crumbly mass slid down his throat was indescribable.

FITTING TIME

When I was growing up (again), my mother's best friend in the neighborhood was a lovely lady named Adrian Anderson. Her husband, Johnny, was a tall, easygoing presence of Scandinavian-derived Minnesotan stock who happened to work in the business of motion pictures. Johnny was a wardrobe master. The walls of his modest den were covered with signed photos from some of the biggest names in Hollywood whom he'd dressed for multiple pictures.

Among these was one Elvis Presley, noted star of motion pictures and sometime singer. After certain pictures, Johnny was required to dispose of certain no longer needed items of attire. The result was local garage sales of no uncertain significance. As a teenage boy, I was of course above such déclassé bourgeois enterprises and blew past them on my way to the local touch football games with nary a glance.

One day my mother presented me with a pair of white jeans she had bought at one of Johnny's sales. She noted that they had been worn by Mr. Presley, and even mentioned the particular picture. I was no fan of Elvis, but the pants were nice, and I wore them until I wore the legs out. Then I cut them off at the knees and used them for beach shorts. Eventually, I threw them away.

*To this day, my wife has never forgiven me for this—
nor has any woman who has ever heard the story.*

———————

Rohrbach was in a particularly good mood as he
rode the elevator to his office. He was alone except for
Spike. No mother actually named her newborn Spike, of
course, and his Spike was no different. His real name
was Nicholas Spianski, but at six foot six and three
hundred and twelve pounds, Spike seemed a much better
fit. An ex–semipro tackle, he'd been Rohrbach's principal bodyguard for six years. Rohrbach had several
bodyguards, of whom Spike was the only one who accompanied him everywhere. Rohrbach needed several
bodyguards.

He was publisher and editor-in-chief of the *Truth*.

You've seen the *Truth*. It slaps you in the face every
time you check out of your local drugstore, or supermarket, or twenty-four-hour convenience store. You've
probably watched its half-hour syndicated television
counterpart that airs between ten and twelve at night. It's
hard to miss, the *Truth* is.

LOCH NESS MONSTER
Attacks Scottish Schoolbus,
Eats Six Children Before Horrified Driver's Eyes!

I HAD ELVIS'S LOVE CHILD—
And He's A Serial Killer,
Distraught Mom Says!

Aliens Kidnap Alabama Town—
Two Twelve-Year-Old Girls Impregnated
by Horrible Extraterrestrial Slugs!

No, that last one can't be right. The *Truth* would never use a word as big as *impregnated*. But you get the idea.

As a going commercial concern, the *Truth* was a roaring success. It made a great deal of money for its stockholders, its employees, and most flagrantly, its devoted editor-in-chief. Rohrbach was quite a happy man. The only people who were not happy about the *Truth* were the unfortunate targets of his writers' scurrilous inventions, but there was little they could do about it. If they ignored the paper, it published even more outrageous stories about them, and if they sued and won, the paper got free publicity and several new stories out of the lawsuit. The *Truth* was a no-win situation for its victims, and a win-win for Rohrbach.

Life was good, if not fair, he reflected as he sloughed off Spike and entered his private office.

It had a spacious view of the Florida coast, of palm trees and blue water and surf. Beat the hell out of working for a real paper in New York or Chicago, he reflected as he settled in behind his desk. It was piled high with paper despite the presence of a computer on one side.

It was not piled so high that he failed to see the man seated in the chair off to his right, next to the concealed wet bar.

Rohrbach froze. The man was tall but not thin, with blond hair and blue eyes. The publisher had never seen him before. He wore unscuffed shoes instead of sandals, freshly pressed trousers, and somewhat incongruously, a florid Hawaiian shirt. His mien was not threatening, but Rohrbach knew from experience you could never tell. How he had slipped inside the editor didn't know—but he sure as hell was going to find out. And when he did, some unfortunate was going to pay.

The publisher's hand strayed toward the alarm button

located just under the lip of the desk—and hesitated. The visitor displayed neither weapons nor hostility. Calm and relaxed, he just sat there staring back at the publisher, a serious but unintimidating expression on his face. If he'd had a gun or something threatening he most likely would have brought it out by now.

Rohrbach drew his finger back from the alarm and sat back in his chair.

"How did you get in here?"

The visitor's voice was deep and strong, but not threatening. "You wouldn't believe me if I told you. I only half believe it myself."

Rohrbach glowered. Beneath that glower employees and even successful corporate lawyers trembled. "You'll believe it when I have you arrested for breaking and entering."

"I only entered. I didn't break anything. And you can't arrest me."

"Really?" Rohrbach was intrigued in spite of himself. "Why not, pray tell?"

"Because I'm not really here, in the really here sense."

Oh brother, Rohrbach thought. A nut. Harmless, but a nut. Not even radical enough for a back-page squib. He sighed. His schedule was full and he was wasting time.

"I see," he said slowly. "Well, Mr., uh . . ."

"Johnny," murmured the visitor. "Johnny Anderson."

"Well, Johnny, since you're here, what can I do for you before I have you thrown out by several large people who you'll also no doubt claim won't be able to do anything to you?"

"Elvis sent me."

Rohrbach had to smile. Nothing to start the day like being visited by one of your own headlines. He checked the organizer on his desk. Nothing like starting the day with a good laugh, either, and he had a few minutes left before the morning story conference.

The guy was living proof of what police and newspaper professionals knew well; the real mental cases didn't look like Charlie Manson. They were regular, ordinary folk just like you and me. Taxpayers and churchgoers and PTA members. Which was how they escaped detection and incarceration until they did something sufficiently drastic to bring them to the notice of their fellow citizens. Like this Johnny here. At least he was harmless.

"I see," Rohrbach said slowly. "Why did he send you? To deliver a message, no doubt?"

The visitor steepled his fingers. "That's right. See, he's sick and tired of all these lies you've been printing about him ever since he died. You know the kind I'm talking about. 'Elvis sighted at diner in Rapid City, Iowa.' 'Elvis's adopted teenage daughter goes on rampage at mental hospital.' 'Fans steal Elvis's body, pharmacist reveals Elvis's secret drug list.' Stuff like that. He wants it to stop. He wants you to stop."

"Sure. Uh-huh." Rohrbach fought to repress a grin. "Um, tell me something, Johnny. If the King is so upset, why didn't he come tell me about it himself?"

The visitor shifted in the chair. "It's kind of hard to explain. I don't really understand it all myself. Something to do with a gig. So he asked me to help him out." The visitor smiled. "We spent a lot of time together."

"Oh, right. Don't know why I didn't think of that." Rohrbach rose. "Well listen, Johnny, I don't know about you, but I've got quite a day ahead of me." The visitor nodded and stood. "I really want to thank you for bringing this to my attention, and I promise you I'll get right on it."

The visitor smiled softly. He certainly was harmless, Rohrbach thought. Have to have a talk with the people

in the outer office, though. Can't have strangers just
wandering into the inner sanctum whenever they felt
like it.

He escorted the tall caller out, shutting the door behind him, and returned to his desk shaking his head. It
was a wonderfully wacky world, which was fortunate
for him because he had pages to fill.

By charming coincidence one of the *Truth*'s northern
California stringers had filed a nice, juicy little rumor
suitable for a bottom front-page banner. At the story
conference they settled on "Elvis's Gay Lover Comes
Forth in San Francisco! Broke and Dying of Aids!" for a
headline. The story was accompanied by several conveniently blurry photos of some poor skeletal figure laid up
in a hospital bed.

They put the weekly issue to bed the next day, and by
the weekend Rohrbach was ready to play. There were
many who firmly believed that being a bachelor million-
aire in south Florida was one of the planet's more envi-
able existences, but you couldn't party every weekend.
Bad for the constitution. So Rohrbach settled for making
a day of it Sunday at Joe Robbie Stadium with a couple
of friends, where from the *Truth*'s private skybox they
watched the Dolphins beat the Bears 24–21 on a last-
minute field goal.

It was as they were leaving for the limo that the
pain stabbed through Rohrbach's chest. He winced and
clutched at himself. His friend Nawani, who owned a
little less than a hundred of the Sunshine State's finest
liquor stores, was by his side in an instant.

"Rob, man, what's the matter?" He waved. "Hey, get
a doctor, somebody get a doctor!"

Even as a crowd started to gather, the pain faded.
Rohrbach straightened, breathing hard, his heart flut-
tering from fear rather than damage.

"It's okay. I'm . . . okay now."

"You sure?" Nawani eyed him uncertainly. "Looked like you couldn't get your breath, man."

"Just for a few seconds. Felt like my shirt shrank about six sizes. But it's all right now."

"Yeah, well, you better see a doctor, Rob. Doesn't pay to fool around with stuff like that. My brother Salim passed away two years ago. Went just like that. A quick pain, grabbed his chest, and *boom*, he was gone."

Though still scared, Rohrbach was feeling much better. "I'll check it out, don't worry."

He did, too. First thing Monday morning. The doctor found nothing wrong with him, no evidence of a heart attack or anything relational. "Probably just a muscle spasm, Rob. Happens all the time."

"Not to me it doesn't," Rohrbach told him.

That night he was sliding into the custom, oversized bed at the mansion when he abruptly sat bolt upright.

The visitor was sitting on the lounge next to the built-in plasma TV. "Hello, Mr. Rohrbach."

There was a six-shot Smith & Wesson in the end-table drawer. Also, Spike was watching game shows two doors down the hall. A buzzer on the end table would bring him running. The bodyguard would make chicken parts of this intruder, only—how the hell had he managed to get inside the estate's heavily guarded, stuccoed walls?

He was wearing white pants now, with matching white loafers and a pale yellow, embroidered shirt. Far better dressed than the average nut. The kind anyone would be proud to introduce at their next party.

Steady, Rohrbach told himself.

"Are you going to ask me how I got in here again?" the figure inquired.

"No, but I know how you're going to go out. In

cuffs." He reached for the intercom, watching the intruder warily.

"Chest feeling better?" The man seemed genuinely solicitous.

Slowly, Rohrbach leaned back against the thickly padded satin headboard. "How did you know about that?"

"I told you. Elvis wants those stories to stop. I was his friend; he couldn't take care of this himself, so he asked me to step in for him."

"Poison." Rohrbach was thinking furiously. "At the stadium. Somehow you got something into my drink." The publisher recalled having downed a number of drinks, not all from the same bottle.

The visitor shook his head. "I'm a very nonviolent individual, Mr. Rohrbach. I couldn't do something like that. I couldn't poison a fly, or shoot anyone, or use a knife. I wouldn't know what to do. All I have any control over while I'm here is that which I know best."

"Then how'd you hurt me like that?"

"Does it matter? I didn't enjoy it. But Elvis was my friend, and I told him I'd help out on this. Are you going to stop the stories?"

"Yeah. Yeah, I'll stop them. I promise."

"That's good." The visitor rose, and Rohrbach reached toward the end-table drawer. But the man didn't come toward the bed. He simply let himself out, quietly.

As soon as he was gone Rohrbach leaped from the bed and locked the door. Then he was on the intercom like paparazzi on a senatorial assignation.

"Spike! Dammit, get your lazy ass in here!"

A half-asleep voice echoed back. "Boss? What's the trouble, boss?"

"We've got an intruder!"

"Intruder? But boss, Security hasn't said nothin', and the alarms—"

"Get your head out of your ass! About six-one, blond, white male. White slacks, yellow shirt. *Get on it!*"

The intercom clicked off. Spike was in motion, and Rohrbach pitied the intruder if the bodyguard found him first.

He didn't. No one did. Security swore that no prowlers had been seen on the estate, and every alarm was quiescent. Rohrbach ranted and howled, but it didn't do any good. He had the mansion's security checked and rechecked, as well as warning people at the office. And he put Danziger, one of his best researchers, onto finding out anything he could about a man named Johnny Anderson who just might, just possibly, have once had some kind of peripheral connection, as a dedicated fan or whatever, with Elvis.

The next week, with grim deliberation, he caused to have printed on the inside front page of the *Truth* a story about Elvis's disfiguring birthmark and the surgery that had failed to cure it, as well as a follow-up on the gay housemate story that purported to show Elvis's male lover being buried in a cemetery in San Jose.

Then, with his entire staff alerted, he sat back and waited.

Nothing happened the next day, or the day after that. He began to relax.

On the third day, he was stepping out of the limo outside one of Miami's finest seafood restaurants, where he was to meet for dinner with an extraordinarily beautiful and admirably ambitious new editorial assistant, with whom he anticipated discussing little having to do with newspaper work of any kind. Spike wasn't with him.

Bedford, the chauffeur, opened the door to let him out. It was warm but not overly humid, a gorgeous night that he expected to end rather steamier than it had begun. He took a step toward the mahogany-and-leaded-glass doorway of the restaurant.

His feet spun him around to face the sidewalk and hustled him irresistibly forward.

He opened his mouth, but nothing came out. What could you say when your feet suddenly took off with you, utterly indifferent to every mental command and imprecation? No, that wasn't right. It wasn't his feet that were running away with him: It was his shoes.

Down the sidewalk he went, flailing wildly with the bewildered Bedford yelling in his wake. Off the curb and out into the street.

Straight into the path of a pumped-up, oversized, bechromed pickup truck thumping out Tupac as deep and low as the pounding of a sauropodian heart.

Rohrbach screamed; oversized all-terrain tires squealed; Bedford gasped. A chrome pipe bumper whacked Rohrbach in the chest, sending pain shooting through his ribs and knocking him down. A trio of terrified teenagers piled out of the truck to gather anxiously around him. If possible, they were more scared than he was.

"Shit, mister, I didn't see you!"

"He stepped right in front of you, Don! I saw him! Right in front of you!"

"I'm all right." A shaken Rohrbach climbed to his feet, brushing at his suit. His ribs ached, but it didn't feel like anything was broken. "Forget it. We'll all pretend it didn't happen. It was my fault."

"Yeah, man," the third boy blurted. "Damn straight it was your fault! You—!" His friends grabbed him and dragged him away, back into the truck.

Bedford was at his side, at once angry and concerned. "Are you all right, Mr. Rohrbach, sir? What possessed you to dart out in the street like that?"

"I'm really not sure, but I'm okay now. Forget it. Just forget it." He glanced down at his shoes. When he started back toward the sidewalk they obeyed. Why shouldn't they? They were just shoes.

Carefully primping his thinning hair back into place, he pushed past the chauffeur and strode into the restaurant.

She was as attractive and eager as he'd expected. Not that she had a lot of choice if she expected to move up the ladder under him. The food was excellent, and the wine made him forget the near-fatal incident out in the street.

They were waiting for dessert when his briefs started to tighten up.

At first it was merely uncomfortable. Smiling across the table at her, he squirmed uncomfortably in his chair, trying to free up the kinks. At first it seemed to work.

Then they tightened afresh. Much tighter.

His eyes bulged, and his expression grew pinched as he jerked forward. His date eyed him with concern.

"Robert, is something the matter? Are you . . . ?"

"Be right back," he told her hastily. "Something in the stone crab . . ."

He straightened and headed for the men's room. Halfway across the floor his briefs suddenly seemed to contract to half their normal size. He bent double, a sickly green expression on his face, and fought to keep from grabbing himself. Several well-dressed diners seated nearby looked at him askance. Somehow he staggered the rest of the way to the hall, then slammed through the door into the elegant men's room.

He didn't even bother to close the stall door behind him as he desperately unbuckled and unzipped his slacks and looked down at himself. So deeply had his briefs dug into his flesh that blood was showing in several places around the elastic. He pulled at the material. It wouldn't give.

The pain increased, and he slumped onto the stool, still clawing frantically at his briefs. Just when he thought he was going to pass out, some give finally returned to the elastic. Making no effort to get up, he sat there breathing long and slow in deep, shaky gasps, waiting for the pain to go away.

How long would his conquest-to-be wait for him? How cooperative would she be later if she thought he was suffering from some unknown disease? If he had a hope of salvaging the evening he had to get back to the table.

He rose and pulled up his pants around the torn briefs, hoping they wouldn't show. The dinner jacket should cover any lines. He stepped out of the stall and took a deep breath.

It was cut off halfway as his tie tightened around his throat.

Wide-eyed, turning blue, he wrenched at the tie. It was very expensive silk, custom made, blue and crimson, and it didn't fray or ravel. Staggering wildly around the bathroom, he banged off the wall, the sinks, the stalls, his fingers fighting to find some space between the silk and his flesh. Eyes bulging, lungs heaving, he fell to the floor and lay there kicking and fighting. Everything was getting blurry and hot, as if he'd spent too much time in the pool with his eyes open underwater.

Dimly, he was aware of the door opening, of a figure bending over him and yelling. He wanted to respond, to explain, and tried to, but he couldn't get enough air, not enough air to . . .

They let him out of the hospital the next day, around lunchtime. It had been a near thing, and he was more fortunate than he could imagine. Not every executive in Miami carried a pocket knife to their favorite restaurant. While someone else had called 911, his savior had severed the asphyxiating necktie. The sole reminder of the experience consisted of a small bandage on the publisher's throat. It covered the tiny nick the knife had made. So constricted had the necktie been that Rohrbach's rescuer had been unable to slip even the narrow blade cleanly between silk and skin.

He responded to every inquiry that greeted him on his return to the office, even to those from individuals he knew hated or despised him. He didn't get much work done the rest of that day, or the next.

By the third morning after his release from the hospital he was feeling much more like his old self, and friends commented freely on his recovery. It wasn't the near strangulation that had slowed him down, he explained. Unless you've experienced something like that you can't imagine what it's like; the loss of air, the knowing that Death is standing next to you, just waiting to reach down and take you for his own. It's the mental recovery, he explained, that takes longer.

Awaiting his sage perusal were stories about crop circles in Wales, a two-hundred-pound twelve-year-old in Rio, a woman who had won three sweepstakes by using astrology, a man in Bombay who claimed to grow the only genuine aphrodisiac in the world and who had eighty-three children, a nuclear worker who glowed in the dark, and . . . a freelancer in New Orleans submitted a story about a shrimper who claimed that Elvis Presley had been living in the swamps outside Lafayette and had been working for him for years, and that he'd married a local Cajun gal and lived only on gator meat and red beans and rice.

The assistant editor who'd brought in the story looked

expectantly at his boss. "Mr. Rohrbach? I thought maybe page five, opposite the breast enlargement ad? Mr. Rohrbach, sir?"

The publisher only half heard him. Still fresh in his mind was the remembrance of choking, the silken garrote tight as a steel cord around his throat, the wheezing sounds, the screaming in his lungs, the . . .

"No," he said.

A look of pained disbelief came over the assistant's face. "Sir? It's a good story, sir. They can't check very well back in that swamp country; it just meets our possibility criteria, and the food tie-in offers some intriguing advertising possibilities."

"I said no." He blinked and looked around the table. "Kill it. No Elvis stories. Not . . . now. My gut feeling is that Elvis is . . . overexposed. Get me something fresh. Cher. We haven't had a good lead on Cher for a month. Come on, gang, get on it!"

A few of them eyed him strangely after the story conference, but no one said anything. Feeling slightly queasy, he returned to his office, speaking only to a couple of people on the way back. When he settled down behind his desk his thoughts were more than a little confused.

His researcher buzzed for admittance, and Rohrbach let him in.

"What is it, Danziger?"

"Sir. You remember that man you wanted me to try and trace? Anderson?"

Rohrbach looked up sharply, his mind now crystal clear. "Don't tell me you found something on him?"

The researcher looked pleased. "Actually it wasn't that hard, sir. His connection with Elvis is more than peripheral." While Rohrbach looked on, Danziger glanced down at the notepad he carried. "Apparently he's quite well known in the business."

"The 'business'? You mean, movies?"

Danziger nodded. "Knew Elvis real well. Did ten—no, eleven films with him."

Rohrbach hesitated. "He's an actor?"

"Nope. And the operative verb is *was*. He passed away in December of 1991."

Rohrbach said nothing, just sat there behind the big desk, gripping the edge with unconscious concentration.

"In a way he was probably 'closer' to Elvis than just about anybody the King worked with." Danziger was grinning, pleased with himself. "He was a wardrobe master. Whipped up all of Elvis's costumes on those pictures, did the fittings, took the measurements, made—" Danziger stopped, mildly alarmed. "Are you all right, sir? Maybe you should think about getting some new shirts. That collar looks awfully tight."

[*Johnny Anderson and his family were my next-door neighbors two houses removed when I was growing up in California. Johnny was a great guy; everybody loved him. Johnny knew Elvis a long time. They got along great then, and I expect they do now.*

There's a picture of Johnny on page 144 of the Elvis Album.]

WE THREE KINGS

I love monsters. You love monsters. Everybody loves monsters. The literary and movie kind, of course—not the real ones who unfortunately inhabit our day-to-day world. It's interesting that we like to read about invented monsters because they help us to forget about the real ones. Kind of like people who watch soap operas because they help them to forget about what they don't have in their own lives.

But who do monsters love? Or do monsters love? Is there inevitably mutual admiration and respect, or must they of course fear one another? It's a truly monstrous matter to contemplate.

Obviously the basis for a Christmas story.

It was overcast and blustery, and the snow was coming down as hard as a year's accumulation of overdue bills. Within the laboratory, Stein made the final adjustments, checked the readouts, and inspected the critical circuit breakers one last, final time. There was no going back now. The success or failure of his life's work hinged on what happened in the next few moments.

He knew there were those who if given the chance would try to steal his success, but if everything worked he would take care of them first. Them with their primitive, futile notions and dead-end ideas! All subterfuge and smoke, behind which they doubtless intended to claim his triumph as their own. Let them scheme and plot while they could. Soon they would be out of the way, and he would be able to bask in his due glory without fear of theft or accusation.

He began throwing the switches, turning the dials. Fitful bursts of necrotic light threw the strange shapes that occupied the vast room in the old warehouse into stark relief. Outside, the snow filled up the streets, sifting into dirty gutters, softening the outlines of the city. Not many citizens out walking in his section of town, he reflected. It was as well. Though the laboratory was shuttered and soundproofed, there was no telling what unforeseen sights and sounds might result when he finally pushed his efforts of many years to a final conclusion.

The dials swung while the readings on the gauges mounted steadily higher. Nearing the threshold now. The two huge Van de Graaff generators throbbed with power. Errant orbs of ball lightning burst free, to spend themselves against the insulated ceiling in showers of coruscating sparks. It was almost time.

He threw the final, critical switch.

Gradually the crackling faded and the light in the laboratory returned to normal. With the smell of ozone sharp in his nostrils, Stein approached the table. For an instant, there was nothing more than disappointment brokered by uncertainty. And then—a twitch. Slight, but unmistakable. Stein stepped back, eyes wide and alert. A second twitch, this time in the arms. Then the legs, and finally the torso itself.

With a profound grinding sound, the creature sat up, snapping the two-inch-wide leather restraining straps as if they were so much cotton thread.

"It's alive!" Stein heard himself shouting. "It's alive, it's alive, it's alive!"

He advanced cautiously until he was standing next to the now seated Monster. The bolts in its neck had been singed black from the force of the charge that had raced through it, but there were no signs of serious damage. Tentatively, Stein reached out and put a hand on the creature's arm. The massive, blocky skull swiveled slowly to look down at him.

"Nnrrrrrrrrrgh!"

Stein was delighted. "You and I, we are destined to conquer the world. At last, the work of my great-grandfather is brought to completion." His voice dropped to a conspiratorial whisper. "But there are those who would thwart us, who would stand in our way. I know who they are, and they must be . . . dealt with. Listen closely, and obey . . ."

Outside, the snow continued to fall.

In the dark cellar Rheinberg carefully enunciated the ancient words. Only a little light seeped through the street-level window, between the heavy bars. Seated in the center of the room, in the middle of the pentagram, was the sculpture. Rheinberg was as talented as he was resourceful, and the details of his creation were remarkable for their depth and precision.

An eerie green glow began to suffuse the carefully crafted clay figure as the ancient words echoed through the studio. Rheinberg read carefully from the copy of the ancient manuscript in a steady, unvarying monotone. With each word, each sentence, the glow intensified, until softly pulsing green shadows filled every corner of the basement studio.

Almost, but not quite, he halted in the middle of the final sentence, at the point when the eyes of the figure began to open. That would have been dangerous, he knew. And so, fully committed now, he read on. Only when he'd finished did he dare allow himself to step forward for a closer look.

The eyes of the Golem were fully open now, unblinking, staring straight ahead. Then they shifted slowly to their left, taking notice of the slight, anxious man who was approaching.

"It works. It worked! The old legends were true." Unbeknownst to Rheinberg, the parchment sheet containing the words had crumpled beneath his clenching fingers. "The world is ours, my animate friend! Ours, as soon as certain others are stopped. You'll take care of that little matter for me, won't you? You'll do anything I ask. You must. That's what the legend says."

"Ooooyyyyyyyy!" Moaning darkly, the massive figure rose. Its gray head nearly scraped the ceiling.

Within the charmed circle something was rising. A pillar of smoke, black shot through with flashes of bright yellow, coiling and twisting like some giant serpent awakened from an ancient sleep. Al-Nomani recited the litany and watched, determined to maintain the steady singsong of the nefarious quatrain no matter what happened.

The fumes began to thicken, to coalesce. Limbs appeared, emerging from the roiling hell of the tornadic spiral. The whirlwind itself began to change shape and color, growing more manlike with each verse, until a horrid humanoid figure stood where smoke had once swirled. It had two rings in its oversized left ear, a huge nose, and well-developed fangs growing upward from its lower jaw. For all that, the fiery yellow eyes that glared out at the historian from beneath the massive, low-slung brow reeked of otherworldly intelligence.

"By the beard of the Prophet!" al-Nomani breathed tensely. "It worked!" He put down the battered, weathered tome from which he had been reading. The giant regarded him silently, awaiting. As it was supposed to do.

Al-Nomani took a step forward. "You will do my bidding. There is much that needs to be done. First and foremost there is the matter of those who would challenge my knowledge, and my supremacy. They must be shown the error of their ways. I commit you to deal with them."

"Eeeehhhhzzzzz!" Within the circle the Afreet bowed solemnly. Its arms were as big around as tree trunks.

Stillman was cruising the run-down commercial area just outside the industrial park when he noticed movement up the side street. At this hour everything was closed up tight, and the weather had reduced traffic even further. He picked up the cruiser's mike, then set it back in its holder. Might be nothing more than some poor old rummy looking for a warm place to sleep.

Still, the vagrants and the homeless tended to congregate downtown. It was rare to encounter one this far out. Which meant that the figure might be looking to help itself to something more readily convertible than an empty park bench. Stillman flicked on the heavy flashlight and slid out of the car, drawing his service revolver as he did so. The red and yellows atop the cruiser turned steadily, lighting up the otherwise dark street.

Cautiously, he advanced on the narrow roadway. He had no intention of entering, of course. If the figure ran, that would be indication enough something was wrong, and that's when he'd call for backup.

"Hey! Hey, you in there! Kinda late for a stroll, especially in this weather, ain't it?"

The only reply was a strange shuffling. The officer

blinked away falling snow as something shifted in the shadows. He probed with his flashlight.

"Come on out, man. I know you're back there. I don't want any trouble from you, and you really don't want any from me. Don't make me come in there after you." He took a challenging step forward.

Something vast and monstrous loomed up with shocking suddenness, so big his light could not illuminate it all. Officer Corey Stillman gaped at the apparition. His finger contracted reflexively on the trigger of his service revolver, and a sharp crack echoed down the alley. The creature flinched, then reached for him with astounding speed.

"Nnrrrrrrrrrr!"

Stillman never said a word.

His head was throbbing like his brother's Evenrude when he finally came around. Groaning, he reached for the back of his skull as he straightened up in the snow. Memories came flooding back, and he looked around wildly; but the Monster was gone, having shambled off down the street.

Eleven years on the force and that was without question the ugliest dude he'd ever encountered. Quick for his size, too. Too damn quick. He was sure his single shot had hit home, but it hadn't even slowed the big guy down. Wincing, he climbed to his feet and surveyed his surroundings. His cruiser sat where he'd left it in the street, lights still revolving patiently.

His gun lay in the snow nearby. Slowly he picked up the .38, marveling at the power that had crushed it to a metal pulp. What had he encountered, and how could he report it? Nobody'd believe him.

A figure stepped into view from behind the building. He tensed, but big as the pedestrian was, he was utterly

· different in outline from Stillman's departed assailant. Seeking help, the officer took a couple of steps toward it—and pulled up short.

The enormous stranger was the color of damp clay, save for vacant black eyes that stared straight through him.

"Good God!"

Startled by the exclamation, the creature whirled and struck.

"Ooyyyyyyyyyy!"

This time when Stillman regained consciousness he didn't move, just lay in the snow and considered his situation. His second attacker had been nothing like the first, yet no less terrifying in appearance. He no longer cared if everyone back at the station thought him crazy; he needed backup.

Too much overtime, he told himself. That had to be it. Too many hours rounding up too many hookers and junkies and sneak thieves. Mary was right. He needed to use some of that vacation time he'd been accumulating.

Body aching, head still throbbing, he struggled to his feet. The cruiser beckoned, its heater pounding away persistently despite the open door on the driver's side. Recovering his hat and clutching the flashlight, he staggered around the front, pausing at the door to lean on it for support. The heat from the interior refreshed him, made him feel better. He started to slide in behind the wheel.

The seat was already occupied by something with burning yellow eyes and a bloated, distorted face straight out of the worst nightmares of childhood. It was playing with the police radio scanner, mouthing it like a big rectangular cookie.

He'd surprised it, and of course it reacted accordingly.

"Oh *no*!" Stillman moaned as he staggered backward

and an unnaturally long arm reached for him. "Not *again*!"

"Eehhhzzzzzz!"

The wonderful profusion of brightly colored street and store lights slowed the Monster's progress, mysteriously diluted its intent. The lights were festive and cheerful. Even as it kept to the shadows, it could see the faces of smiling adults and laughing children. There were the decorations, too: in the stores, above the streets, on the houses. Laughter reached him through the falling snow: childish giggles, booming affirmations of good humor, deep chuckles of pleasure. Invariably, it all had a cumulative effect.

Memories stirred: memories buried deep within the brain he'd been given. The lights, the snow, the laughter, candy and ebullient chatter of toys: It all meant something. He just wasn't sure what. Confused, he turned and lurched off down the dark alley between two tall buildings, trying to reconcile his orders with these disturbing new thoughts.

He paused suddenly, senses alert. Someone else was coming up the alley. The figure was big, much bigger than any human he'd observed so far that night. Not that he was afraid of any human, or for that matter, any thing. Teeth and joints grinding, arms extended, he started deliberately forward.

There was just enough light for the two figures to make each other out. When they could do so with confidence, they hesitated in mutual confusion. Something strange was abroad this night, and both figures thought it most peculiar.

"Who . . . what . . . you?" the Monster declaimed in a voice like a rusty mine cart rolling down a long-neglected track. Speech was still painful.

"I vaz going ask you the same qvestion." The other figure's black eyes scrutinized the slow-speaking shape standing opposite. "You one revolting-looking schlemiel, I can tell you."

"You not . . . no raving beauty yourself."

"So tell me zumthing I don't know." The Golem's massive shoulders heaved, a muscular gesture of tectonic proportions.

"What be this, pbuh?" Both massive shapes turned sharply, to espy a third figure hovering close behind them. Despite its size it had made not a sound during its approach.

"Und I thought you vaz ugly," the Golem murmured to the Monster as it contemplated the newcomer.

"Speak not ill of others lest the wrath of Allah befall thee." The Afreet approached, its baleful yellow eyes flicking from one shape to the next. "What manner of mischief is afoot this night?"

"Ask you . . . the same," the Monster rumbled.

The Afreet bowed slightly. "I am but recently brought fresh into the world, and am abroad on a mission for my mortal master of the moment." It glanced back toward the main street, with its twinkling lights and window-shopping pedestrians blissfully unaware of the astonishing conclave that was taking place just down the alley. "Yet I fear the atmosphere not conducive to my command, for what I see and hear troubles my mind like a prattling harim."

"You too?" The Golem rubbed its chin. Clay flakes fell to the pavement. "I vaz thinking the same."

"I think I know . . . what is wrong." The other two eyed the Monster.

"Nu? So don't keep it to yourself," the Golem said.

"I have been pondering." Eyes squinted tight with the stress of the activity. "Pondering hard. What I think is that the season," the creature declared slowly, "is the reason."

"Pray tell, explain thyself." The Afreet was demanding, but polite.

The Monster's squarish forehead turned slowly. "The brain I was given . . . remembers. This time of year—the sights I see—make me remember. The time is wrong . . . for the command I was given. All . . . wrong. Wrong to kill . . . at the time of Christmas."

"Kill," the Afreet echoed. "Strange are the ways of the Prophet, for such was the order I was given. To kill this night two men: one of art and one of learning. Felix Stein and Joseph Rheinberg."

The Monster and the Golem started and exchanged a look. "I vaz to stamp out Stein alzo," muttered the Golem, "as vell as a historian name of al-Nomani. Rheinberg is my master."

"And Stein . . . mine," added the Monster.

"Fascinating it be," confessed the Afreet. "For al-Nomani is the one who called me forth."

"He is one whom I was to . . . slay," the Monster announced. "And this Rheinberg . . . too."

The formidable, and formidably bemused, trio pondered this arresting coincidence in silence while cheerful music and the sound of caroling drifted back to them from the street beyond. Though least verbal of the three, it was again the Monster who articulated first.

"Something . . . wrong . . . here. Wrong notion. Wrong time of . . . the year. Everything . . . wrong."

"Go on, say it again," the Golem growled. "Not just Christmas it is, but Chanukah also. Not a time for inimical spirits to be stirring. Not even a mouse."

"The spirit of Ramadan moves within me," the Afreet declared. "I know not what manner of life or believers you be, but I sense that in this I am of similar mind with you."

"Then what . . . we . . . do?" the Monster wondered aloud.

They considered.

Stillman blinked snow from his eyes. By now there wasn't much left of his cap, or his winter coat. He fumbled for the flashlight, somehow wasn't surprised to find that the supposedly impregnable cylinder of aircraft-grade aluminum had been twisted into a neat pretzel shape.

He saw the cruiser in front of him and began crawling slowly toward it. Nothing inside him seemed to be broken, but every muscle in his bruised body protested at the forced movement. The rotating lights atop the car were beginning to weaken as the battery ran down.

He was a foot from the door when he sensed a presence and looked to his right.

Three immense forms stood staring down at him, each all too familiar from a previous recent encounter. It was impossible to say which of the trio was the most terrifying. A clawed hand reached for him.

"Please," he whispered through snow-benumbed lips, "no more. Just kill me and get it over with."

The powerful fingers clutched his jacket front and lifted him as easily as if he were a blank arrest report, setting him gently on his feet. Another huge hand, dark and even-toned as the play clay his little girl made mud pies with, helped keep him upright. Trembling in spite of himself, he looked from one fearsome face to the next.

"I don't get it. What is this? What are you setting me up for?"

"We need . . . your help," the Monster mumbled, like a reluctant clog in a main city sewer line.

Stillman hesitated. "*You* need *my* help? That's a switch." He brushed dirty snow from his waist and thighs. "What kind of help? To be your punching bag?" He blinked at the Monster. "Uh, sorry about shooting you. You startled me. Heck, you still startle me."

"I . . . forgive," the Monster declaimed, sounding exactly like Arnold Schwarzenegger on a bad day.

"Yeah . . . okay, then. Well . . . what did you . . . boys . . . have in mind?"

The Afreet's eyes burned brightly. "In this time, praise be, is it still among men a crime to set another to commit murder?"

Stillman stiffened slightly. "Damn straight it is. Why do you ask?"

The Afreet glanced at its companions. "We know of several who have done this thing. Should they not, by your mortal laws, be punished for this?"

"You bet they should. You know where these guys are?" All three creatures nodded. Stillman hesitated. "You have proof?"

The Golem dug a fist the size and consistency of a small boulder into its open palm.

"You shouldn't vorry, policeman. I promise each one a full confession vill sign."

"If you're sure . . ." Stillman eyed the stony figure warily. "You're not talking about obtaining a confession under duress, are you?"

"Vhat, *me*?" The Golem spread treelike arms wide. "My friends and I vill chust a little friendly visit pay them. Each of them."

Stillman delivered the three badly shaken men to the station by himself. There was no need to call for backup. Not after his hefty acquaintances warned the three outraged but nonetheless compliant tamperers-with-the-laws-of-nature that if any of them so much as ventured an indecent suggestion in the officer's direction, the improvident speaker would sooner or later find himself on the receiving end of a midnight visit from all three of the . . . visitants. In the face of that monumentally understated threat, the would-be masters of the world proved themselves only too eager to cooperate with the police.

Stillman presented the thoroughly disgruntled experimenters to the duty officer, together with their signed confessions attesting to their respective intentions to murder one another, a collar that was sure to gain him a commendation at the least, and possibly even a promotion. It was worth the aches and pains to see the look on the lieutenant's face when each prisoner meekly handed over his confession. It further developed that all three men were additionally wanted on various minor charges, from theft of scientific equipment and art supplies to failing to return a six-year-overdue book from the university's Special Collections Library.

The members of the unnatural trio who had propitiated this notable sequence of events were waiting behind the station to congratulate Stillman when he clocked off duty. He winced as he stretched, studying each of them in turn.

"So . . . what're you guys gonna do now?" he asked curiously. "If you'd like to hang around the city, I know for a fact you could probably each get a tryout with the Bears."

"Bears?" the Monster rumbled. "I like to eat bear."

"No, no. It's a professional sports team. You know? Pro football? No," he reflected quietly, "maybe you don't know."

"If it be His will, we shall each of us make our way to a place of solitude and contentment. For such as we be, there is a special path for doing so. But we must wait for the coming of day to find the true passageways."

Stillman nodded. "Seems a shame after what you've

done tonight to have to hang out here, by yourselves, in this crappy weather."

Mary Stillman came out of the kitchen to greet her returning husband. She was drying a large serving dish with a beige towel spotted with orange flowers.

"Mary," Stillman called out, "I'm home! And I've brought some friends over for a little late supper. Do we have any of that Christmas turkey left?"

"Urrrrr—Christmas!" the Monster growled like a runaway eighteen-wheeler locking up its brakes at seventy per, and his sentiment if not his words were echoed by his companions.

While the Golem skillfully caught the dish before it struck the floor, the well-mannered Afreet performed the same service for a falling Mary Stillman. When she recovered consciousness and her husband hastily explained matters to her, she nodded slowly and went to see what she could find in the kitchen, whereupon they all shared a very nice late-night snack indeed, wholly in keeping with the spirit of the Seasons.

NASA SENDING ADDICTS TO MARS!

Giant Government Cover-up Revealed!

Okay, so I inhaled. Twice. That's all, honest. Not that I have anything against the stuff. It's just not my baggie.

Hypocrisy is as all-American as burgers and fries, apple pie and ice cream, Washington and slaves. For all the good things we espouse in America, we can't seem to get beyond wanting others to do as we do—whether they want to or not. When it comes to the business of recreational pharmaceuticals, the jury is still out. Cocaine is bad, coca tea is good. Opium is bad, morphine is good. Too much alcohol is bad, just enough is okay, none is better—have a Bud.

Now state after state teeters on the cusp of legalizing marijuana for medical use. My own feeling is that if I've got cancer, it doesn't matter if some stiff-nosed specialist in the Surgeon General's office proclaims the scientific virtues of THC or not—I'm gonna smoke and drink and pop whatever I damn well please, and don't let it bug you 'cause I'll likely be dead soon enough.

On the other hand, if the medicinal virtues of the weed turn out to have a firm foundation scientifically, so much the better for those who suffer from lack of it. No telling to what good it might be put . . .

"Ladies and gentlemen, the president of the United States!"

Someone in the presidential party had thoughtfully brought along their CD of "Hail to the Chief," just in case one happened to be lacking at Mission Control. The familiar music filtered through the intercom system as the tight knot of Secret Service men escorted their charge into the room, not unlike a cluster of nervous remoras convoying a shark. Played back over the intercom system, the march sounded tinny.

An unpatriotic thought at what should be a moment of great national pride, Hepworth knew. A glance at MacDonald and Tetsugawa showed that they shared his nervousness.

Following the initial curious look at the chief executive, the members of the mission team had returned to work, their attention focused purposefully on their instrumentation. Not all of them shared the secret that had been so strenuously guarded by Mission Command. With luck, that secret might be maintained for another day, another week. A great deal depended on how the president reacted.

Time enough to worry about that later. At the moment there were greetings to be exchanged, additional preparations to be made. Hepworth was making his own notes on what the president was wearing, whether his shoes were shined, how firm his handgrip was, and how genuine the easygoing, down-home grin so familiar from hundreds of telecasts was. It was important for Hepworth to memorize these details because his kids were sure to grill him on them the moment he got home. Not every kid on the block could boast about the day his dad met the president.

He thought Tetsugawa and MacDonald handled it better. Older and more experienced, they were used to the diplomatic niceties required on the bureaucratic circuit. To MacDonald, the president was only an ex-senator with bigger lifts in his heels. To Tetsugawa, he was a banker with access to unlimited largess.

A voice interrupted his reverie. "We're ready to transmit, Mr. Hepworth."

"Thanks, Rusty." Stepping forward, he found it surprisingly easy to pull the president away from the circle of sycophants into which he'd been drawn like a ship in a maelstrom. "We're ready for you now, Mr. President."

"Thank you, Warren." You were instantly on a first-name basis, which made you feel at once important and at ease, Hepworth noted admiringly. Just like his cheery next-door neighbor Steve Beckwith inquiring yet again if he could borrow the power mower.

Extracting his notes from a coat pocket, the president quietly cleared his throat and regarded his audience as the engineers concluded their final tests. Only when all was in readiness did he advance slightly in the direction of the microphone and begin to read from his prepared statement.

"Gentlemen and lady of the first manned mission to Mars, it is my very great pleasure to greet you on this first morning of the greatest achievement in the history of America and mankind's space program. By now the whole world has thrilled to the story of your successful landing on that ancient and mysterious world, which henceforth must be mysterious no longer. As in the coming weeks you probe its dusty red secrets . . ."

Hepworth listened with one ear. Certainly it was a speech of considerable historical import, one right up there with "One Small Step for Mankind," but other concerns preyed on his mind. He should have been relaxed. The interminably long spiraling journey out to the Red Planet, the anxiety attending the descent when unexpectedly strong winds threatened to turn the touch-down at Hellas to tragedy; all were behind them now. Nevertheless, the future of the expedition was far from assured.

The president droned on, relishing the moment. Hepworth automatically scanned the readings on the most important screens. To his relief, one in particular remained monotonously unchanged. Only the Mission Command physicians would be sensitive to the elevated readings of certain gauges, to the unusual respiratory patterns everyone at Command had grown accustomed to since the *Barsoom*'s departure from Earth orbit. Certainly there was no one in the president's immediate entourage knowledgeable enough about such matters to notice that anything might be amiss.

Eventually, the president concluded his official message of congratulations. Now they had to wait for the crew to compose their response. Ah, the response. Hepworth suddenly wished he were somewhere else. But he was the voice of Mission Control, and there was nowhere for him to hide.

While waiting, he paced aimlessly among the instrumented aisles, trying to avoid members of the official party. Let MacDonald and Tetsugawa make small talk with them. He leaned over one console festooned with dials and readouts and half a dozen flat-screen monitors. The operator checked an earphone and turned to grin at him.

"Fuentes just scored on a five-yard plunge. We're tied with Pittsburgh twenty-one all going into the fourth quarter."

"Thanks, Mel." Hepworth moved on, feeling better. So far it had been a rough season for the local team. You'd think that with a hundred-plus screens in Mission

Control someone could figure out a way to rig one to secretly pick up network broadcasts.

All of a sudden it was time; by the clock, and by simple physics. He took his place and waited. The big monitor on the wall crackled and cleared. They had to use the big screen this time. The president's team had insisted, and as a result there was no way to avoid it.

The panoramic view that materialized was remarkably sharp and detailed. It did not look especially alien. Rocky, ochre-tinted hills poked into a pink sky. Overhead, a single fragile cloud struggled to keep from dissipating in the rarefied atmosphere. As always, there were a few gasps from the newcomers in the audience. A live television picture from Mars, especially when viewed on the big projection screen, was still a sight to inspire awe in the most jaded viewer.

A figure wandered into view and waved at the camera pickup. Hepworth immediately recognized the lanky form of Gregorski, the mission geologist. The lightweight Martian suit clung to parts of his frame, reminding everyone how far removed the environment of the Red Planet was from barren Luna.

Gregorski waved again, then executed another gesture that distance fortunately rendered ambivalent. Glancing to his left, Hepworth saw MacDonald wince. One of the president's aides squinted uncertainly at the big screen but held his peace when no one else said anything.

The geologist did a slow forward roll in the light gravity and landed triumphantly on his feet. So far not too bad, Hepworth thought. The president was murmuring to an assistant and looking content.

There was a flash-interrupt. It was followed by a second, and then the screen cleared again. They were inside the lander now, the camera panning to show the interior of the main cabin. Food and equipment lay strewn about, poorly stowed. That was to be expected, though. Everyone on Earth knew how rough the wind-whipped touchdown had been.

Then a face was grinning into the pickup. Several onlookers started involuntarily. The sudden appearance of a five-foot-high nose can be disconcerting. The nose was quite red, but brief exposure to Martian sunlight could do that. It could, Hepworth told himself insistently.

The nose retreated, to find itself surrounded by the other facial features of Mission Commander Swansea. The colonel rubbed his burgundy-hued proboscis, unaware that in the process he'd slightly smudged the expensive pickup lens, and grinned.

Behind him they could see the two other members of the landing team, Oakley and Preston. For a moment, Hepworth thought everything was going to be all right. Then he saw that Oakley's flight suit was unzipped all the way to her thighs. It wasn't obvious because she was facing away from the pickup, but Hepworth's trained eye picked up the telltale clues immediately. Nearby, he heard Tetsugawa inhale sharply.

Please, he thought frantically. Say thank you, give greetings, be profound if you must, but get off camera as fast as you can.

Preston turned from his console to face the pickup, weaving only slightly. A condition fortuitously ascribable to the light gravity, Hepworth knew.

No such luck.

"Heyyy, good buddy!" Preston was smiling at Swansea, neglecting to address him as commander. "Whatta you know? It's the president. The goddamn farking president." The colonel swayed toward the pickup. "Yo, Pres! How's it goin', man?"

Hepworth found that he had begun to sweat.

Swansea pulled back. "Farrrrr outtttt. What's happenin' down yousaways, noble Earth creatures?"

Perhaps, Hepworth thought desperately, the president would ascribe the mission commander's response to a personal desire on the part of a famous minority American to address his own community in colloquial fashion at a moment of personal triumph.

The president was frowning uncertainly at an aide. He couldn't reply, of course. He'd delivered his own message of greeting earlier. Because of the time delay all he could do now, all any of them could do, was watch and listen.

Hepworth looked to MacDonald, but the engineer only shrugged. His finger hovered over the button that could halt reception, but it did not descend. An abrupt cutoff would require explanations, and that would invariably be worse than the truth.

They'd all discussed many times what could be done if this happened. The general consensus was that they'd have to ride it out and pray none of the mission members became abusive or insulting. With everyone in mission control watching the big screen, any kind of comprehensive cover-up was out of the question.

Turning, he could see the network reporters behind the soundproof glass. Many of them had been covering the space program for a good portion of their careers, but they'd never heard anything like this. More than one jaw had sagged at Swansea's comments. Behind the television people the print reporters looked torn; uncertain whether to run and file what they'd seen, or wait to see what else might develop.

"He can't tell you what's happening, freako," Preston announced from his station. "Time delay."

"Oh, riiiight." Swansea took no umbrage at the correction. He looked very happy as he turned back to the pickup.

"Say, Mistah President. We wish you was heah. How about a weather report? You want a weather report? We does some baaad-ass weather reports." He looked over his shoulder. "Hey, sweet thang. Lay some weather on the Man."

"Sweet thing?" The president whispered to the secretary of state. "Is that Major Oakley's official nickname?"

Lander copilot and chief biologist Oakley was speaking. "Well, Mr. President, sugar, it's pretty damn cold outside right now, and that's the Nome of the game." She giggled. "If you really want to know, the weather sucks and it'll be a cold day in Hellas before any of us do any sunbathing. Could ski, if we had any snow, which we don't. Lousy friggin' couple centimeters of ice." She swayed slightly as she grabbed at a pickup. It took her three tries to get ahold of it.

"Hey, Hanover, you lazy good-for-nuthin' orbitin' mothergrabber! How come they put us down on a cold slope with no snow?"

This demand was followed by an inarticulate gargle. Somewhere in the vast chamber that was Mission Control, a technician had begun to laugh. He was hurriedly shushed. Meanwhile Hanover, alone up in the orbiter, could be heard singing something about cockles and mussels, alive, alive-ho. Hanover was the possessor of three advanced degrees and a lousy singing voice.

Oakley could be seen batting the flexible pickup aside. "Lazy mothergrabber," she mumbled. "When we get back up there I'm gonna kick his ass." She started to turn and rise.

As she did so, her unzipped flightsuit parted. It was instantly apparent that the major was not wearing her regulation flightsuit undergarments. In fact, she was wearing no undergarments whatsoever. Whistles echoed through Mission Control until a fumbling Preston could organize her accoutrements.

The president stared at the screen in stony silence while upstairs, frantic technicians tried to edit a shot that had already gone out. One Secret Serviceman fought to repress a smile.

"Cool it, sweets," Preston could be overheard telling her. "We're on TV."

"Yeah. The boob tube." Oakley grinned, apparently in no wise abashed by her recent unscientific disclosures.

"It certainly seems to be a happy crew," the president finally commented.

MacDonald ventured a wan smile. "Attitude is crucial on such a long journey, Mr. President."

Swansea had slipped out of range of the visual pickup. Now he returned, puffing on a cigarette and waving lazily at the lens. "Uh, we got to sign off now, Mr. President. Work to be done and time waits for no man, *comprende*? Tell everybody back home that we loves them and that we're givin' our all for the good ol' U.S. of A., hey?" Behind him, Oakley was giggling again. Something about giving it to her instead of to the U.S. of A.

The image began to break up. Faintly, they could see Swansea offering the cigarette to Preston. "It's midmorning, man. You want a regulation toke?"

Then the screen went blank.

The silence in Mission Control was deafening. Only the instrumentation conversed, in soft buzzes and clicks. After a long pause the president turned and began whispering to MacDonald, who nodded as he listened. The president talked for quite a while. MacDonald's expression was grave.

After the chief executive and his entourage departed, the senior engineer beckoned to Hepworth.

"He didn't buy it."

"Who would, after witnessing a performance like that?" Hepworth gestured toward the big screen, now ablink with flight data and other innocuous statistics.

"He'd like to see all senior members of the team in the briefing room. Now."

"Right." Hepworth followed his friend and boss. The flight crew hadn't cooperated. Not that they were expected to, but hopes had run high. So to speak. He consoled himself with the knowledge that it could have been worse. It *had* been, in the course of the flight out from Earth, but that dialogue had arrived via containable, editable, closed channels.

Actually, he thought the crew hadn't performed too badly. Except for some of their dialogue. And Major Oakley's exposure. And Commander Swansea's closing commentary.

Well, maybe they had performed badly.

The president was waiting for them, a measure of his concern. He sat at one end of the desk and bid them join him. As the door closed behind him Hepworth could hear the distant howls of reporters struggling to get past the guards. On a trip to Tanzania, Hepworth had once heard hyenas closing in on an injured impala. The memory came back to him now, unbidden.

The president was quiet, staring down at his folded hands. Hepworth thought the room too brightly lit. Then that familiar face rose to eye each of them in turn. To Hepworth's immense discomfort, it eventually settled on him.

A small eon or two passed in continued silence before the chief executive said softly but firmly, "Well?"

The voice of Mission Control looked to Tetsugawa, then MacDonald, who nodded but offered no support. Hepworth was on his own.

"I guess you'd like an explanation, Mr. President."

"Your observation reeks of understatement, Mr. Hepworth."

So it's no longer "Warren," he reflected. Not a good sign.

He rose and began pacing. He always thought better on his feet.

"The White House science advisor may have told you, Mr. President, that the weight of accumulated research has shown us that long-term exposure to weight-lessness in Earth orbit is not in the same league, physio-logically speaking, with much greater exposure over interplanetary distances. As we discovered several years ago, the illness that develops during such extended trips is persistent, debilitating, and if allowed to continue re-sults in physical problems as well as severe psychological complications."

"I've been briefed," the president replied. "I've kept abreast of the project since before I was elected."

Hepworth nodded, grateful that he wouldn't have to explain every little detail, every nuance of the situation. Compared to his elected brethren on Capitol Hill, this president was technologically sophisticated. It just might make a difference. At the very least, it was bound to help.

"We experimented with every imaginable kind of medication, sir, to alleviate the symptoms attendant on such far-ranging expeditions. The ones we would have preferred to use were too weak, or wore off after a month or so. Anything strong enough to significantly mute the relevant debilitating condition affected indi-vidual performance to the point where it compromised mission safety.

"What we needed was medication which could be taken as necessary but would not impair the crew over a time span of several months. We also needed something that would not damage the crew's mental well-being. As you know, the problem of being cooped up in a small ship over so much time and distance was more difficult for us to deal with than the hard science and engineering.

"In the end it was Ms. Tetsugawa who came up with the right stuff. As you may know, she is our chief design engineer and is responsible for the overall performance of the spacecraft, particularly the lander. She also suffers from inoperable glaucoma in her right eye. Among the medications that have been prescribed for her over the years and that allow her to continue in her career is cannabis."

Tetsugawa gave him a welcome breather as she spoke up. "In the course of preparing for this expedition, Mr. President, we discovered that periodic use of cannabis, or rather, its principal component, ACTH, relieved the majority of symptoms associated with long-distance interplanetary travel while still allowing the crew a sufficient degree of functionality to successfully carry out their assignments. It has the added side benefit of enhancing their mental well-being.

"We considered various methods of application, from pill form to injection, but found that the, um, traditional intake methodology was the most effective. Like everything else on the ship, the *Barsoom*'s ventilation system is overbuilt and redundant. It handles the smoke without difficulty."

"That's nice to know," the president responded dryly.

"I might add, sir, that the necessary material was obtained through legal sources, principally the same pharmaceutical company which supplies glaucoma sufferers like myself. I understand that the raw material comes from wild fields in Hawaii."

The president's fingers were working. "At least it's the product of American agriculture. There was no other way?"

MacDonald shook his head. "I'm sorry, Mr. President. We had the choice of utilizing an effective method of treatment or abandoning the Mars flight until some chemical substitute could be found."

The chief executive looked thoughtful. "What about long-term risks to the astronauts?"

"Compared to the other risks involved in this expedition they were deemed minimal, sir. Their dosage is carefully monitored, though occasionally they can exceed that limit. I'm afraid they may have done so today, though in light of their extraordinary accomplishment it may be understandable. As you may know, when they announced touchdown we had our own little celebration here at Mission Control."

"Testing was rigorous, Mr. President," the diminutive Tetsugawa put in. "The United Tobacco Company was kind enough to lend us their secret laboratory facilities. They had their own reasons for participating, of course. We'd hoped to keep this aspect of the mission quiet until the crew had returned and been through debriefing. Your insistence on this transmission made that impossible."

"The American people have a right to know," the president replied. "They have a right to know what their tax dollars are paying for." Next to him, an aide put a hand to his forehead and groaned.

"I'm surprised you managed to keep it out of the papers this long," another executive assistant exclaimed.

The president rose and turned to stare at the large relief map of Mars that dominated the near wall of the briefing room.

"This is a great day for our country. Nothing must be allowed to take away from that, nor from the accomplishments of that gallant crew. In the time-honored tradition of science and exploration they have made great sacrifices and suffered much."

"Maybe not too much," one aide whispered to another. The secretary of state glared at them.

"Those are our feelings also, Mr. President." MacDonald's spirits rose. It was going to be all right.

"I am sure that once the circumstances are properly explained to them, the public will see things in an understanding light. You can handle the press, can't you, Roy?"

The White House press secretary pursed his lips. "I'll need plenty of supportive material from NASA, sir. It won't be easy. People have been conditioned for so long to think that—"

The president glanced over his shoulder. "Putting three men and a woman on Mars hasn't been easy either, Roy."

The spokesman swallowed. "No, sir."

Hepworth was breathing easier. He marveled at the president, admiring the skill of a consummate politician at work. There was no anger; only an attempt to find solutions.

"We'll provide all the backup material you need," MacDonald told the press secretary. The president turned to the chief mission engineer.

"I appreciate your striving to keep this aspect of the mission out of the public eye for as long as possible, Mr. MacDonald. At least we have the successful landing to build upon. Had this information leaked earlier it would have greatly complicated funding. You've all done your jobs well. Now it's my turn. Thanks to our idiot economic advisors I've had to justify far more unsettling surprises than this." He turned from the map.

"It will be difficult to spin the press, but we'll manage. Tabloid headlines like 'Potheads Go to Mars' will be the least of our problems. It's the conservative media that worry me." He sighed. "The Moral Majority never wanted any space missions anyway."

"We'll hold up our end, sir," insisted MacDonald.

"I know that you all will." He moved to shake hands with each of them in turn. "It's been an important day, unexpected revelations notwithstanding. Now I'm afraid I have to get back to Washington. As your Commander Swansea pointed out, time waits for no man." He headed for the door. Beyond, a phalanx of aides and Secret Service men were sweeping the corridor clean of reporters.

"One thing comes to mind right away, guys." The press secretary lingered in the doorway. "I think it would be a good idea if future Mission Control press releases at least temporarily stopped referring to it as 'The High Frontier' . . ."

EMPOWERED

Litigious. That's a big word. One I didn't encounter until I was old enough to learn that it referred to a biblical affliction brought forward to modern times. Personally, I'd rather have the plague of frogs or rain of fire. Our legal system doesn't just impoverish people: it withers them. Sometimes literally (see Ally McBeal).

You can't do anything anymore without talking to a lawyer. I prefer the Japanese system, where once you've decided to go to court you've already lost face, therefore it's better at all costs to avoid doing so. It doesn't matter anymore if you're a good guy or a bad guy—just who your lawyer is. Every month, several folks committed to long stays in the penitentiary are released because they're cleared by DNA tests, and every month O.J., who failed his, strides the golf courses of America like some grinning front man for the Grim Reaper himself.

Doing good or doing bad, it hardly matters anymore. It doesn't even matter what kind of suit you wear to work . . .

They'd used too much explosive, but Krieger didn't care. The stuff didn't do anyone any good sitting in the basement of the safe house, and the one thing he sure didn't want to do was use too little and risk blowing, as it were, the whole job. So he'd told Covey to use all he wanted, and the demolition demon had taken him at his word.

Besides, Krieger liked big explosions.

Covey had certainly orchestrated one. As he and Krieger and the rest of the gang hunched down behind the truck, the force of the blast blew out the whole back of the building. Even before the dust had begun to settle they were up and running, masks and filters enabling them to breathe where others could not while simultaneously disguising their identities. Across town Joaquin and Sievers were faking their bank break-in, drawing the majority of the police to their nonexistent robbery. By now those two should be on their way to freedom via the carefully plotted escape route through the town sewers.

Meanwhile, except for its now numbed and bleeding private security force, the special Colored Gem exhibition at Vaan Pelsen's was open to anyone who chose to saunter in without buying a ticket. Needless to say, Krieger and his team didn't have any tickets. They never paid for admission.

Some gems lay scattered like electric gumdrops among the rubble, but Covey's careful placement of the explosives the previous night had only destroyed the back third of the store. Save for shattered glass and bodies, the front portion was largely intact. One guard had somehow survived uninjured. He was quickly taken down by Pohatan, wielding his Uzi.

Not being averse to physical labor, Krieger carried his own canvas sack. While Pohatan and Covey kept watch over the street, where dazed pedestrians were stumbling about looking for assistance, Krieger and the rest of the team efficiently and methodically helped themselves to the necklaces and rings, watches and bracelets, settings and loose gems from the demolished display cases. No alarms rang in their ears. The explosion had destroyed them as well.

Anything worth obliterating, Krieger mused as he worked, was worth obliterating well.

Having rehearsed the heist for months, they worked fast, intending to be long gone before the first of the duped city police could make it back across town from the faked bank robbery. Still, Krieger urged his people to move more quickly, and to leave nothing behind. Ignoring the shocked and moaning injured among the store's staff, they roughly shoved bleeding bodies aside in their quest for the last of the regular stock and special exhibition. In less than ten minutes they had reassembled and were heading for the remnants of the back door.

Where a lanky green figure waited to confront them.

"Who the hell is that?" Pohatan gaped at the caped, emerald silhouette.

"Doesn't matter," Krieger snapped. "Waste him."

Reflexively, Pohatan brought the Uzi up and squeezed the trigger. The compact automatic crackled.

Before the bullets could strike home, a giant oak sprang full-grown from beneath the crumbled tarmac to interpose itself between the gunman and the green figure. Slugs thudded harmlessly into the thick wood.

Krieger's jaw dropped. His carefully prepared plan contained no contingencies for this kind of inexplicable interference.

The green-clad man stepped out from behind the tree. Lean muscle rippled beneath his tight suit (spandex, Krieger wondered dazedly?), and he wore a green band across his eyes.

"Give it up, Krieger. It's all over."

"Like hell." Krieger turned to his men. Already the distant complaint of sirens could be heard approaching rapidly from the north. "Get him!"

Pohatan threw his massive bulk at the figure, only to run headlong into a dense grove of new-sprung spruce that hadn't been there when he'd started his charge. Brownlee succeeded in reaching him, whereupon the figure's arms seemed to metamorphose into long vines. They wrapped around the startled assailant, lifted him effortlessly off the pavement, and flung him clear over the ruined store into the street beyond.

While the rest of his team rushed the floral fighter Krieger raced for the truck, the sackful of jewelry bouncing against his back. A glance rearward showed that the rest of his gang were having no better luck than their already incapacitated colleagues.

Krieger jammed the key into the ignition and fired up the big engine, slamming the truck into drive. Turning the rig, he accelerated as he bored down on the green shape, who had just disposed of the last of Krieger's associates. There would be no time for the green stranger to get out of the way, Krieger saw. He grinned broadly. He liked running people over almost as much as he liked big explosions.

Giant roots erupted from the ground immediately in front of the truck. Wide-eyed, the gang boss tried to swerve. The roots twisted and grabbed at the truck, coiling around both axles and lifting it off the ground. As the solemn-faced green man looked on, they heaved the vehicle sideways. It smashed into a pair of parked cars, rolled over, and came to rest among the tables of an outdoor restaurant whose patrons had fortunately run inside and remained there when Covey's explosives had first gone off.

The first patrol car to arrive in the parking lot behind the smoking ruins of the jewelry store disgorged a pair of stunned officers, who gratefully took delivery of the still alive (but badly damaged) Krieger and the rest of

his gang. As the cops looked on, a brace of flexible willows emerged from the earth to lightly grasp the green
figure. Bending their crowns to the ground, they aimed
him skyward.

"Wait a minute!" yelled one of the officers. "Who are
you? *What* are you?"

"Call me 'Earth Spirit,' " the green man intoned. "I
was once one of you, one of the teeming masses. Now,
because of an industrial accident, I'm somewhat more,
and this is what I intend to do with my newfound
powers. Spread the word among lawbreakers and pol-
luters. Let them know that no matter where they try to
hide, they are safe no more!"

With that the willows sprang forward with tremen-
dous velocity, sending the green man soaring out of sight.
No doubt another tree or bush was waiting somewhere
to catch him and relay him on his way. The officers exchanged a glance, then positioned themselves to watch
over the battered gang until backup and medics could
arrive.

Meanwhile, they had plenty to talk about.

"You know, you're a very difficult person to locate."

"How did you find me?" Earth Spirit stepped back
into the cave. "And how did you get past all the thorn
bushes and poison ivy I caused to spring forth to dis-
courage intruders?"

The small, heavyset man set himself down in a high-
backed chair that was growing right out of the cave
floor. He mopped at his sweat-streaked brow with a
monogrammed handkerchief. "Nice place you got up
here. Spacious, but a little dark for my taste." He smiled
apologetically. "I'm mildly claustrophobic."

"And hugely puzzling," Earth Spirit declared. "You
haven't answered my questions."

"I put out the word quietly. Announced a reward for information. Local farmer noticed a lot of sudden growth up on this mountaintop and got in touch with a regional contact of mine. At that point I decided that a personal visit was in order. May I call you 'Earth'? It's a lot easier, I prefer to be on a first-name basis with people, and besides, the other half's copyrighted."

"If it will make you feel more at ease." The green one settled himself into a chair opposite. A compliant vine handed him a drink.

"As for the thorns and the ivy, as you can see, I dressed accordingly. Willis and Geiger. I'm not used to this kind of gear. Silk three-pieces are more to my taste."

"You're from the government," Earth Spirit surmised.

"Not at all, though I'm sure they'll get here sooner or later. My name is Lemuel French. I'm a lawyer."

The green-clad man frowned. "What would I need with a lawyer, Mr. French?"

The smaller man stared at him in disbelief. "You really don't know? Well, maybe not. Ever since the Vaan Pelsen debacle you've kept pretty quiet, except for vine-wrapping the occasional mugger."

Earth Spirit smiled. "My actions seem to have had a deterrent effect on local crime."

"That they have. It's one of the problems you're going to have to deal with."

"Problems?" The vine held the drink steady.

"You're really out of touch up here on this mountaintop, aren't you? No paper, no cable, no broadband."

"I prefer the company of the natural world," the green man replied stiffly.

"You want to live like a granola that's fine with me, but your activities impinge on the real world. That's why I sought you out. See, I believe in what you're doing and I want to help." He smiled broadly. "For a fee, of course. We really need to discuss your putting my firm on retainer."

"I told you, I have no need of a lawyer."

"So you said." French popped the polished brass clasp on an elegant eelskin briefcase and removed a thick sheaf of papers. "These are copies. You'll be served as soon as they can find you. That gives us some time."

Earth Spirit eyed the papers in spite of himself. "What is all that?"

"Let's see. Where to start?" French shuffled the sheaf as smoothly as a Vegas dealer handling cards. "The first suit is from Vaan Pelsen, Inc."

"Vaan Pelsen? Why would they want to sue me? I saved their merchandise."

"But a lot of it was damaged in the gang's escape attempt. Fancy goldwork, that sort of thing."

"They wouldn't have it to fix if I hadn't stepped in."

"I agree completely, and I'm sure the court will take that into account." French had his reading glasses on now. "Here's another: 'Mildred Fox, plaintiff for Sissy and Michael Fox, juvenile principals.' "

The green man looked baffled. "I've never heard of these people."

"They were dining in the restaurant where you threw Mr. Krieger and his stolen truck. Ms. Mildred Fox is the mother of the two named children. She claims that her kids suffered severe emotional distress from nearly being struck by the escape vehicle, and that among other things they now refuse to ride in the family minivan, thus forcing Ms. Fox, a working mother, to sell it at a loss and buy an ordinary car. Claimant further deposes that her children now experience uncontrollable fits at the sight of any large delivery vehicle."

"This—this is ridiculous!" Earth Spirit sputtered.

"I heartily concur, and we'll make Ms. Fox and her

well-coached little schemers look that way in court." As if by magic more papers appeared.

"Is there much of this?" Earth Spirit regarded the phone book–sized pile with growing trepidation.

"Depends on your definition of *much*. A Mr. Colin Hvarty is suing you for medical expenses pursuant to a broken leg and sprained back, plus possible concussion."

"I never broke anybody's leg, not even one of the robbers'!" the green-clad man protested.

French looked up and smiled regretfully. "Apparently Mr. Hvarty was standing in the street opposite Vaan Pelsen's when he was struck by a flying crook. Did you happen, in the course of your work, to perhaps fling one or more of the miscreants in that direction?"

"I didn't mean to hit anybody."

"Well, you did." French adjusted his glasses. "We'll have to see about getting you some liability insurance, though after the business at Vaan Pelsen's you'd better be prepared to deal with an outrageous monthly premium."

"Superheroes don't need liability insurance."

French peered over the top of his glasses. "Is that so? You want to perform good deeds in this country, you'd better make sure you're fully covered before you start.

"The owner of the parking lot behind Pelsen's has presented a bill for the following: to wit, expenses directly related to removing a large oak tree and a number of smaller growths from his property, and repaving the damaged area. The owner of the restaurant where Ms. Fox and her offspring suffered their purported trauma is suing for damage to eight tables and chairs, shade umbrellas, decorative railing, landscaping, and assorted crockery, glassware, and utensils.

"A Mr. Loemann and a Mr. Kelly are suing for damage to their respective vehicles. Those are the two cars you unfortunately hit with the getaway truck. Or rather, their insurance companies are suing you. A local nature organization has filed a writ to prevent you from utilizing any vegetation of any species whatsoever in your crime-fighting activities until you can present them with an acceptable environmental impact report demonstrating beyond reasonable doubt that your work does not involve the use of dangerous chemicals, stimulants, or scientifically unapproved bioengineering. The regional office of the Food and Drug Administration wants to talk to you about essentially the same thing."

"Go on." Earth Spirit's expression was grim.

"Thank you. The municipal police have a warrant out for your arrest for interfering with police activities. I don't think we have to worry about this one. They don't want to jail you; just co-opt you."

"I don't work for anybody. I'm independent."

"Then you're going to be butting heads with the local law enforcement bureaucracy from now till doomsday. Bureaucrats don't like outsiders poaching their turf. They're afraid you might apply for and get a government grant intended for them."

"But I'm helping them in their work, fighting evildoers."

"You're not going to have enough time to fight the local school bully. See these?" French waved another entire sheaf of papers. "Subpoenas. Calling you as a witness in the Vaan Pelsen case. Each robber has requested and been granted an independent trial, so you'll have to give testimony in all of them. Also, at least two members of Vaan Pelsen's gang are suing you, including Krieger. They claim that since you're not a member of any recognized law enforcement department, you had no right to interfere, and that they've suffered irreparable mental and physical damage as a result of your unauthorized activities."

"I was making a citizen's arrest."

"They claim use of excessive force. Among other things."

"That's outrageous! They had explosives and automatic weapons."

"Maybe we can cut a deal. I'll speak to their people."

The green man's chest expanded proudly. "I don't have to belong to an official organization. I represent the Earth."

"Not in this county you don't. And don't go on boasting that you're some kind of foreigner. This is a conservative community." He murmured half to himself. "We can use temporary insanity in at least half these cases, if we have to. I mean, just look at you."

Earth Spirit blinked down at himself. "What's wrong with me?"

"Grown man living alone in a cave atop a mountain? Talking to plants? Running around in green spandex?"

"It's not spandex," Earth Spirit protested, a mite defensively.

"Whatever. So long as there's no brand-name infringement involved." French sighed tiredly. "Then there's the government."

"What about the government?" Earth Spirit said darkly. "I'm trying to help them."

"Why do you think the local police bureaucracy is so afraid of you? If some superhero starts dropping out of the sky on local criminals and the crime rate falls to zero, what do you think happens to their budget? Not to mention their jobs. They're terrified you'll stick around.

"As to helping the government, the spin on the street is good, but they're wary. Nobody knows which party you belong to."

"I belong to no party. I belong to—"

"The Earth—yeah, yeah, you told me, already. Even

worse. A third-party iconoclast. They want to know your name."

"I am Earth Spirit!"

"Right, sure, okay." French made pacifying gestures. "But they can't find anybody named 'Earth Spirit' anywhere. You're not on the tax rolls, so they want to know if you've filed any returns. You may be 'of the Earth,' but if you want to practice your profession in the U.S. you'd better be able to prove that you're a citizen. Or else have, you should pardon me, a green card. Do you even have a Social Security number?"

Earth Spirit looked away, clearly uneasy. "If I give up that kind of information I'll have to reveal my true identity. I can't do that. Criminals could threaten me and my work through family and friends."

"There's always the witness protection program, but I don't think it would work very well for superheroes. Eventually you'd forget yourself, make a redwood sprout in a mall or something."

"This is all that Krieger's fault," Earth Spirit growled.

"Could be. You can't do anything about him, though. He's had a restraining order put out against you. You can't go near him."

"Why would I want to go near him? He's in jail, where his kind belong."

"Are you kidding? His lawyers had him out of the hospital and back on the street in forty-eight hours. Bail."

Earth Spirit rubbed at his forehead, above the mask. "Is there much more of this?"

"Cheer up. It's not all bad news." French inspected fresh paper. "Mattel wants to start a line of 'Earth Spirit' toys. Two major fashion houses want to license your costume as the basis for new lines of men's clothing. Oprah, Jay, Conan, Jerry, and 'Blind Date'—not to mention CNN and the networks—all want you for interviews.

Time and *Newsweek* are preparing features—you can't buy that kind of publicity. CAA and William Morris are vying to represent you on the Coast, and each claims to have multipicture deals already cut and waiting for your signature. Personally I'd go with CAA. They already have De Niro committed to play Krieger.

"There are book offers all over the place, and I think that with your okay I can get this incipient Kitty Kelly exposé nipped in the bud. We'll also make arrangements to protect you from the people at 'Hard Copy,' 'Inside Edition,' and 'Geraldo,' though even I can't do much about the tabloids. Have you seen the *Enquirer* or the *Star* this week? No, of course you haven't."

Earth Spirit looked up. "That's the good news?"

"Impressive, isn't it? You stand to make millions. Of course, there's the matter of my firm's fee, but I'm sure we can come to an equitable arrangement. Oh, one other thing."

"I can't imagine."

"The FAA wants you to cease and desist all this flying about. They're worried about your influence on air traffic patterns. Better you should take a cab."

"To fight crime?"

"Why not? The cabbies in this state can get around pretty good."

"What about the government? Why should I have to worry about tax returns? I have no income."

"You're going to. You might as well cash the checks as they come in, because nobody'll believe you don't have any income anyway. It's un-American. Don't worry. The accountancy firm that's associated with us will make it effortless for you. And you can use the leftover money to fight crime in whatever way you wish. If there is any."

"Crime?" Earth Spirit murmured uncertainly.

"No. Leftover money."

The green one rose dynamically from his chair and began to pace, fingers flexing like questing stems behind his back. "All I wanted was to help people and battle the forces of evil."

"And you can, you can," French insisted soothingly. "It's just a question of going about it in a careful, intelligent, sensible way—and making sure all the proper forms are filled out and filed beforehand."

Earth Spirit halted abruptly, and French flinched. After all, the fellow did have superpowers—and was doubtless a few cards short of a full deck to boot. That bizarre outfit . . .

"All right," the verdant one responded finally. "I'll hire your firm. On a per-case contingency basis. Get me clear of this Vaan Pelsen business, and then we'll see."

"That's fair enough." French rose and they shook hands.

"Would you like me to have my friends help you down the mountain?" Earth Spirit offered in parting. "It's kind of a rough hike."

"Tell me about it," French grumbled. "I'll walk, thanks. Even though I think I shook the couple of paparazzi who followed me from the city, you'll be safer if I don't draw attention to myself. You needn't apologize for your naivete. It'll be much easier now that I know you're not some nut and that you understand what it means to have to work within the system."

Earth Spirit waved. "Oh I do, Mr. French, I do. Now."

Six months later the first deposition arrived on Tonga, advance scout of an irresistible media army, but by that time Earth Spirit had already moved on once again, to a land where lawyers were less numerous still.

Passport problems were already beginning to dog him,

though, and in Singapore he barely escaped having his suit and mask garnished for nonpayment of one claim. He made his escape, though, always keeping one step ahead of the media. No matter what else happened, one thing he had resolved.

There was no way they were going to tree him.

THE KISS

When this was submitted to the redoubtable Jane Yolen for an anthology she was editing, she rejected it, referring to it as a horrible little story. Despite the turndown, I took that as high praise for a low tale. Remember what I said earlier about not doing the obvious? About trying to make old ideas contemporary? That doesn't necessarily mean making them nice.

There are lots of things in this world that aren't nice. Why should fantasy be any different? This story is for all the women out there who have kissed frogs—and had them turn out to be something other than a prince.

Crisp small memories of autumn, a few leaves clung to the naked branches of the trees, dry and brown as stale oats. Whiteness blanketed the park, silent snow dancing in tiny pinwheels across the shoveled walkways like tenebrous toys exhaled from some spectral workshop. Tapered icicles parasitized the bright, hard metal of a water fountain, bearding chrome. Over everything the first week of January lay, pregnant with chill.

Jenny blinked away the snowflakes that swirled about her like stoned white mosquitoes as she sighted a path through the open places, taking the shortcut home from work and disdaining the bus stop immediately outside

the office. The short walk would allow her to avoid
having to make a connection in a less-congenial section
of town. After eight hours in the limpid atmosphere of
the sterile cavern in which she worked, the air outside
was rejuvenating to her lungs as well as her legs.

This morning the weather pundits had proclaimed
that the storm had arrived, but it had taunted them by
stalling just outside the metroplex, teasing the inner city
with wild gusts and cold laughter. Just for me, she
thought. Just to save me fifteen minutes I don't have to
spend now waiting in a bus shelter rank with the scent of
slept-upon newspapers and clotted urine. Grateful for
the respite, she lengthened her stride, not wanting to
miss the cross-town bus. Bucking the wind, trifles of ice
as beautiful as they were capricious tickled her rosy, exposed cheeks, only to be turned to simulacra of tears as
they were instantly metamorphosed by the bundled fur-
nace of her body.

A little louder the squall sang, urgently warning. She
shielded her eyes as she searched for the pedestrian
bridge that spanned the central pond, blinking against
the bite of the incoming blizzard. There it was; a russet
arch of brick and mortar spanning the gray, half-frozen
water, solid and familiar. Careful there on the tricky rise
lest she slip in her slick, shiny black boots, whose tops
were feathered with damp fake fur.

She had only just started across when she heard the
soft croaking.

Why she paused she never knew, but pause she did, to
shove snow from the railing with a gloved hand as she
turned to peer over the side. Nothing to be seen below
but liquid as hard and gray as old slate shingles. Frowning, she started to turn, to continue on her way, when the
rough noise came again.

She hesitated. There was nothing nearby save snow

and trees stark as tombstones, looking like brown lightning rammed into the earth. Uncertainly, she retraced her steps from bridge to pond's edge, her boots leaving behind in the snow deep, oval echoes of her passing.

A small shape crouched on an exposed, ribbed slab of weathered granite that protruded out of the slushy surface. Curious, she bent, then crouched closer still.

"Why you poor thing, what are you doing out this time of year? You're shivering!"

Ordinarily she would have walked on, would have ignored the small, insignificant blob of drab olive-hued flesh. The sticky, moist mass, resembling a sock soaked in cold phlegm, repulsed her. But she had on gloves thick with plastic and fleece, fashionable artificial skins that would keep her fingers inviolate. She plucked the baseball-sized creature from its cold, hard perch and cradled it in one palm, sheltering it from the wind with the other.

Bulbous eyes visceral with anger rose to meet her own and so startled her she almost dropped it. After that, the voice itself was almost anticlimactic.

"I am a prince, real and true. If you will but kiss me I will whole again become."

Snow flecked her cheeks, sought crevices to chill within her layers of protective clothing, pinked her cheeks and nose.

Looking around, she saw that she was still alone. Sensible citizens had gone to cover. Twilight served notice on the approaching storm. Perhaps, she thought, she was not quite alone.

This is ridiculous, she told herself. Ridiculous and absurd!

Within her cupped, sheltering fingers the amphibious lump lurched clumsily forward. "A single kiss and you will see the reality that is me."

Kiss that blob of mucousy flesh? Press her own sensitive lips against that thin blubbery slit of a mouth? Still, she had on heavy lipstick, a wind-prophylactic that had been applied prior to leaving the office. What better time and place than here and now, isolated and unobserved, to indulge just once in a brief, lunatic folly?

Suppressing the rationality that normally mapped her waking hours, she leaned impulsively forward and touched her lips to the flabby face, withdrawing almost immediately and wrinkling her mouth. Enough of a witless winter's dream! If she didn't hurry she was going to miss her bus. Not ungently, she returned the creature to its rock and turned to leave.

In the center of the bridge, at the apex of its arch, a twinkling made her turn—a tempest glow silhouetting a presence that was now solid where a moment before had been nothing. Flakes of black silver, tarnished by time and circumstance, shaped a massive figure behind her. It had arms and legs, and it moved with purpose in her direction, clad in thick coat and pants, heavy shoes laced with dead snakes, and a wide-brimmed hat that shadowed the downturned face.

Her mouth opened when she saw the knife, long and lean as its master. Edge keener than her deepest fears, blade brighter than the luminant snow that fell anxiously now as if embarrassed at its delay, it rose toward her like a live, twisting, animate being. A coldness that was not of isobars and pressure fronts congealed within her gut, a ball of frozen jelly heavy as hopelessness.

Thick and gnarled and powerful, his hands were upon her, freezing her as effectively as if she'd been overrun by and entombed in a glacier. The knife described a Gothic arc, and blood bright as pomegranate juice shocked the pristine snowbank in which the two of them stood locked in unholy embrace. She blinked and expelled a querulous trauma.

"Why . . . ?"

His gaze and expression were as one, as cold-clammy and pigmentless as the greasy flesh of a cave salamander wrenched up suddenly from the abyss and left to shrivel in the sun.

"Someone of your age and experience should know by now," the voice croaked. "Before you embrace it, make sure you know what kind of prince you're kissing."

Later, when he was done and fresh snow tenderly went about blotting up the crimson bloom, he abandoned the park and headed purposefully deeper into the city, knowing there would be other princesses. Princesses who would also be searching for him. Real and true.

THE IMPOSSIBLE PLACE

The first World Science Fiction Convention I ever attended was in Berkeley, California, in 1968. I was a senior at UCLA and looking forward to meeting, actually meeting, some of the writers whose stories I had grown up reading. My first day, I climbed onto one of the minibuses that were used to shuttle fans from the several convention hotels to the main venue, only to find myself sitting next to Fritz Leiber.

Now, if you've never seen a picture of Fritz Leiber, he was one of the few writers of SF who actually looked the part. His father was a well-known actor (viz the chief inquisitor in The Hunchback of Notre Dame, 1939), and Fritz had inherited his father's looks. I recall mumbling something inconsequential, to which Mr. Leiber replied pleasantly enough, whereupon I did my level best to squeeze down into the crack between the cushion and the back of the seat.

I was later astonished to discover that these giants of the genre, whom I had always envisioned climbing unscalable mountains and hacking their way through impenetrable jungles, rarely went anywhere or did any such thing, with but few exceptions. I was immensely disappointed, because all I had ever dreamed of was visiting such impossible-to-get-to places like my hero, Sir

Richard Francis Burton. Oddly enough, over the past third of a century or so, I've actually been able to do so.

This story is about one such real impossible place. To get there, fly to the Kunene River, which forms the border between Namibia and Angola, hop in your Land Rover, head south—and keep your eyes peeled.

———————

"But I could *swear* I heard singing last night!"

Matthew Ovatango scratched the place on his forehead where his short, tightly kinked hair began as he gazed out across the night-swept vastness of Kaokoland. They had camped in the shadow of a smooth hillock of gray granite that very much resembled a gigantic ball of elephant dung. Beyond the battered but indestructible Land Rover lay the immense reaches of the Hartmann Valley. Sere yellow grass carpeted the endless plain. Not far to the west, the southern Atlantic Ocean gnawed remorselessly at the lonely sands of the Skeleton Coast.

The nearest town, if such it could be called, was Opuwo, a two-hundred-kilometer drive to the east over a barely detectable dirt track. In these barren reaches survived few trees, and fewer people. Howard had come, deliberately and with photography aforethought, to one of the most godforsaken corners of the Earth in search of solitude and marketable photos. Thus far the latter consisted entirely of landscapes. No one lived in this lonely corner of Namibia except a few wandering Himba and their cattle.

So how could he have heard singing in the chill and perfect night?

"Perhaps it was a pied crow." His guide stirred the fading fire with a stick. The bark of Bushman's candle collected earlier in the day flared briefly at the fringes, the waxy exoskeleton of that remarkable plant perfuming the night air as it burned.

Rising, Howard turned to gaze into the darkness. Half a moon transformed the nearby inselberg, a mountain of sculpted granite boulders like the one beneath which they were camped, into a fantastic imaginary fortress. It reminded him of the massive walls of Sacsahuaman, the plundered Inca fortress above Cuzco, in Peru.

But this was only a pile of rocks. The people who had first inhabited this land had raised up nothing more elaborate than crude, temporary huts of shattered rock and reed, of straw and mud and cow dung.

He was turning back to the fire when he heard it again.

This time he whirled sharply and took a couple of quick steps away from the crackling blaze. "Don't tell me you didn't hear that! Your ears are sharper than mine, Matthew."

The guide eyed him appraisingly. "A pied crow, Mr. Howard, sir. If you trust my ears, then trust my words."

The photographer strained to hear more. "That cry wasn't like any crow call I've ever heard."

"And the pied crow most likely isn't like any crow you've ever seen, either, sir." Patiently the guide stirred the pulsing embers, cajoling them to renewed life. "You sit yourself down and get warm, sir. Tomorrow we will drive down toward the Hoarusib and look for the desert elephants."

Howard let his glance linger a moment longer on a landscape that seemed to fade away into the stars. Then he disappeared into the tent. Moments later he reemerged with electric torch, canteen, and camera.

Ovatango's lips tightened in the soft glow from the fire. "You shouldn't leave camp, sir. Especially at night. Easy to get lost here."

"I know what I'm doing, Matthew." Howard slung

the camera strap over his neck, hooked the canteen to his belt. "I've done plenty of night photography in strange places, just last month in Etosha. I can always follow the fire back to camp. Get some rest yourself. You're going to be doing a lot of driving tomorrow."

"This isn't Etosha, sir. This is the Skeleton Coast. Etosha is civilized country compared to here. There is a reason for its name, you know. Just last year two men illegally prospecting for diamonds on the Coast got lost. They had been here before, they 'knew' the country, and they were well equipped. A private plane spotted their Land Rover, and a government patrol came out to look for them.

"They had become lost in the fog and driven around in circles. When their radio didn't work they tried to walk out. It took two weeks to find the bodies. The jackals and hyenas had been at them."

"Don't worry about me." Howard started off in the direction of the looming inselberg. "I'm not afraid of hyenas." He grinned. "Maybe I'll catch the sunrise from the top of the rocks. I like being on my own, Matthew."

The guide didn't smile back. "No one comes to this place who doesn't, sir. Please be careful. You are my responsibility. I am not worried about you meeting a hyena. But what if you step on a horned adder or a dancing white lady?"

Howard kept his eyes on the circle of ground illuminated by the flashlight. "I won't be climbing any dunes, Matthew. This is all rock and gravel here. And a dancing white lady," he added, speaking of the ghostly white tarantula of the Namib sands, "would be more frightened of me than I of it."

The fire didn't shrink behind him so much as it was swallowed up. The immense dark stones that he soon found himself scrambling among all looked exactly alike, sleek and rounded as if polished in some titanic gem tumbler. There were no trees, of course, not even a salt bush. Only by the sand rivers could trees find enough subterranean water with which to sustain themselves.

The shifty weight of his canteen was a reassuring presence on his hip. The damp chill of night would give way to the rising heat of early morning. He found himself slowing, the guide's words shadowing his thoughts. What if the fog did advance this far inland tonight? The famous mists of the Namib could instantly reduce visibility to zero. No fire could light a way through it back to camp. Furthermore, there was no water to be found in this country for a hundred kilometers in any direction, from the Kunene River up on the Angolan border to Cape Frio camp—and maybe not water there, either.

But the night was crystal clear, the stars devoid of flicker, and though his athletic years were behind him, he felt confident he could outjog an advancing fog, even on unfamiliar terrain.

It was the lack of landmarks that gave pause. Even in broad daylight it was easy to get disoriented out here. Many did, and many died. He dug in his pocket and relaxed a little. It was unfair of him not to have shown Ovatango the luminous compass, but it would be amusing to see the guide's face when he strode confidently back into camp.

He was ascending now, using the pale starlight to find his way. Here he had to be extra careful. A deceptively gentle, smoothly weathered ascent could terminate abruptly in a sheer drop of a hundred meters or more. Sand whispered under his hiking shoes, each step a small voice telling him to shush, shush, as if the land itself were admonishing him to respect the unparalleled silence and solitude.

He thought he must be nearing the summit when

moonlight suddenly broke through the rocks off to his left. There was an opening there, and he turned toward it. Over a black granitic curve that bowed up into the sky like a black clavicle he trod, then down, down into a frozen stream of sand, and up once again.

Then he stopped, his lips parting in wonder. It was not a gap, a break in the rocks he'd come upon, but an arch. An absolutely lunatic geological phenomenon.

He'd seen many natural arches before, and photographed them. In the American Southwest, in Australia, in Morocco. Always they were fashioned of sandstone, the rock easily eroded through by the wind. But he was not looking at sandstone now. He stood within a garden of solid, impermeable granite.

The Namib was the oldest desert in the world, and the wind here had had eons in which to work. No more than seven or eight feet high at its maximum, the opening in the rock was longer than a football field, tapering in height to mere inches at either end. The bridge of rock itself was fifty or sixty feet thick and at least as broad, a sleek-flanked rope of black stone flung by the hand of a perverse geology across the crest of a low hill. The result was a long window in which a man could stand with his head scraping the rock ceiling while gazing out across an endless flat valley. Moonlight bathed the horizonless reaches in pale silver.

His fingers throbbed from gripping the camera too tightly. He let it hang from the sturdy strap and rest against his chest. There was no way he could capture the phenomenon spread out before him at night. Photography would have to wait for daylight, and a wide-angle lens. Very wide.

Then he heard the singing again, and knew despite Ovatango's disclaimers that it did not arise from the throat of any crow that had ever lived.

Crouching without knowing why, he advanced toward the upper end of the fantastic arch. As he ascended the slight slope, a figure strode unexpectedly into view. He froze, watching and listening. So mesmerizing was the unexpected sight that not once did he think of his camera. For Howard, this was unprecedented.

The woman was short, no more than five feet tall, and naked save for a modest strip of cloth that encircled her loins. Her skin was not black, but a very beige or dried-apricot color. Her black hair was cut short in a neat crewcut, and her eyes were almond-shaped. Though she looked almost Mongolian, he knew she was not. He had seen her people before, though more often in the southern part of the country.

She had a beautiful voice, though he recognized neither her words nor the language from which they sprang.

Arms outstretched, she was half singing, half chanting. At first he thought she was singing to the moon, but she was too far beneath the arch for that indolent disc to be visible from where she stood. She had to be singing to the rock itself. Or to something on the rock.

The song stopped, the delicate hands lowered, and suddenly she was looking straight at him. She made no move to cover her nudity, nor did she seem in the least afraid of him. This too was typical of her people, who from his brief acquaintance he knew to be bold and confident.

"Hello, big darling. You have found me out, so you might as well come up here." Her English was rich and supple, as if she were pronouncing every vowel with her whole throat.

He hesitated, wondered why he was hesitating, and then resolutely climbed up to stand beside her. She had taken a seat on the curved floor of the arch. Feeling it was the polite thing to do, he crossed his legs and sat down next to her. Despite her seminudity she gazed back at him openly, frankly. The smooth skin of her breasts hovered beneath the slim arms she rested on her knees, their sleek curves mimicking that of the rock itself.

"I heard you singing. My guide didn't want me to come."

"But you are a man who does not like to be told what he can and cannot do. I like that."

He coughed gently, the cold invading his throat. "You're very direct."

"It is a characteristic of my people."

"You're San?"

"No. Khoikhoi, or as most people say today, Nama. The Bushmen-San are very close to us." For the first time since he'd sat down, her eyes left him, to question the darkness from which he'd emerged. "Your guide is not Nama."

"No. Herero."

"Ah. That explains it. A Nama guide would not have brought you anywhere near here. This place is sacred to the Khoikhoi. Only a very few know of it. My grandfather was one who did. Also," she added with a startlingly white smile, "the Herero and the Nama do not get along. It goes back a long ways, and has a lot to do with cattle."

He smiled back. "Trouble in Africa often does."

"You are an interesting man, Mr. . . . ?"

"Howard. Howard Cooperman. My friends call me Howie."

"Howie is too weak a name for this place. I will call you Howard."

"Your English is very good. Surely you don't live around here?"

"No one does. Only memories live in this place. I am

an accountant for the First National Bank of Windhoek." She waved a hand toward the southeast. "That way."

"I know. Hundreds of miles of nothingness. That's why I'm here. There aren't many places left in the world where you can find real nothingness."

They were both quiet for a while then, sharing the kind of total silence Howard had only experienced before inside a cave. Not a bird called, not an insect chirped, not the muted roar of a distant aircraft disturbed the upper atmosphere. Civilization of any sort was very far away.

"You want to know what I'm doing here, dressed like this. Or rather, undressed like this, singing on a rock in the middle of the night. But you're too polite to ask." She traced an outline on the bare rock. "I am singing praise songs. The old songs, which my grandfather taught me."

"It was very beautiful," he told her. "You sing to the rock?"

"No." She giggled softly, and her laughter was like water in the desert. "Why sing to a rock? Look above you."

Tilting back his head, he brought the beam of the electric torch up—and his breath momentarily failed him.

The underside of the arch was completely covered in the most exquisite primitive paintings he'd ever seen. Both the ancient Bushmen and their cousins the Khoikhoi had left such paintings all over Namibia and Botswana, planting pigment at sacred places throughout the Kalahari and Namib Deserts. Only weeks ago he'd spent several days photographing the most famous of them at Twyfelfontein.

But this was grander, much grander. Everything had been executed on an overpowering scale. Their outlines

incised into the rock and then filled with color, hundreds
of animals paraded across a canvas of a million tons of
flying granite. Pacing the great herds on either side were
the famously fluid stick figures of the ancient hunter-
gathers who had lived side by side among them.

The animals and people and paintings dated from a
time long ago when this part of southwest Africa was
much wetter and lusher, when the people called the
Strandlopers hunted oryx and springbok and impala on
the beach, and rivers like the Secomib and Nadas still
reached the sea. Ten thousand and more years ago, when
the game and the grass had covered the land as far as the
eye could see. Before the Namib took over this part of
the continent and the South African army slaughtered
what animals remained.

"No one's ever photographed this before." He stood
awestruck by the skill and accomplishments of the ancient painters. "I know: I would have seen pictures." Despite the chill, his fingers were moist against the hard
body of the camera.

"No. You can be the first. Or—you can help me."

He blinked and turned back to her, the light flashing in
her onyx eyes and making her turn away sharply.

"Sorry." He lowered the beam and then, on impulse,
clicked it off.

"Thank you." In the shade of the arch she was a
shadow herself now. "I need a man."

"You really *are* direct."

The bubbling laughter echoed again. "Not like that,
though I wouldn't refuse you. I need a man to dance for
me. It has to be a man. The women sing the praises. The
men dance."

"I don't understand, but if you need a man to dance
for you, why not one of your own people?"

She leaned toward him. "Because they are all afraid."

The cold of the Namib night jumped suddenly closer, like a dancing white lady spider on the hunt.

"What are they afraid of?"

"They have been told that the old ways are wrong and that they must all become modern. I am modern; I have a good education and a modern job, but I also had a grandfather. He brought me to this place when I was a little girl, and showed me the dances, and because of him I was never afraid. My grandmother taught me the songs.

"When I was old enough I started coming here as soon as I could get away. First from Gibeon, where I was born, then from Keetmanshoop where I went to school, and now from Windhoek, where I work. Sometimes a boy or a man would come with me, but they wanted to dance a different dance. Sometimes I danced with them, sometimes not." Eagerness infused her voice.

"You come from a far-off land. You have no fears of the old ways, no prejudices. You heard the singing and came of your own free will. I think you are special, Howard. Special to this place and special to me. If I sing, will you dance?"

He shook his head. This was too bizarre. But if he could get her to pose for him in the morning, she would make a magnificent image, framed in the impossible arch with the great valley stretching out before her.

"I'm not much of a dancer, Ms. . . . ?"

She didn't stand so much as flow to her feet. "I am Anna Witbooi. My grandfather was the greatest of the Khoikhoi elders, a direct descendant of Heitsi Eibib, who was the first of our people. I will sing the true praise songs and you will dance. I can show you the steps, but I cannot dance them myself. The women sing; the men dance.

"First you must take off your clothes."

It seemed crass to be self-conscious in so pure a setting. He folded his clothes and laid them in a neat pile—all but his briefs, which she told him he could retain. It was cold, and he hoped he wouldn't start shivering. The damp chill didn't seem to bother her at all.

"Like this." Standing so close he could feel the warmth of her, she started to dance.

The movements were simple and not impossibly precise. More of a rhythmic stamping and turning than anything else. All he had to do was keep time to the chanting.

"All right," he finally told her. "I'll give it a try. Just don't expect too much. But I want something in return. Tomorrow, when there's light, I want to take some pictures of you."

"Yes." She was teasing him. "Tomorrow you can take pictures of me."

"Just one question. Why do you do this, come out here year after year, to sing to a bunch of old paintings?"

"Because the praise songs need to be sung. Because of tales my grandfather told to me. Because I know in my heart that there can be nothing to fear from a place as breathtaking as this."

Having said that, she began to sing.

At first he felt silly, prancing about in the altogether, but the feeling passed quickly. There was no one here to laugh at him or point accusingly. The steps felt natural, and he entered into the unbounded spirit of the moment with increasing enthusiasm. Dancing pushed back the damp night and warmed his body. He began throwing his arms up and out, careful not to scrape his fingertips against the unforgiving ceiling.

He hoped he was doing well, but he couldn't tell. Anna

had her eyes half closed and her own arms outstretched as he'd first seen her. Her voice echoed and quivered with words so ancient they had never been written down. They bounced off the smooth rock as he twisted and twirled, his feet rising and falling, the bare soles only occasionally smarting from the isolated pebble that marred the otherwise perfectly smooth floor of the majestic gash in the mountain.

A gleam caught his eye that did not come from his torch. Just a little to the left of his head, a family of giraffe etched in eternal stone and tinted white and red was glowing with a ghostly light all its own.

"Don't stop," she whispered urgently, somehow working the admonition into the singsong of the chant.

He missed a step but managed to recover. The glow within the rock was the palest of efflorescences. Head tilted back, he strained on tiptoes until his face was only inches from the ancient painting. He couldn't tell if the light was emanating from the primordial pigment or the granite beneath.

"Faster!" she hissed at him, snapping him out of his awed stupor.

His knees lifted with her voice. Muscles long disused strained to comply. He found himself whirling with an abandon that verged on madness, the self-control of a lifetime fled, as if he no longer cared for anything save keeping step and time to her singing. The light in his eyes was internal, but that which had begun to illuminate the entire underside of the arch pulsed within the living rock itself as each painting, each patiently rendered etching, began to throb with the glow of a dozen candles.

Bushmen's candles.

It was a toss-up as to whether his legs or his balance would give out first. It turned out to be his legs. Calves aching, thighs trembling, he settled slowly down onto the smooth rock like a tin top winding down. The pure air refreshed his lungs as he drew in long, deep breaths. He was utterly, completely exhausted.

"Sorry . . . ," he managed to wheeze. "I'm—sorry, Anna. I can't go any longer."

"But you did fine, Howard. You did very fine." As she knelt beside him, her warmth spread over his ribs like a blanket, burning where she placed her hand on his shoulder and squeezed with the strength of old iron. "Look."

He raised his eyes. As far as he could see, the Namib night was alive with massed game. Like runaway construction cranes, giraffe clans loped along above great herds of gemsbok and blue wildebeest. Rare black-faced impala mixed freely with zebra while families of wart-hogs scurried about underfoot. Four-legged phantasms, a clutch of albino springbok cropped contentedly at the thick grass. Somewhere a lion coughed into the night and a leopard cried lonely.

Thousands of them there were, surging and bawing and mewling and eating, the endless veld on which they trod a carpet of muted green in the moonlight. Close by but hidden a river flowed, its own special music sweet behind the stark curtain of night. Eden it was not, but it was close.

"What . . . ?" he started to say, but she put a firm finger to his lips, hushing him as she tucked her body against his.

"The men dance; the women sing," she whispered. "This is the picture my grandparents wanted me to paint. Look at it, drink it, keep it always with you. Me too, if you want. You're a distinct man, Howard Cooperman, and me—I'm tired of being an accountant."

"What's that?" He pointed excitedly. Graceful as ballerinas, the small herd paraded into view from amongst the wildebeest, elegant heads bobbing in time to their rumps. The front half of each body was striped, the back portion an unbroken shade of roan.

"Quagga," she told him. "They say that the last ones became extinct in the nineteenth century, but my great-grandparents saw them in this country as late as the 1920s. Another secret of the Khoikhoi."

Howard gaped. A quagga stallion turned to consider him and snort challengingly before moving on. It showed no anxiety at their presence. No fear of ever having been hunted. The stallion was a sublime and noble memory of recent Earth, of not-so-very-long-ago Africa. Howard forgot about his camera, useless in this light anyway, and used his eyes.

Eventually he returned his attention to his companion. It was the dancing, he knew. The dancing and the music. They had placed him in some sort of trance; a trance he wished would never end but that he knew soon must.

"Will they still be here when the sun comes up? Will you?"

Her face, redolent of both Asia and Africa, turned up to him, and she offered him that utterly natural, thoroughly guileless smile. "If you want me to be, big darling."

Somewhere far away, in a place of mystery and wonder, he heard a voice saying, "Of course I do," and realized it was his own. He commended that voice for its honesty, just as he commended his lips to hers.

Matthew Ovatango looked all the next day and well on into the evening before getting on the radio and calling for help. Planes flew out from Sesfontein and scanned from the air, but it was a couple of days before two Land Rovers full of rangers could arrive from Otji-warongo and begin to search on foot.

They found a well-equipped Toyota Land Cruiser reg-istered to an Anna Witbooi of Windhoek. Its tank was a quarter full, and there were three jerry cans of petrol in the back end. Protected from the omnipresent dust and grit by a plastic laundry bag, a severe black business suit with fluted white blouse hung like a shed exoskeleton from a hook above the passenger seat. From the empty vehicle they tracked petite footprints to the base of the inselberg, and from there climbed up and discovered the great arch. But there was nothing to indicate that Anna Witbooi or Howard Cooperman had ever climbed that far.

Eventually the search was called off, as were many in that part of Kaokoland and the Skeleton Coast, and the friends and relatives of the respective missing parties were officially notified. But the place was not forgotten, for awed anthropologists came to study the magnifi-cent etchings that decorated the underside of the impos-sible granite bridge. They took measurements and made drawings and carefully photographed the deft incisions that extended from one end of the arch to the other, wishing only that more than a few lingering flecks of paint had adhered to the stone.

Sprinkled among the hundreds of animal etchings were the fragile, yet easily recognizable silhouettes of people, the ancient hunter-gatherers who had always followed the now vanished herds and whose most ac-complished artists had decorated a thousand similar lo-calities throughout southern Africa, though perhaps none so expertly as this. The images carried baskets and babies, spears and throwing sticks.

The youngest member of the largest party of visiting

specialists pointed out that the berry-gathering basket being held by one male figure looked suspiciously like a Nikon. She and her colleagues had a good chuckle over it around the campfire that night, and their laughter lingered in the pure and empty air like a fragment of song.

THE BOY WHO WAS A SEA

I adore the ocean. I love the way it feels against my skin, the way it envelops me in another medium when I'm diving, the loving yet ferocious force with which it tumbles me end over end when I wipe out while boogie boarding or bodysurfing. When asked, I'm prone to say I have saltwater in my blood.

And to think that would-be writers worry about where to get ideas . . .

"I think I've found the trouble. Your boy has saltwater in his veins."

George Warren turned uncertainly to his wife. Eleanor Warren put a protective arm around their son Daniel, who continued to play contentedly with his transformer robot toy while blissfully ignoring the adult conversation.

"He's always liked the ocean, but I don't see how that explains what's wrong with him."

"You don't understand. I don't mean that he's attracted to the sea. I mean that he really has saltwater in his veins. And not just plain, ordinary saltwater. Seawater. See?" Taking a thumb-sized vial from a pocket of his white lab coat, he passed it to George Warren, who held the small glass tube close to his face and up to the light.

After a moment's contemplation he passed it to his wife. "There are things moving around in it."

Kindly Dr. Lowenstein nodded sagely. "Very unusual things. Exceptional things. One might even go so far as to say extraordinary things. Things without precedent. Tell me; when was the last time Daniel suffered a severe cut or laceration?"

Mr. and Mrs. Warren looked at one another. "Daniel's never had a bad cut, Doctor," his mother replied uneasily. "Is there something wrong with his blood?"

"Wrong? Dear me, no, Mrs. Warren. There can't be anything wrong with your son's blood because he hasn't any. Not in the conventionally accepted sense, anyway. His circulatory system is full of seawater. Ordinary, standard-issue, Pacific-normal seawater. Furthermore, it is inhabited."

George Warren was a hard worker and a devoted husband and father, but he was not an especially imaginative man. He was having some trouble following the doctor's explanation.

"You mean Daniel's veins and arteries are full of ocean water instead of blood?"

Lowenstein nodded again, solemnly this time.

"Then how can he live?" an understandably concerned Mrs. Warren inquired.

"Deuced if I know." The doctor rubbed the little patch of white whisker that clung like a paralyzed moth to his lower lip. In his spare time, infrequent as it was, Dr. Stephen Mark Lowenstein liked to play the trumpet. This in no way inhibited his work or made him less kindly. He was quite a very good pediatrician. "Along with other minerals, there's a lot of iron in seawater. In the case of your son there seems to be enough to supply adequate oxygen to his system with the aid of some as-yet-undetermined hemoglobin supplement. It's all really quite fascinating. For consultation, I don't know whether to call in a biochemist or a marine biologist."

"But will he be all right?" Mrs. Warren asked earnestly.

Dr. Lowenstein's shoulders rose and fell. "So far he acts like any ordinary, healthy boy of six. I don't see why he shouldn't continue to mature normally."

"But the chills," George Warren wondered, alluding to the reason for the office visit in the first place.

"It's not unusual for a child to have chills. Not in Chicago in January. What is unusual is the way your son's, uh, blood, seems to be responding to the change in climate. There are what appear to be tiny ice floes forming in his bloodstream. Seastream."

Mr. and Mrs. Warren exchanged another glance.

"As you might expect, they're most prevalent at what we might call his polar extremities. I suspect that's why his feet are always cold and he has these headaches when it snows. There are also definite signs of a small glacier forming in the upper region of the superior vena cava. Many of these ice floes are the result of the berg calving which is taking place in the chest cavity." At the alarmed look on Mrs. Warren's face he added, "I don't foresee any danger at this time. They appear to melt before they enter the heart. But it's certainly a matter of concern."

"What can we do?" a worried George Warren asked.

Lowenstein scratched his lower lip. "Your blood, Eleanor, is normal Type A, and you, George, are AB. Daniel appears to be type TS."

" 'TS'?" George Warren echoed.

"Tropical Sea. I would suggest that you consider a move to a warmer climate. His specialized internal biota seem more closely related to the kinds of organisms one would be likely to encounter in the vicinity of the equator. There is evidence of coral-like building from the aortic arch on downward, as well as throughout the jugular. As soon as this, um, reef building reaches maturity, growth appears to cease, thus posing no danger to the boy's general circulation. It's calcification of the arteries to be sure, but not the sort that results from an excess of bad cholesterol. The rest of his remarkable internal biota seems not only benign, but quite healthy."

"What sort of 'internal biota,' Doctor?" Mrs. Warren was still concerned, but less anxious.

"Most astonishing. I've observed evidence of schooling by more than twenty separate varieties. There is also a healthy population of sedentary forms. Everything seems to be thriving. Your son is a most beneficent host."

" 'A warmer climate.' " George Warren looked thoughtful.

"Indeed," Lowenstein murmured. "Somewhere on the ocean."

"I'm a manager for Kmart. It may not be easy to get a transfer to a place like that."

"I'll write you a prescription." Dr. Lowenstein smiled encouragingly.

"Remember when he was two?" Mrs. Warren gazed fondly down at her son, watching him reassemble the transformer. "When we went to Florida and he swallowed all that water and didn't even gag?"

"That wouldn't cause something like this." Her husband hesitated and turned back to the doctor. "Would it?"

"Nothing should cause something like this," Lowenstein replied assuredly. "But so long as the boy is healthy, why worry? Marvel, yes; worry, no."

The Kmarts in Florida were all at full strength, personnel-wise, and had no need for the services of

George Warren. But the family persisted, and kindly Dr. Lowenstein (*kindly* being an anomaly in these days of munificent malpractice suits and individual medical corporations) was there to help at every turn.

So it was that the family came to settle in Kahului, Maui, the largest town on the second-largest island in the placid and agreeable Hawaiian chain. No longer did Daniel suffer from annual shivering. They knew they'd made the right decision the first time he splashed excitedly into the shallows at Makena. His condition had been thoroughly explained to him, and he had come, as boys are wont to do, to simply accept it.

"I'm in the sea and the sea's in me—yippie!" he said as he threw handfuls of warm water into the air. Sitting on the beach, a smiling George Warren took his wife's hand in his own and squeezed reassuringly.

Just as Dr. Lowenstein had predicted, Daniel grew into a strong, healthy young man, handsome and with an air of the faraway about him that proved very attractive to the ladies. Students at the college did term papers on the singular liquid that ebbed and flowed through his body, competing to see who could be first to identify the next new microspecies. One transfer student even qualified for her thesis by providing evidence of seasonal migration within his veins, showing that at least two Danielian species migrated from his arms to his legs every spring, returning to his arms in the winter.

Displaying an abiding interest in oceanography that understandably exceeded that of all but the most avid graduate students, Daniel did his best to assist the professors at the college, willingly volunteering samples of his life-fluid whenever it was requested for study. A serum derived from his veins helped to save the life of an especially beloved orca at Sea World in San Diego, and another dose did wonders for a sick dolphin at Honolulu's seaquarium.

Doctors decided that his heart forced water across the microscopic reefs in his system in much the same way that daily tides refreshed atolls and reefs in the Pacific and Caribbean. At the college and hospital they came to speak of the tides of Daniel, and tried to determine if his heartbeat was affected by the phases of the moon. When one day he was admitted suffering from dizziness and weak spells it was decided that his system needed the sort of replenishment supplied to normal seas by land-based rivers. Upon further analysis, a weekly dose of specified minerals matching precisely those found in the benthos were prescribed, and sure enough the spells soon went away.

It wasn't that he had no aptitude for academics. It was just that he couldn't bear to be long away from the water. So despite his more-than-adequate grades, additional college was dropped in favor of vocational studies, and in due course he received his ship captain's license and divemaster's certificate.

Desirous of seeing other seas, he initially spent some time in the merchant marine, always acquitting himself honorably and amazing seasoned sailors with his ability to pick a course through challenging waters without the aid of GPS or chart. After some years exploring the world's oceans he returned to live permanently on Maui, preferring to work as a divemaster with an established concern instead of opening his own business.

"I'd rather not have the responsibility," he told his now-retired parents when they questioned this decision, "and have more time free to dive on my own."

They understood, of course. Urged on by his mother, he gave serious consideration to marriage, but there was some concern as to the physical status of prospective children, and despite his modest fame he had a difficult time with serious dating. No spray or mint could mask his breath, which smelled now of kelp, now of sargassum, and at its worst, of a weathered planktonic bloom. So he had ample female company, especially out on the water where such things were not as noticeable, but few amours.

There came a day, fine and sunny and not at all in any way ominous, when he was working in the dive office out on the pier and Fredo came running breathlessly from town to lean exhausted against the open portal.

"Have you heard?"

Everyone, including Daniel, looked up. "Heard what?" owner John Renssalear inquired on behalf of them all.

A junior divemaster, Fredo hugged the entrance as if reluctant to let loose of it. "Come and see for yourselves!"

Some curious, some concerned, everyone in the office shuffled out of the building onto the pier. Fredo pointed them not toward the bustle and haste of nearby Lahaina but south toward Kahoolawe. In between Maui and that uninhabited source of constant contention lay the tiny volcanic crescent of Molokini, famous as a dive site and marine sanctuary. There was next to no vegetation on the rocky outcropping, which made the smoke rising from its northeast flank very puzzling.

"It's a tanker!" Fredo informed them breathlessly. "The *Comco Sulawesi*. She was bound for the refinery at Honolulu with sixty thousand barrels of Indonesian crude aboard when she went aground!" He swallowed, his throat dry. "I was monitoring the Coast Guard channels. She's afire, and the crew's preparing to abandon ship."

"They can't do that!" Martine Renosa exclaimed.

"What about the tug at Kahului?" Renssalear's voice was calm, but tension caused his weathered face to crinkle like brown tinfoil.

Fredo shook his head sharply. "There're no ships due in the harbor today, so the crew went over to Hilo for a break. They're sending three oceangoing tugs from Honolulu."

"They'll never get here in time," someone muttered angrily. "What the hell's a tanker doing in the channel anyway? Especially at this time of year."

"Nobody's sure," Fredo explained. "They think the captain wanted to see the islands close up." From the back of the crowd someone groaned.

"Sixty thousand barrels." John Renssalear had been a commercial diver on wells in the North Sea and the Gulf of Mexico, working deep water under potentially lethal conditions. It took a lot to shake him.

"If she breaks up, that much crude could kill all the reefs on this side of the island, all the way from La Perouse Bay up to Kapalua. Not to mention everything around Kahoolawe, Lanai, and maybe even Molokai."

"What about Molokini?" someone asked abruptly.

"Molokini?" Renssalear barely had the energy to shrug. "Molokini's as good as dead. That oil will smother the coral and turn the diving sanctuary into an underwater desert."

"Never mind Molokini," Renosa growled darkly. "What about the whales?" No one said anything. Everyone knew it was the height of the calving season and that the channel was full of migrating humpbacks and their newborn young.

"Say, John." Renssalear turned to Daniel Warren, who was staring evenly at the rising plume of black smoke. "Can you run me out there?"

The owner of the dive operation cocked his head slightly to one side as he regarded his most valued employee. "What did you have in mind, Dan?"

"Just run me out there. Maybe—maybe I can do something."

Wide-eyed, Fredo looked from one man to the other. "Are you two crazy? That ship's on fire. She could blow at any minute!"

"Or not," Dan Warren whispered. "She might just burn until her tanks burn through."

Renssalear didn't hesitate. "Let me get my gear."

The powerful little boat crashed through the swells, heading south toward the burgeoning pillar of doom. They sped around fleeing yachties, dodged the Coast Guard cutter that had positioned itself to keep back curious tourists, shot past the two big lifeboats that looked like fat waterborne grubs and that were carrying the multinational crew of the tanker to safety.

The emergency ladder the tanker crew had left behind flapped and banged against the side of the stricken ship. Maneuvering with the skill and experience born of many years at sea, Renssalear put the dive boat close alongside. Still, it took three tries before Dan Warren was able to make the short but dangerous leap to the dangling ladder.

Renssalear backed off, watching tensely as Daniel ascended the treacherously flapping rungs.

Long moments passed. The Coast Guard was screaming at him on three different frequencies. Renssalear ignored it, acknowledging his radio only when it crackled on a prearranged channel.

"I'm in the pilothouse, John."

Renssalear murmured a silent prayer. "Nice going, Dan. What now?"

"I'm going to try and back her off the reef. I know it better than that Indonesian captain ever could. I know its bumps and ridges, where the hollows are and every twitch of the current. I know where the sand is deep and where the coral grows shallow. I can feel it, John! Its just something . . . I've got in me. Now, give me some space."

Renssalear waited as the immense diesels rumbled to life within the belly of the tanker. Props bigger than his dive boat churned the water, sending bottom dwellers like rays and flounder flying.

At first nothing happened. Then a deeper groaning became audible. Not many people would have recognized that noise, but Renssalear did. It was the sound of a steel keel grinding against coral and stone.

Spewing smoke like a drunken volcano, the mortally wounded *Comco Sulawesi* slowly backed off the eastern horn of Molokini. Once safely behind the islet, above the dive site known to locals as the Edge of the World, with 350 feet of water under the hull, Dan Warren turned the injured vessel south and headed for the open Pacific.

"Put her on autopilot and get off there!" Renssalear shouted into the radio. "I'll pick you up."

"Sorry, John," came the steady reply. "No can do. I've already tried that. The autopilot doesn't respond. Maybe I can find something to lash the wheel."

Time elapsed. Too much time. The *Comco Sulawesi* cleared the southern tip of Maui and then Kanahou Bay on Kahoolawe, passing through the Alalakeiki Channel on its way out to open ocean. Renssalear followed grimly, battling the rising seas in his small boat.

Finally, a response. "Got 'er!"

"What'd you use?" Renssalear shouted into his radio mike.

"Duct tape." Renssalear could almost see his friend grinning. "Advanced technology can't function without duct tape."

"I'm going to tie you up in duct tape and mail you off on a forced vacation!" Renssalear wiped a tear from one eye. "I'll come around and pull up to the ladder. The swells are pretty high. Find a life jacket or preserver and jump in if you have to. Don't worry, I'll get to you."

"I know you will, John. I'm on my way!"

Two minutes later the *Comco Sulawesi* blew up in a spectacular shower of hot metal, burning wood, and flaming oil, bringing to mind for a few minutes the far greater but no more terrifying eruption of Mount Saint Helens. A cursing, screaming Renssalear fought with the wheel of his wildly bucking dive boat, angling it into the backwash and somehow keeping it upright and afloat. Crude drenched his skin, his deck, his equipment, but he didn't care. He kept wiping it from his eyes as he fought his way to the place on the water where the bloated tanker had floated only moments before.

"Didn't need to worry about the damn autopilot," he muttered to himself as he searched the spreading sheet of burning debris for signs of life. "Should've got off when he had the chance. The brave, dumb son of a bitch should've got off."

It was counted a minor miracle when they found Dan Warren clinging to a piece of shattered decking, badly burned and semiconscious. The Coast Guard cutter that had been monitoring the disaster threatened to burn out its own engines as it put on speed for Kahului Harbor, the medics on board doing their best to subdue the pain and keep their patient alive. But there wasn't much they could do. They had not been trained to treat the likes of Dan Warren.

At the hospital they knew him better, but despite their best efforts he continued to lose ground. Or rather, water. While his parents and friends crowded the waiting room and spilled out into the halls and even the street, stricken physicians caucused outside the operating theater.

"There's nothing we can do," one mumbled. "The stuff is all through him. He just ingested too much of it."

"His circulatory biomass is dying," another declared sorrowfully. "He's suffering from an internal oil spill. All the specialized organisms, the unique quasi-coraline structures—the oil's killing them all. He needs a transfusion. Of blood."

"We can't do that." The head of surgery eyed his colleagues, voicing what they all knew. "You know what his system is like. A normal transfusion would kill him as effectively as the petroleum."

"I wonder why the solution didn't work?" muttered another. They had tried replacing Daniel's singular body fluid with a saline solution blended to duplicate that of seawater. Even the pH was correct to a dozen decimal points. But it hadn't worked.

"It doesn't matter." Another doctor was insistent. "We have to try real blood. There's no other way."

"Maybe one." Surprised, they all turned to the head nurse. "Wait for me." Running outside, she dialed the emergency room. Everyone there knew what had happened. Everyone knew how Dan Warren had sacrificed himself in his desperate attempt to save the island's underwater patrimony.

"Is Jimmy Wakamao there?" she asked. He was. "Jimmy, this is Gena Pukalani. I want you to go up to Point Waihee. There's a little reef there. Take the ambulance and don't let anybody or anything stop you. I want you to bring back five gallons of water off the reef, where the current is strong and the water is clear. Yes, you heard me right. Five gallons. Take Steve Portugas with you."

While they waited, the doctors continued to do what they could for Dan Warren. They were arguing over whether to proceed with a transfusion of type AB when the ambulance driver and his assistant burst into the conference room. Between them they carried the plastic container of precious seawater.

"What's this?" the chief of surgery asked. "We've already tried a saline substitute."

"A *sterile* saline substitute," the head nurse argued. "Dan Warren's body fluid isn't sterile. It's full of life, of living things. It's the sea in miniature. Only the sea can restore him."

"Or kill him," insisted the doctor who was in favor of trying real blood. He indicated the plastic jug. It smelled of open ocean. "Who knows what kind of toxic microorganisms are floating around in there?"

The head nurse looked back at him. She was a local, and had more confidence in the sea than did the good doctor only recently arrived from Philadelphia.

"Nothing more dangerous than has been living in him for his whole life, I'll bet."

Everyone looked to the head of surgery for a decision. If he decided wrongly, he would be accused of letting a state hero die. Finally, he said somberly to his head nurse, "Let's try it."

The clean seawater flushed out the oil. There was damage, but with time and therapy Dan Warren's system gradually rehabilitated itself. The coraline structures that lined his veins and arteries slowly rebuilt themselves; the unique microspecies once more swam and thrived in the inlets and fjords of his legs and arms.

The state gave him a medal, and the locals threw the granddaddy of all luaus in his honor. After a while all the fuss died down. There were pineapples to be gathered, and protea to harvest, and golden macs to box and ship. Tourists needed looking after, and gods old and new required the usual propitiation.

Dan Warren is still there, working out of Lahaina. You can go diving with him if you like. You can't miss him. He carries the aroma of the sea about him like a halo. His eyes are blue, of course.

But like no blue you've ever seen.

UNDYING IRON

When non-SF people ask me what got me started reading SF, much less writing it, I have to tell them it was the Sense of Wonder inherent in so many of the stories. Then I have to stop and explain Sense of Wonder to them; what it is and why it's always capitalized. Sometimes it's easy. Other times, no matter how long I talk or how many examples I give, they just don't get it. It's like trying to explain Beethoven to somebody who only listens to country-western. The terms of reference simply aren't there.

Every once in a while I get tired of trying to give a contemporary spin to stories. I yearn for the innocent reading days of my youth, when every Asimov story widened my eyes, when each new Sheckley I encountered made me gasp with its sheer inventiveness, and when Leinster left me so locked in one of his tales that I was afraid I'd hurt my eyes if I looked away from the printed page.

But most of all I miss the ability of stories to make my thoughts soar, to make my mind bear witness to wonders no other form of literature can approach. To take me to places and show me things beyond the bounds of this tiny, familiar world we ethnocentrically call Earth.

Sometimes, I even try to do it myself.

Ory was frightened.

She'd been frightened like this only twice before: once when a silimac had torn its way through Corridor Eighty-Eight, barely missing her but killing twenty of the Flatt family, and once when Jonn Thunder had consumed something unwholesome and had gone into convulsions that had lasted nearly a whole week.

But this was different. Perceiving no threat to her person, she did not fear bodily harm. This new fear rose from the depths of herself, as if she were being poisoned by her own mind. It was new and incomprehensible, this irrational fear that something awful was about to happen.

She was terrified.

Drifting aimlessly down Twenty-Four Tunnel, she gazed vacuously at the pale haze that clung to the inner lining and wondered what to do next. Fear had given rise to a throbbing in her brain. Of that she was certain. Still, she had tried to ignore the persistent discomfort. Headaches were a corollary to her specialty. They came and went like feeding time.

But this one lingered, unresponsive to all the usual treatments. Refusing to dissipate, it impaired her ability to cogently cogitate, robbed her of relaxation time, and had started to affect her even when she slept. It was a dull, insistent pounding that refused to abate.

I can't go on like this, she thought worriedly. I have to talk to somebody.

Selecting a Downtunnel chute, she boosted herself westward. Cousins, aunts, uncles, and nonrelatives waved greetings or shouted cheerily to her as they rushed past. Some were fellow Checkers, others bound on important business of their own. The Brights illuminating Twenty-Four Tunnel glowed softly all around, bathing her in their reassuring refulgence. Colors changed as the Brights tracked her position.

Ory ran an Alpha shift. More than half her routine checks remained to be made, but she contrived to schedule them so that they would bring her close to Tamrul's cubicle. With luck, he might have some helpful suggestions to offer concerning headache treatment.

Used to be, Tamrul could always be counted on to provide satisfactory answers to her questions, but not anymore. The past ten years had exposed the onset of a creeping senility the Philosopher could no longer hide. Knowing of his gathering infirmities, he was still her first choice. Less lucid he might be than in earlier times, but he remained unfailingly kind and understanding. Unlike some of the others, he would not laugh at her, nor treat her with unbecoming brusqueness.

She slipped out of Twenty-Four Tunnel and headed north to Two Hundred Twelve Corridor. Several Dispatchers accelerated to pass her, barely observing minimum clearance. Full of self-importance, they wore their rudeness like combat medals.

"Hey, slide over!" she shouted at them.

"Do you hear something?" the one in the lead queried his companions.

"White noise," a companion ventured.

"With twitchy probes," another added for good measure.

They raced onward up the tunnel, chuckling nonstop and holding hands. Dispatchers were incorrigibly incestuous in their relationships, keeping to themselves as much as possible even though their jobs required frequent contact with others. Ory ignored their taunts. It was their way of dealing with individual insecurities. When it came to instigating original conversation, they were not very interesting anyway.

Two Hundred Twelve Corridor, Section Nine-One. Waving politely to a passing Inspector, she banked around a tight corner and buzzed Tamrul's cubicle. In the old days he got out more often. Now if you wanted his advice, you had to go to him. No more house calls, he'd posted one day. That did not trouble Ory. A Checker had plenty of freedom. So long as she completed her shift schedule she could roam pretty much where she pleased.

The Corridor Brights stood down behind her as she buzzed a second time. She could sense him inside, whining to himself the way he often did when he was alone. It was sad to hear. She felt sorry for Tamrul. Not that he was any better or worse than any other Philosopher, but he had always regarded her with more than just a polite eye. She felt that he saw something special in her, though he was too formal to come out and say so. Just as well. It could never have worked out. As a Checker, she led much too active a lifestyle for him. They were reduced to delighting in the pleasure of one another's conversation.

At last she was admitted. He greeted her with the informality that came from long acquaintance. "Good day, Ory. It's nice to see you again. What brings you up into my neck of the woods?"

"Your beneficent face. What else?"

"You flatter my expression, which I am quite aware rarely expands beyond the mournful. No wonder I like you so much. Sweet Ory, always ready to take the extra step to make others feel better about themselves."

Sounds of amusement rose from nearby. A couple of guys from Maintenance were streamlining a recalcitrant photon flow, their compressors humming. Clearly, they found the private conversation a source of unexpected mirth.

"Moderate your volume, Tamrul." To show she was not upset with him, Ory offered one of her famous smiles. "Half the Family think you're senile already. No need to add fuel to the rumors."

"You're right. I should render my verbalizations more circumspectly. I'm too direct for a Philosopher."

"And get off this self-pity kick. When did you start with that? It doesn't become you."

"It is simply that I am bored, Ory. That's all. Do not commit the error of others by mistaking ennui for senility. This old mind is as sharp as ever. But a brain is no different from any other tool. Gets rusty if it isn't used. I miss the group discussions of the old days." He made a visible effort to rouse himself from his self-induced stupor.

"Now then: You still haven't told me what brings you here. What troubles you? What would you like to discuss? The nature of Existence? The secrets of the Universe? The reversal of entropy?"

"I have a headache."

"Oh." Tamrul was crestfallen. "Is that all? Then why come to me? It sounds like you need to pay a visit to Doc."

"I thought I'd get your opinion first, Tamrul. The idea of going to see Doc doesn't thrill me."

"Perfectly normal reaction. Nobody does."

"I wouldn't mind if his reputation was better, but on my shift they're saying he has a tendency these days to overprescribe. It's only a headache."

"Well then, why don't you drop down to Twenty-Eight and see Marspice instead? Maybe his diagnosis will suit you better."

"Come on, Tamrul. You know the physicians. They'd run a consult on me automatically, and I'd end up worse off than if I'd gone to see Doc in the first place. Marspice is out of my section."

"Consultation is performed to ensure more accurate

diagnosis—or so they say. Still, I suppose you're right. Someone in Administration might raise hell if you purposely avoided Doc Welder in favor of Marspice. What is so remarkable about this particular headache that it brings you to me in the first place? You have them all the time."

"I know. But this one is different."

"Different how?"

"They usually fade away after a day or two, without ministration from Doc or anyone else. Not only isn't this one going away, it keeps getting worse. It's really bothering me, Tamrul. Bad enough to cause me to miss two checks: one in Underlying Physics and the other in Biosearch. Pyon covered for me both times, but she has her own schedule to keep. She can't back me up forever. Pretty soon I'm liable to mess up on something important, and Admin will take notice." She quivered slightly. "You know what that could mean."

"No need to be so melodramatic. I swear, you have a particular flair for it, Ory. In your own words, this is only a lousy headache, albeit a persistent one." He softened his tone. "Much as the idea displeases you, I don't think you have any choice except to see Doc."

"That's not what I wanted to hear from you." Disappointment flashed across her face.

"Sorry. I provide honest opinion, not salving balm." He was regretfully inflexible, as she had feared he might be.

"I know." She sighed resignedly. "I guess I just needed confirmation from someone else. It makes a difficult decision a little easier, somehow."

"At least I can commiserate." He touched her gently. "You stop by again sometime, and we'll have a nice debate on the nature of karma, okay? And remember that no matter how low you're feeling, we're still on course for undying iron."

"I know we are, Tamrul. Thanks for your time. And for your personal concern."

Reversing from the Philosopher's cubicle, she let herself drift back out into the corridor. With an effort, she turned her thoughts to completing the rest of her shift. Neither the visit nor her determination did anything to alleviate the pain in her brain.

But she did not go to see Doc. Instead, when she had finished her shift, she returned to her rest cubicle. Other Checkers were heading out, speeding past her, intent on making good work of the Beta shift. Pyon was already in her own resting place, curled up tight in sleep position. She blinked when Ory, unable to turn her thoughts off, entered silently. From above and below came the soft whispers of other Alpha shifters discussing the events of the day.

"Lilido down in One Sixty-Five went crazy today," Pyon quietly informed her visitor.

"Wonders! That's the third in six months. What's the matter with those people down there?"

"Don't know." Pyon shrugged. "Nobody else seems to, either. Apparently she was working normally when she just started spraying everyone and everything in sight. Finally turned the flow on herself and choked out. Nasty business, they say. Took a whole Maintenance crew the rest of the shift to get the mess under control. Routing had to shift traffic around the clogged Tunnel. Admin was pissed and didn't try to hide it."

"If everything you're telling me is true, then you can't blame them." Ory snuggled close to her fellow Checker and tried to relax. "Personally, I never thought those Lilidos were all there upstairs anyway. Always sucking

up that gunk they work with. That'd make anybody go
crazy after a while."

"Yeah, I guess." The cubicle was silent for several moments before Pyon inquired, "How's your headache
tonight?"

It was hard to prevaricate while the back of her brain
throbbed. Not that Ory felt any need to evade with Pyon.
She was her best friend.

"It's still there. Gets better, gets worse, but won't go
away. I went and told Tamrul about it today. He told me
what I already knew and didn't want to hear: that I
ought to go see Doc."

Pyon's soft whistle echoed eerily in the enclosed space.
"Sounds pretty serious, for a headache. I think Tamrul
may be right. How long have you been trying to cope
with this?"

"Longer than normal."

"I have some medication. Want to try it?"

Ory hesitated only briefly. "No, thanks. I'd better
not. I could get into real trouble if anyone else found out
that I was using an unauthorized prescription. You can
imagine the reaction from Admin."

"I won't tell."

Ory smiled. "I know you wouldn't, Pyon, but if there
were persisting side effects or if it only made my head
worse, it would come out during a deep-probe examination. It's not worth the risk."

"Up to you. You're the one who's suffering."

By now the voices of the other Alpha shifters had
stilled, and the resting chamber was suffused with the
soft hum of sleep.

"Thanks for covering for me yesterday."

"Forget it," Pyon insisted. "What are friends for? Are
you going to see Doc?"

"It doesn't look like I've got much choice. I'm about

out of ideas, and I have to do something. I can't take much more of this. Sometimes the pressure gets so bad my whole brain feels like it's going to explode. I've had headaches before, but never anything like this. This one is unprecedented."

"You know what Doc will want to do." Tension and unease had crept into Pyon's voice. "He'll suggest a purge of your system. They say that's his remedy for everything these days. Diagnosis be damned, purge the system!"

"Not this Checker's system, trouble blotter." But beneath Ory's bravado she feared that her friend was right. "It's not *that* serious yet."

Pyon turned reflective. "I know it sounds awful, but maybe a system purge wouldn't be such a bad idea. Everyone says that you feel like a new person after a purge."

"Everyone says that you *are* a new person after a purge. They also say it hurts like hell. No thanks."

Pyon yawned. "Well, I'm glad it's a decision I don't have to make. *My* head feels fine. I hope you find some other way of treating the problem. I don't mean to kick you out, but it was a long day and I'm feeling about half unconscious. Sleepwise we're already significantly behind the others. Good rest to you, Ory. Go to the undying iron."

Ory tried, but sleeping was next to impossible. Desperately as she tried to ignore it, the headache did not go away, and it was worse by the time the next shift start rolled around. The internal pounding was so intense it was a struggle to keep from crying aloud several times. Despite her self-control she drew questioning stares from several patrolling Mokes and had to force herself not to hurry too quickly past them.

There was no avoiding it any longer. System purge or not, she would have to go see Doc.

His oversized cubicle was as spotless as ever, and his departmental insignia glistened beneath the painfully bright lights. So did his attitude.

"Well hello there, Alpha shifter. You're a Checker, aren't you? I don't get to see many Checkers. You're a conspicuously tough bunch. What can I do for you?"

She sidled carefully into the cubicle, keeping her distance from him. Her hesitation made him chuckle.

"Take it easy, Checker. Despite my reputation, I don't bite. Not unless it's required by diagnosis, that is."

The comment typified his sense of humor. Maybe another physician would have found it funny. Ory didn't. Half panicked, she wanted out, but she was already inside. Recognition committed her. If she fled without allowing herself to undergo examination, Administration would be notified.

"I have a headache."

He frowned slightly. "Is that all?" His expression critical, he turned and drifted across to a cabinet. "You want a repress injection? That should take care of it."

Despite the temptation to accept the offer and get out of that stark white place, she plunged onward with the truth. "I've had headaches before. I don't think a repress will do the job this time."

Doc shook his head and looked sympathetic. "You Checkers: always worrying, always offering suggestions. I think you should all take more time off, but then I suppose you'd probably worry about someone else running your schedule incorrectly. Headaches are congenital with you, or at the least, an occupational hazard." He pondered. "Very well—so you don't think a repress will do the trick. What makes you believe this headache is different from any you've had before?"

"I can tell," she replied with certainty. "Not only hasn't it gone away, but it hurts worse than anything I've ever experienced previously. And there's something else." She hesitated. "A feeling, which also won't go away."

His gaze narrowed. "What kind of 'feeling'?"

"That something exceptionally out of the ordinary is going to happen."

"Dear me! That sounds ominous. Are you contemplating a change of specialties, perhaps? Thinking of applying for a Prognosticator's position? Iron knows there are plenty of vacancies."

"No, it isn't that," she replied impatiently. "I couldn't be a Prognosticator anyway. That's too much like Tamrul's work."

"So you've been talking to that old fraud. Filling your head with chatter about anticipatory emotions, has he?"

Ory leaped to her venerable friend's defense. "This has nothing to do with him, Doc. These feelings originate entirely with me. I didn't get anything from him. Tamrul's just old and tired and . . . bored."

"Maybe so. In any event, he is beyond my help. What he needs I cannot give him. Whereas you, on the other hand . . ." His lenses sparkled. "If you refuse a repress, that leaves me with only one sensible alternative. System purge."

She eyed him distastefully. "You enjoy your work, don't you, Doc?"

"Yes, and a good thing it is, too, since there's been so much of it lately. Well, what is your decision?"

She slid away from the examination brackets and along the back wall. "I think I'll hold off for a while yet. I was hoping you might be able to prescribe a third course of treatment."

"I just told you: There isn't any third course. Repress

or purge, those are your choices. What else would you have me do?"

It was difficult even to form the words, but with the threat of a system purge looming over her she forced herself.

"Ask Mother."

All traces of Doc's ready, if slightly ghoulish humor, evaporated abruptly. "You're not serious. That's a joke, right? A poor joke."

"I'm serious, Doc. I wouldn't joke about a request that serious." Pain flared in her brain, momentarily numbing her perception. She waited for it to subside. "I think we need to ask Mother about my headache."

The physician's response was stern and unbending. "As you are well aware, Mother is sound asleep. She is not to be awakened because some lowly Checker has a bad headache. Where's your common sense? Maybe you need that purge more than I thought. Maybe this is no longer a question of alternatives." He was staring hard, almost accusingly, at her.

She found herself backing away from that unrelenting, no longer sympathetic gaze. "I understand what you're saying, Doc. My head seems better now. I think I'll be okay. Really."

"So you claim. That's what worries me. I don't think there's any question about it. You require purging. In fact, based on this interview, I'd say that it is long overdue." He reached out for her, and she barely managed to skip past him.

"Be sensible about this, Ory. I know what's best for you. It's my job to know. Now, are you going to cooperate, or do I have to call a couple of Mokes?"

"Rest easy, Doc. You were right all along. It was just a bad joke." She laughed. "I really had you going for a minute there, didn't I? You think you're the only one in this section with a low-down dirty sense of humor?"

Eyeing her uncertainly, he hesitated with one digit hovering over the Call switch. Finally, he drew back. Calling in the Mokes was a serious step, one that the caller had better be able to justify. Her laughter seemed spontaneous enough.

"First another Lilido goes off, and now a Checker plays jokes." A warning tone pervaded his voice. "Don't play these kinds of games with me, Ory. It's too serious. Suppose I *had* called the Mokes?"

"Then the joke would be on you. Really, Doc, can't you spot a gag when it's being played on you?" She resumed her methodical retreat toward the entrance.

"Hmph. Say, what about your headache? Was that made up, too?"

"No, but it's far from being as serious as I made it out to be. This visit wouldn't have been funny if it was. Let's give it another couple of days and we'll see if it goes away of its own accord."

"And if it does not?" He was watching her closely. "Suppose the joke doesn't stay funny?"

"If it doesn't go away then I'll certainly let you run a system purge on me."

He looked satisfied. "Now, that's being sensible. Very well, we will hold off another couple of days. But I am going to have your shift monitored, so don't think you can fool me about this. I'll know if it gets serious."

"Of course you will. How could I hide something like that?"

She practically knocked over a couple of passing Chelisors in her haste to escape from the white, threatening cubicle. The ambling pair recovered quickly and tried to peddle their zings and thomes, but she wanted nothing to do with their wares. Not now. All she wanted was to put plenty of distance between herself, the medical cubicle, and Doc's eager, grasping hands. Most certainly she did not want to be purged by him. It seemed to her that he was growing a little senile himself.

But her time for exploring options was running out. He was going to put a monitor on her shift, and her head hurt so bad she was near tears.

There was one more close friend whose advice she could ask, one more independent party who would not prejudge her. She rushed heedlessly down Eighty-Five Tunnel, hardly bothering to acknowledge the greetings of puzzled friends and acquaintances. At the speed she was making it was not long before she entered restricted territory.

Keeping her eyes straight ahead, she maintained her pace.

Checkers could go most everywhere. She would be all right if she didn't have the bad luck to run into an Inspector.

That was what nearly happened, but the one who had been coming toward her stopped to bawl out another Checker Ory did not recognize, and so she was able to slip past and blend in with a crowd of maintenance workers. Jonn Thunder's section was always busy.

The rising heat began to affect her as she made her way through several sealports well striped with warnings. A Lilido or an unshielded Moke would soon overheat here, but Checkers were equipped for travel anywhere. As Doc had noted, they were built tough. She could stand the local conditions for a little while.

Then she was through the last protective sealport and there he was: immensely powerful, confident of his strength and ability, hardworking and tireless. Not for the first time, she thought she might be a little bit in love with Jonn Thunder. Her feelings for him seemed to go beyond simple admiration. For his part he sometimes treated her like an infant, infuriating her. She knew this amused him, but she could never get used to it. Her personality demanded that she be taken seriously. Perhaps, she thought, that was one reason why so many Checkers suffered from bad headaches.

She didn't think he would toy with her this time. He had the ability to sense seriousness in a visitor.

"Hello, little Ory Checker," he rumbled pleasantly. "What brings you to Purgatory?"

"I'm running a check on its unstable inhabitants. Making sure they haven't been guzzling any more hydrogen than they're entitled to."

"Who, me? Do I look drunk? Hey boys: Do I look drunk?"

Overhead, Matthew Thunder belched conspicuously. "Yeah, come to think of it, you do, but you always look drunk to me, Jonn."

"Been stone drunk these past hundred years straight, that's my opinion," Luke Thunder declared from another region of Purgatory. At the moment he was sweating over an uncommonly delicate adjustment. "He just camouflages it well, don't he, Checker?"

"You're all making fun of me." She would have admonished them further, but a bolt of pain made her yelp. Instantly, Jonn Thunder was all sympathy and concern.

"Hey, little nosey-mote, what's wrong?"

She unburdened herself to him, telling him all about the headache and the persistent fearful feeling that accompanied it, about her talk with Tamrul and her encounter with Doc, and lastly of the suggestion she'd made that had nearly caused her to be short-listed for a system purge.

Jonn Thunder was very quiet when she had finished. For a moment she thought he was going to berate her just as Doc had, and suggest a purge, but he had no such intention. He was thinking. Jonn Thunder might not be very deep, but he was methodical.

"Did you make the same suggestion to Tamrul?"

"No. My head wasn't bothering me as much when I went to see him. Besides, I know how he'd react, what he'd say. He's a dear old thing, but in his own way quite inflexible. That always struck me as a strange quality for a Philosopher to have."

"He's getting old," Jonn Thunder muttered. "We're all getting old. Except you, Ory Checker, and a few of the others. What do you think, boys? Where ought she to go from here?"

They debated, in the manner of Thunderers, and it was a fascinating thing to observe. When they had finished, it was Jonn who spoke. "Do what you think you have to do, Ory. We can't help you. I'm for sure no Doc, but you don't look or sound to me like you need purging. Not Doc's variety, anyhow. But you're going to have to do whatever you decide to do on your own. Me and the boys have a lot of pull, but it's useless where something like this is concerned.

"You'd better be careful. If Administration finds out what you intend they'll have the Mokes down on you straightaway. They'll haul you right back to Doc, and this time he won't bother to ask your opinion before he goes to work. You know that."

She didn't want to believe what she was hearing. "You could help."

"No we can't, Ory. I'm sorry. We have our own status to worry about. If I neglected my work for a minute just to help a Checker with a bad headache, there'd be a serious scandal. If anyone found out, they'd put me down for a system purge too."

Ory was shocked by the very notion. She could not imagine such a thing, and said as much.

"It's the truth," he told her. "You're on your own, Ory."

"But this is important." She was insistent. "Something's happened. I can feel it—inside my mind. Mother has to be awakened."

"Then you'll have to wake her by yourself, Checker. Wish I could believe in the necessity of waking Mother as strongly as you seem to, but my head's fine. We won't do anything to stop you. By rights, we should notify Admin ourselves." She froze. "But there always was something about you, nosey-mote. Something special, though I'm damned if I can define it. So we won't interfere." A chorus of agreement echoed from his hard-working relations.

"But we won't help you, either. If you're challenged, you'll have to deal with Admin by yourself."

"Thanks for listening to me, Jonn Thunder. I guess that's about all I could hope for."

"Don't be bitter, Ory. I consider myself brave, but not a fool. Maybe you're a little of both. Good luck." He sounded wistful, but unyielding.

She backed out of Purgatory, leaving them to their work. More time had passed than she'd realized. Already, she'd risked a great deal in coming here. Now her own schedule was going unattended. Doc and his talk of setting a monitor on her had forced her hand as much as the pain in her brain. The Mokes would be looking for her soon enough, if the search hadn't commenced already. All it would take would be one frizzing station to pass the word and she'd find herself being prepped for purging before you could say spindrift.

She could not let that happen. She couldn't. Something

she could not explain—something much deeper than the constant, fluctuating pain—drove her onward. If Jonn Thunder and his relatives had thrown in with her she would have had a better chance; it would have improved the odds. Despite what he had told her, she did not really believe Admin would risk purging any of them. But they believed otherwise, and so had refused to help her.

She was alone.

Pain shot through her mind, making her convulse. She couldn't wait any longer. She knew what she had to do. Steeling herself, she hurried up the tunnel. If they caught her, the worst they could do to her was run a total purge. By now she was starting to believe even that might be better than the unrelenting pain.

She had embarked on her present course of action with little forethought and no preparation. Even if she succeeded in placing herself in sufficient proximity, how was she, a lowly Checker, going to wake Mother? And what would she say if she was successful? There was every reason to believe that Mother might react to the unscheduled awakening with outrage and fury instead of understanding. None of Ory's memories contained anything about waking Mother. She did not know anyone who had actually seen the ritual performed. It simply was not done.

But she could think of nothing else to do. And however unnatural, however outrageous, something about it somehow struck her as right.

It was a long journey up to Administration territory, and her initial resolution weakened as she neared the control zone. Overbearing Supervisors, intense Inspectors, and armed Mokes were everywhere. Pain and not prudence had driven her this far. She realized with a start that if someone confronted her, she had no reasonable excuse to offer for being this far out of her section.

She found herself pausing at the entrance to the tunnel. The longer she hesitated, the more likely it became that some patrolling Moke would accost her with a demand for an explanation of presence, an explanation she would be unable to provide. After that there would be harder questions and then—a trip to Doc's, under escort.

Sure enough, one of the armed watchers was drifting toward her right now, his armor glistening in the pallid light. Her mind spun, thoughts whirling frantically as she fought to see and think clearly despite the throbbing in her head. If only the pressure would relent and give her a few moments of respite.

Then the Moke was hovering over her, glowering, and it was too late to consider retreat.

"Checker," he growled, "what check thee here?"

"I—I . . ."

"Please to mumble not. I've already a Lilido acting strange who needs a looking-at."

"I—I'm here to check on Mother's status." Could she have said anything more blatant? Motionless and scared, she awaited the Moke's reaction.

"Stupid Lilido is going crazy," he muttered as he backed off. "Get on with it, Checker." In obvious haste he slid past her, brushing her aside so roughly that she wobbled in his wake. The threatening hum of his powered-up weapons system faded with his departure.

In a daze, she hovered in the Tunnel, recovering her determination and marveling at the unexpected ease of her escape. A little brass goes a long way, she decided. Of course, it probably helped that the Moke was trying to deal with two problems at once. Thus confronted, he had chosen the tangible trouble over that which was merely nebulous. Pushing on, she soon found herself deep within the solemn bowels of Administration.

Clerks and Controllers swarmed all around, ignoring her, intent on assignments of self-evident importance. No one else stopped to query her or question her presence. The assumption was made that because she was already there, she had a right to be where she was. Carefully, she picked her way through the bustling mob. There was an urgency of movement in Administration, a sense of power and purpose that she had never encountered anywhere else, not even in Jonn Thunder's Purgatory. The intensity frightened her a little.

Fright brought you here, she reminded herself. Fright and pain. Time to risk all in hopes of alleviating both.

Mustering all her confidence, she boldly intercepted a speeding Termio and blocked his path. He eyed her irritably but waited for questions. When at last she moved aside to let it pass, she had her directions.

Still, no one thought to confront her, despite the fact that she was traveling through highly sensitive territory. After all, she was a Checker, and it was presumed that she was going about her lawful business. Her profession was her only protection. She prayed that she would not meet another Checker, one authorized to operate within Admin.

Then she was There, and that was when she really almost turned and fled.

Projections and Brights, Terminals and Secures towered ten corridors high before her. Termios waited patiently at their assigned stations while Clerks and Controllers dashed to and fro with seemingly reckless abandon. There were no Mokes in sight.

Oblivious to all the activity around her, Mother slept on and on through the endless night.

For one last time Ory wondered if she was doing the right thing. She feared a total purge worse than anything. Fire burned her brain, and she winced. Well, worse than almost anything. Hesitating no longer, she commenced to ascend the awesome escarpment. Espying a vacant station on the epidermis of the great structure, she angled toward it. Locking in, she proceeded to establish contact as if she were running a standard, everyday check.

What do I say? she found herself wondering. How do I act?

She was working furiously even as she worried, executing the necessary commands with speed and skill. The enormous somnolent bulk behind her seemed to let out a vast sigh. Clerks began to cry out while the Controllers set up a fearful hooting. Showing obvious alarm, a squadron of Mokes came charging into the room. A frantic Termio pointed to the source of the disruption.

"There she is—it's that Checker! No authorization for that position. *Get her!*"

"Please," she whispered desperately into the link she had strained to establish. "Please help me, Mother! I didn't want to do this, I didn't! But my mind hurts so bad. Tell me what to do, please!" She was sobbing out her hurt and confusion even as the Mokes came toward her. The arming telltales on their weapons pulsed menacingly, tiny bright points of paralysis promised.

Suddenly, a powerful, all-encompassing, golden refulgence appeared directly above her, while a warm voice not to be argued with boomed the length and breadth of the chamber.

"Off, Moke!"

The guards slammed to a stop, banging into one another and muttering uncertainly among themselves. One started forward anyhow, aiming a blunt, glassy tube at the cringing Checker.

A white wash of fire flamed from above. When it dissipated, the Moke could be seen free-floating and inert. His companions held their positions and eyed the body of their motionless comrade with dawning understanding.

When the voice sounded again, it was comforting, reassuring, and softer. "A moment, Checker." Crowding together, the reverent inhabitants of Admin watched and waited to see what was going to happen next. Even the Supervisors were cowed, a sight Ory had never thought to see.

When at last the voice of Mother returned, the Checker felt a great relief. In the fury of the Mokes' approach and her own desperation she had nearly forgotten her purpose in coming here. Now it came flooding back to her, and suddenly seemed no more threatening than a bad dream.

The pain of many days, the pressure of multiple moments, was gone. The hurt had been banished.

"It is all right, Ory Checker. You have done well. Now, come to me."

Ory did so, instinctively choosing the right path. In place of pain there was now understanding and revelation. She marveled at the revealed complexity of Mother, and saw her own self revealed anew. The rush of comprehension was so great she nearly fainted.

"Thank you, Mother. Thank you for your compassion, and for your insight."

"Not to thank me but that I must thank thee, child. Feeling better now?" It was impossible to imagine so much warmth, so much solace, emanating from a single entity.

"Better than ever." Ory frowned internally. "Except . . ."

"Except what, child?"

"I still have this unshakable feeling that something significant is soon to happen."

Comfort flowed out from Mother, comfort and warmth enough to send Controllers and Clerks and even Mokes contentedly back to work.

"Your perception is wonderfully accurate, Checker. Something important is indeed about to happen. Thanks to you. Thanks to your programming. You came to me all by yourself?"

"I did. There was no other choice. I had a terrible headache."

"Ah, yes. Well, I suppose one is enough. It is, after all, the result that is important." She sighed, a vast mental exhalation that rushed through the chamber like a cool wind. "So much time wasted. Almost dangerously much." Mother paused for a while. "A hundred years spent idling in orbit; doing nothing, going nowhere. If not for you, all might well have been lost. I praise your headache even as I regret your discomfort. All I can tell you is that if you had not acted as you have, all would have been far worse."

"All what, Mother? And what was that about my programming?"

"Your headache. It was programmed, of course. But I see that you do not yet understand. Do not worry. You shall, I promise it. But first there is much to do. I have my own work to execute that has been too long neglected. Stay by me, watch, and learn." Once more the voice rose to dominate the chamber.

"Observer!"

One of the little Observers promptly materialized from somewhere in the vicinity of Control. Despite Mother's gentle urging, Ory hesitated before plugging in and making use of the floating eye's abilities.

She gasped. She was looking *outside*. Outside Mother, outside . . . everything.

In a direction she could only classify as *below* lay an immense, shining, mottled globe. And then as she continued to watch—oh, wonderful!—Mother began to give birth.

Thousands of offspring consisting of tiny pods burst free from beneath her. Gathering themselves into an extended swarm, they began to drift rapidly toward the softly radiant sphere. The birthing continued for some time, and a fascinated Ory watched it all.

When the last pod had vanished, swallowed up by the thick fluffy band of atmosphere, Mother let out another great sigh and spoke to her again.

"You see, little one, to what purpose I am. It is all part and parcel of what your friend Tamrul has tried and not had the ability to convey to you. Tamrul is more complex than he seems, and not as easily renewed in spirit and purpose as are Checkers and Mokes and such, but fear not. Now that I am awake, I can recharge his spirit. In rescanning your conversations with him, I see how right he was. You *are* special. Despite what you may think, with a little education you would make a good Prognosticator."

From somewhere up in Control those honorable worthies responded to this evaluation with a murmur of discontent, but they were quickly silenced by reassurances from Mother.

"Would you like that, child? You could stay here and work beside me."

"I—I guess I'd like that very much. I never really thought such graduations were possible."

"All things are possible," the soothing voice reassured her, "now that I am awake again."

Ory tried to understand all that she had seen and been

told. It was a lot to comprehend and absorb in such a short time. "They say that changing specialties is a little like undergoing a purging. Will it hurt?"

Mother laughed—a delicious, summery sound. "No, little one. It may confuse you some, at first. But it will not hurt. And it is something that you deserve." There was a pause before she continued, during which Ory thought she could almost hear Mother thinking.

"A hundred years wasted dreaming in orbit because initial activation sequence failed. There will be much animated discussion among my minions in Control as to what went wrong. And only a single operating fail-safe felt strongly enough to act, at the risk of her own stability. So fine is the line between success and disaster."

"Fail-safe, Mother?"

"Your headache, little Checker. It pushed you to check on something you did not even understand. Fortunately for all, you did. For you see, those little pods hold both my children and my parents."

"That doesn't make any sense."

"In time and with education you will come to understand. Those pods contain a hundred thousand carbonites, Ory. Not people like you and me and Tamrul and Doc. Things called human beings. They slept the longlong sleep so that I could bring them safely to this new world, to this new homeland. To found a new colony and a new life far, far from Earth."

What strange echoes that last word generated in Ory's mind. The faintest of memories of distant, long-forgotten things. Not bad things. Simply . . . so strange.

"A ship." She heard herself whispering aloud. "I remember a little, now. Olden of memories comes back. Tamrul spoke sometimes of such a thing. He said—he said that we were on a ship, going to undying iron. He never could make it clear to me."

Again came that gentle, all-knowing laugh. "Do not blame poor old Tamrul. He did his best. His job was to keep your psyches clear and healthy. Despite serious degeneration of his reasoning programming, he has done an admirable job these past hundred years. That century of delay was not provided for in the original programming. I know there have been problems he has been unable to handle recently. The breakdowns among the Lilidos, for example. I can deal with that now."

Ory was simultaneously excited and confused, overwhelmed by revelation and explanation. "Then what he said is true. We are on a ship."

"No, no, little Checker. You still do not see it all. I have given you back some of the bits that time took from you, but you have yet to piece them properly back together. We are not on a ship. We *are* Ship. You and I, Doc and Tamrul, all the Controllers and Servos and Clerks and Mokes and yes, even Jonn Thunder and his brothers."

Ory tried to grasp the concept, but it was too much to digest all at one time. Pods and people, new worlds and old, being *of* something instead of being something that was apart—she struggled to make sense of it all. She had always considered herself an individual, just like Pyon and all her other friends and acquaintances. Yet how could she dispute Mother?

"I sense your confusion, Checker. You *are* an individual. So is Pyon. Your programming and your physical self are individualized for optimum performance and flexibility. But you are also Ship, Ory, just as I am. Use the Observer. Look upon thyself." Lowering an exceptionally highly polished portion of herself, Mother held the component steady.

Fearfully, Ory complied, and in so doing, relaxed. Because she saw nothing frightening, or remarkable. Reflected back at her was a floating, meter-high metal ovoid, lined with flashing red and yellow and blue lights, from which trailed a dozen slim, sensitive metal probes for plugging into and checking the status of multiple stations. She had seen her own reflection many times in the smooth-sided walls of corridors and tubes and tunnels. She was an Alpha shift Checker, normal in all respects.

"You are a component, Ory. As am I. The only difference between us is shape, function, and capacity. You have nothing to be ashamed of."

"I'm not ashamed, Mother."

"Good! You will make a fine Prognosticator when you have been reprogrammed and had your memory capacity and reasoning circuitry supplemented. And you will retain your identity. Have no fear on that account. My children, our parents, programmed us well. They made only one mistake, and you have resolved that most excellently."

Ory hesitated, uncertain, wanting to be sure that she understood. "Now that you have given birth to these human beings, what are we to do? Go back to this 'Earth' for more of them?"

"No, little one. Earth is too far to go, impossibly distant. So far that you cannot imagine it. And we cannot sleep the longlong sleep as do the humans. One shift must always be on station. The Universe is a big place, full of dangerous surprises. Humans need to know about them so they can avoid them or otherwise deal with them in their future. But while we can give birth but once, we can continue to provide information that will be useful. Even as we speak, I am waiting for permission from below to leave orbit."

Ory remained, excused from her shift at Mother's direction. Activity in Admin picked up, then returned slowly to normal. There was a new sense of purpose to the movements of Clerks and Termios and Controllers, a feeling of a task well done. And there was something else, something new. A sense of anticipation.

"Ah, there," Mother announced with satisfaction quite some time later.

"There what?" asked Ory sleepily. She had spent much of her time alongside Mother catching up on sleep that had been lost to headache pain, and she was cramped from holding one mental position for so long.

"Coding for release. Supplies and equipment are all delivered, and the colony's self-sufficiency is assured. We have been congratulated."

Without knowing exactly why, Ory suddenly felt very proud.

"We can relax a little now," Mother told her. "It is time to embark upon that which we do best and fluidly, Ory. The gathering of knowledge. We will go on and on, Checker. On until we can accumulate and gather and relay no longer. But that time is a long ways off. We are liberated to go."

"To the undying iron?" Ory asked uncertainly.

But Mother did not reply. She was suddenly very busy. Activity around her rose to a frenzy. New directives were issued, orders passed, instructions relayed. Slowly, majestically, the great grand colony seeding ship shifted position. It must have been a wonderful and yet poignant sight to the inhabitants of the newly settled world below. From somewhere aft and south, Jonn Thunder and his brothers roared with reinvigorated pleasure at the prospect of the new task assigned to them.

When all was said and done and they were once more, after a hundred years of accidental idleness, on their way, Mother remembered the Checker hovering patient and uncomplaining beside her lower-level input terminus.

"Poor Tamrul." The matronly intelligence voiced concern. "I really must cleanse and recharge his memory. We do not go to undying iron, little Ory Checker. We *are* undying iron.

"We are going on to where our destiny takes us—under Orion . . ."

THE QUESTION

And now, as the Pythons were wont to say, for something completely different.

I've always said that a good writer should be able to make a story out of anything. Anything at all. Who says there's nothing new under the sun? Looked at sufficiently askew (some might prefer the term wacko), everything is new under the sun.

Sitting around one day searching for a story idea, I could only come up with the ancient, the hoary, the venerable to the point of fossilization. The key came when I determined to tell the tale seriously.

Consider it a philosophical precursor to a certain noted (and most excellent) film of recent vintage . . .

Even had they known, it was unlikely anyone would have tried to stop him. A very few might have sensed he intended something; the majority simply ignored him. Had they known the truth they would have been indifferent at best, at worst afraid. There were those who would have thought him mad. Most would have been merely bemused.

He did not ask for their advice on the matter because they had none to give. What he envisioned had never been tried before; there were good reasons why. And only a fool risked death for no good reason.

Or was there at the bottom of it, after all, a reason? Lach'an wasn't sure himself. He only knew that he burned to find out.

To leave the Home. Why in Creation would anyone want to? What reason even to contemplate such a bizarre thought? It wasn't as if there was anything Outside to make life more enjoyable. There was nothing beyond the Wall save death, and it was only the truly mad who desired to hurry that meeting. Within the Home was warmth, food, shelter, companionship, succor. Its protected, patrolled territory was extensive enough to give home to thousands without crowding. Life was simple, straightforward, and fulfilling. An individual could live off by himself or participate in polite society. It was a matter of choice, a commodity present in the Home in sufficient quantity to please even the most discriminating.

There wasn't even need to work. The Servants took care of that.

It was they who produced and served the food, kept the Home clean, saw to the people's medical needs, maintained the buildings and the community's mechanical infrastructure. Tremendously strong and of immense stature, they nonetheless moved with care lest they accidentally injure the feeblest citizen. They were especially gentle with the young, often playing with them and bringing them special treats. If a Servant did injure one of the people, it devoted itself immediately thereafter to restoring the harmed one to health.

When the seasons changed and the weather turned bitter it was the Servants who made certain that the Home was properly heated. Many's the time Lach'an had seen them rouse themselves from sound sleep in the midst of a bad storm to repair a leak or clean a clogged drain while the people slept on oblivious to the damage. It was the Servants who did battle with the carnivores that prowled beyond the Wall and occasionally tried to force themselves inside. The clumsy beasts were no match for the Servants and their advanced weaponry.

Thus protected and cozened, why would anyone think of leaving the Home?

Lach'an had no ready answer to that. He could not have explained what drove him to contemplate madness. Therefore he said nothing; merely watched, and waited, and bided his time.

His own doubts aside, the Wall was his principal obstacle. There was no need for another. Narrow but invulnerable, a marvel of engineering, it towered above the Home. The Servants patrolled it regularly to ensure its integrity. It kept the sanctuary secure from the killers who prowled the wild lands Outside. As to what else might lie beyond, no one cared. No one except Lach'an.

One could easily see between the woven metal cables that formed the Wall. Frustrated carnivores broke their teeth on it, wore themselves out trying to surmount its great height, exhausted themselves in their attempts to excavate an entry beneath. The people smiled at their futility. The Servants had done well. The Home was impenetrable.

How could Lach'an expect to succeed where powerful, determined killers failed repeatedly? It was the problem he contemplated daily, without finding a solution. Until the coming of the big rain.

It began without warning or scouting thunder one sultry summer night. The humidity increased until water seemed not so much to fall as straightforwardly condense out of the surrounding air; fat, heavy drops that arrived like the opening salvo of a military bombardment. They pounded the Home and gouged the dry earth. The lower levels of the Home quickly flooded as drainage channels overflowed, unable to carry off the rain as fast as it fell.

Aroused Servants stumbled from their quarters and worked frantically to stave off serious damage while the people looked on, safe and secure inside their homes. The Servants labored miserably in the downpour, but none of the people moved to help them. That would not only have been contrary to tradition, but undignified.

It took the struggling Servants some time to get the flooding under control. Only when the ferocious storm began to ease did they allow themselves time to rest, eventually returning tiredly to their own segregated quarters.

As the water level went down the people gradually emerged. They chatted excitedly, commenting on the damage and how the unprecedented deluge had altered the landscape in the vicinity of the Home. Having nothing better to do, Lach'an joined them. As was his wont, he ranged farther than his companions, wandering alone to the farthest reaches of the Home as he strove to memorize every detail of the terrain beyond the Wall.

That's when he saw his chance.

When he came across the gully he could hardly contain his excitement. He did so because he had to. If anyone else noticed the freshly cut arroyo they would immediately call it to the attention of the Servants, who would respond by rushing to repair the egregious breach in the Home's security.

Lach'an looked around anxiously. For the moment he was alone. He stood there thinking hard and fast. More time to prepare for this moment would have been desirable. It would, for example, have been better to have eaten his fill before going, since there was no way of knowing what he might find in the way of food on the

Outside. He was not nearly so concerned about finding water, not after the recent storm. It would have been better to have had a plan and followed it accordingly.

Still, how did one plan for the unknown? Lach'an was a creature of impulse, an individual used to making quick decisions. Did he know what he wanted or not? The gully was there *now*, an inviting gape beneath the Wall. There was no one around to argue with him. No reason to hold back. And the longer he hesitated, the greater the likelihood someone would see him and cry out.

He turned for a last look at the Home, at his home; the only one he'd ever known or ever might know. For an instant he doubted his purpose. He never doubted himself. The invulnerable arcology towered behind him, drying in the early light of morning. From within came the voices of waking people. Some he recognized, others he did not. The Home was far too large to know personally all who dwelt within. Now he intended to abandon that security and comfort for the mystery and possible quick death of the Outside, where there would be no roof to shelter him, no soft heat to warm him at night, no attentive Servants to see to his every need.

Perhaps I *am* mad, he thought as he turned and raced for the gully.

No one saw him: not any of his friends, no strangers, nor the Servants. The conduit he utilized would be discovered soon enough, whereupon the Servants would hastily seal it to prevent the ingress of any dangerous local fauna. That meant that if his determination weakened and he wished to return he might well find himself locked out.

No time now to ponder such disagreeable possibilities. Was he losing his nerve even before he'd fully committed himself? He resolved to think no more about returning.

He was going to be the first of his kind to learn what lay Outside.

It was so easy. A quick dash down into the gully and he was racing along its length, ducking beneath the formerly impassable underside of the Wall, feeling the lowermost cable brush his forehead. A few strides more found him ascending the slight slope on the far side, until he stood once more on level ground.

It was unkempt, the surface untended by Servants. That much was to be expected. Right away he found evidence of the presence of game and knew he would not starve. By turning and straining his neck he was able to see the entire west side of the Home. He could still hear the babble of everyday conversation as his companions awakened to their daily tasks.

Then he tensed. Two Servants were examining the gap that the storm had cut beneath the Wall. Curious citizens arrived to cluster around them, looking on and commenting. He'd made his break just in time. As he stared, one of the Servants happened to glance up—and see him. Startled, it gestured in his direction and made a rumbling noise. Several citizens spotted him at the same time and called out.

He'd been seen. The alarm had been raised.

He shouldn't have stopped to catch his breath and evaluate his situation until he was well out of sight of the Home. Now it was too late. Furious at himself, he whirled and dashed off into the surrounding brush, knowing that behind him the Servants would be on the move. Strong enough to fight off any prowling carnivores, they would not hesitate to do their utmost to "rescue" him. But Lach'an didn't want to be rescued.

There was still a chance to elude their well-intentioned pursuit. The Servants were massive and powerful, but also awkward and slow. Any of the people could run circles around them.

The brush would slow them. Lach'an raced through the dense vegetation, ignoring the branches that took malicious swipes at his face, easily clearing surmounting and protruding roots. He was in excellent condition and ran easily, comfortably, inspired by the knowledge of what he'd already accomplished.

He was certain he'd left any pursuit far behind when he suddenly came up short, staring straight ahead. Here was something he'd never heard of, which was not surprising since he was the first of the people to encounter it. It was astonishing, daunting, and altogether terrifying. No one could have imagined such a thing. It was beyond belief, beyond envisioning.

There was a second Wall.

A Wall that moved.

It was utterly different and far more impressive than the static barrier that surrounded the Home. This Wall was in constant motion, a wide river of brightly colored lethal blurs that would destroy anything foolish enough to try forcing its way through. No wonder so few carnivores ever came close enough to try the interior Wall: they were stopped dead, cut down, by this one. Indeed, he thought he saw fragments, bits of bone and skin, of a razor-tooth that had tried to make it through the barrier only to be smashed to bits by the roaring blurs.

Yet—it was not solid, this second barrier. He could make out gaps that appeared at irregular intervals. Attempting them would be suicidal.

The inner Wall prevented unauthorized entry to the Home. This one was deadly, designed not merely to stop but to kill. It looked robust enough to kill a Servant as easily as a citizen.

Nervously he paced the barrier's boundary, appraising

its power, estimating his chances. Wind blew outward from its depths, warning of the fate that lay in store for anyone foolish enough to consider trying to push through. The better to enhance its effectiveness, the barrier's designers had made no attempt to disguise its purpose. Wind and color and the corpse of the mangled razor-tooth shouted at him: Here lay death.

A noise made him turn. Lurching clumsily through the brush toward him were the two Servants. He knew it would be useless to argue with them. They were incapable of understanding. Their programming was immutable, and his most reasoned protests would not alter their intent. Convinced they were aiding him, they would gently but firmly return him to the Home.

Lach'an damned their good intentions. He'd come this far, had made it beyond the inner Wall. Not the Servants nor anything else was going to keep him from advancing.

They spotted him and altered their course to intercept, emitting coded recognition noises and proffering service. No doubt they expected him to react logically and turn to greet them.

Instead Lach'an pivoted, took a deep breath, and plunged headfirst into the chaos of the second barrier. He could hear the Servants' shocked exclamations behind him and took perverse joy in their surprise.

They accelerated to their maximum speed but were brought up short by the barrier. As Lach'an had surmised, it was just as lethal to them despite their size and strength. Slow they were, but not stupid. He had no time to study their reaction further because every ounce of his being was now devoted solely to trying to pick a path through the destructive field of force.

It was an infernal construct, designed to lull you into a false sense of security before obliterating you from existence. He advanced cautiously, every sense alert, every nerve in his body tingling. No matter what happened now he knew he would not, could not, go back.

The Servants continued calling to him. He could hear the concern in their voices and deliberately shut them out. The violent growl of the barrier was loud in his head as he raced on, running as he'd never run in his life. Sprint, pause and wait, retreat slightly, choose a new direction, and sprint again. The worst of it was not being able to gauge how much farther there was to go. He could only press on, carried forward by strong legs and an unwavering determination.

The movement of the barrier was patternless, death on a scale as random as it was expansive. The trick was to keep moving, if not always straight ahead then to the side or, when prudent, backward. He dared to feel hopeful. He was still alive.

Halfway through he discovered that he could see the other side, the true Outside. Not the bastard mirage that lay between the Home and this hitherto unsuspected obstacle. It was lush with dense vegetation, unrecognizable flora blanketing hilly terrain. It drew him like a half-remembered dream. Ancient emotions rose up unexpectedly inside him. He knew then that no matter what the cost he had to reach that place, had to finish what he'd started. Not just for himself, but for all the smug, self-satisfied, ignorant people he'd left behind.

The emotions that filled him brought with them a power and determination he'd never known he possessed. Confidence replaced fear.

It was a mistake.

Too soon by half to celebrate success. He'd failed to reckon with the insidious subtlety of the barrier's designers.

As he rushed toward his goal, the river of wind and color and destruction abruptly and without warning reversed direction. It was almost as if it had been waiting for him to relax before springing the final trap.

Sensing the mistake he'd made, he threw himself forward at the last possible instant. No one but Lach'an could have reacted so quickly. Nonetheless, he wasn't quite fast enough.

The impact was terrible.

He felt himself flying through the air, the wind completely knocked out of him. Saw the ground coming up to meet him and hit hard. Pain shot up his right leg.

Get up, something inside him screamed. Get up before the false peace you're sliding into claims you completely. Get up or die!

Somehow he managed to gather his feet beneath him and rise. All around him the barrier surged and ebbed threateningly. He knew that if he failed to move, and move quickly, it would finish him any second. Not running effectively anymore, he was reduced to staggering on, stumbling weakly in the direction of the green grail that lay somewhere just ahead. Whereas previously he had put his faith in good judgment and conditioning, he trusted now to whatever luck remained to him.

Several times death missed him by inches, though in the nimbus of pain that ballooned from his injured leg he hardly noticed its grazing caress. He found that his outraged foot would accept some weight. The leg wasn't broken, then. Just painfully sprained. The rest of his body was a single, shaken, mobile bruise, and that from the most glancing blow the barrier could mete out. If it struck him with its full force he doubted he would even feel it. The Outside was close now, so close. He could smell it.

As he staggered onward, a single immense blur bore down on him. He tried one last time to sprint, but events inside the barrier occurred too fast for thought. It was obvious that he wasn't going to make it, that his injured leg would allow him neither to advance nor retreat in time. All he could do was watch the final seconds of his life tick away. Rather than peace or even pain, frustration filled him.

A great roaring rattled his skull as darkness descended. He felt himself being lifted off the ground as the barrier swallowed him completely, spinning him in tight circles preparatory to tearing him apart and spitting him out. He imagined himself becoming part of the irresistible flow, fragments of Lach'an rushing past at high speed to assault the next individual foolish enough to take up the challenge.

And then it was over, as quickly as it had struck.

He lay there breathing hard, several dozen yards from where he'd been engulfed. It took him a long moment to realize that instead of striking him as it had the razortooth, the deadly blur had passed over him, the vacuum created by its passage whipping him along before depositing him in its wake. He was further battered, but still alive and intact. A second such encounter would surely destroy him, mentally if not otherwise.

Not pausing to wonder if any strength remained to him, he fought his way onto his feet and lurched deliberately onward, aching too much to think.

Something solid blocked his path. He blinked, studied it, and realized it was a low containment wall. It marked the far side of the barrier. Uttering a disbelieving cry, he gathered himself and jumped, nearly tumbling back into the lethal slipstream, fighting to keep his balance. Behind him, too close, the barrier thundered.

It no longer mattered. He was through, across, beyond! From somewhere deep inside his soul he found enough energy to emit a cackle of triumph.

Safe now, he allowed himself to turn and regard the

Servants still standing on the barrier's far side. Their
faces reflected the confusion they felt. They simply did
not understand. Nor did they make any move to follow.
Their respect for the barrier equaled his own, but their
courage did not. He was alone now, as alone as one
could be in the true Outside. What dangers lay before
him, what mysteries and threats and revelations, he
could not imagine, any more than he could define the
emotions that raced through him.

Behind lay the security of the Home. Somehow that no
longer mattered. Nothing mattered except that he'd ac-
complished what he'd set out to do. And he'd done the
great thing without really stopping to analyze why it was
so important that he do it. He knew only that everything
felt right.

His leg throbbed. He was going to need food soon,
and a place to rest while he recuperated from his injuries.
With luck and persistence, he would find both. Without
another backward glance, he turned and limped off into
the silently beckoning woods.

On the other side of the barrier the Servants watched
until he vanished among the trees. Only then did the
larger of the pair turn to his companion to voice the confusion he felt.

"Didn't think he was gonna make it. No way, no how.
Damnedest thing I ever saw."

"Yeah." The deeper voice of his stocky companion reflected equal puzzlement, nor could he offer any further
insight into what had just taken place. "I wonder why he
wanted to get to the other side of the road, anyway?"

THE KINDNESS OF STRANGERS

Unless the filmmakers have a particular axe to grind (and I'm not talking about Braveheart), *all too many movies tend to feature the same kinds of people in all-too-forgettable roles. When was the last time you saw an Asian-American male in a major role that didn't involve him kicking or shooting the bejeezus out of somebody? (Okay,* Fargo—*but it was a bit part.) How about an Arab-American in a nonterrorist part?*

Where it should be better, science fiction is often worse. I hate idealized heroes and heroines. That's the movies, of course. Always have been, probably always will be. But SF is, and should be, different. Fortunately, editors are more receptive than producers to what should be their artistic responsibility.

I know guys like this . . .

———

Harry Sandusky wheeled himself out the door of the sun-baked trailer (*mobile home* being far too grand a designation for the place) and down the metal ramp that pointed toward the abandoned gas station. Inside the trailer, the alarm had gone off, signifying the arrival of that rare and precious commodity, a customer. Despite the minimal entrance charge of one dollar per person, not many travelers stopped at the old station on State Route

163 to view Harry's minimuseum of pickled rattlers, scavenged hubcaps, rusting license plates, Lucite-embedded tarantula paperweights, lovingly tended succulents, and other engaging detritus of the desert. But enough did to supplement his Social Security and SSI without drawing the attention of the IRS or any other avaricious government acronyms.

The visitor was tall, in his early thirties, and well-dressed. Overdressed for the high Nevada desert, but not for Reno or Carson City, both of which lay a modest distance yet worlds away to the west. Gamblers sometimes came Harry's way, slumming just long enough to remind themselves how badly they missed room service and air-conditioning. They always had the dollar price of admission. Those that did not, didn't come this way.

The man smiled tolerantly as the bearded occupant of the wheelchair rolled up. "Morning. I was just passing through."

"What else would anyone be doing out here?" Harry cackled. "You're welcome to have a look around. Admission's one dollar." He squinted up at the supercilious visitor. "Guided tour's another dollar."

"Name's Rick Boyes." Already bored, the visitor shrugged indifferently. "Guess I'll spring for the guided tour. I'm trying to kill a morning."

"Gonna make me an accessory to murder, eh?" Tilting back slightly, Harry spun the wheelchair on its axis. "Follow me. But not too close. I brake for critters."

Looking suddenly uncomfortable, the visitor glanced down at his feet, not neglecting to peer behind him. "Your sign didn't say anything about live exhibits."

"Not exhibits." Harry grinned. "Neighbors. There's not much living around here that can't get over, under, or through a chicken-wire fence."

Boyes looked on politely as Harry proceeded to enu-
merate the details and delights of his modest collection.
"That snake in that big jar over there, that's the biggest
rattler I've ever had on the property," he would declaim.
"And that over there is a coyote skull. I'd like to have a
whole skeleton, and God knows there's plenty of the critters around, but coyotes don't like to kick off in acces-
sible places, and until they build one of these grocery
carts with tracks instead of wheels, I'm kind of limited in
my roaming."

The visitor nodded somberly, eying the chair. " 'Nam?"

Harry shook his head. "Bosnia. Land mine. Christ,
how I hated those little suckers. Didn't care who they
killed or maimed. Our side, their side, little kids, some
poor hungry sorry-ass sheep. Step on the wrong spot and
your ass goes ka-boom. Only in my case, it was only
from the ass down."

"I'm sorry," the visitor offered politely.

"Sorry, shit." Harry spun the chair and pushed off in
the direction of the old garage that he had renovated to
hold his indoor exhibits.

They were coming up on his favorite part. The part
that invariably startled and amazed his visitors. While
some were gratified by the sight, and some were indifferent to it, and not a few were openly sarcastic about the
limited appeal of his museum, there was nary a one who
failed to be impressed by the gadget in the box. He called
it a gadget because he had to call it something and he had
no idea what it was. But then, neither did anyone else.

"You strike me as a smart guy," he told Boyes as the
visitor trailed along behind him. "Let's see if you can tell
me what this is." So saying, he parted the wooden doors
to the homemade display cabinet. Revealed within on its
improvised stone pedestal was the gadget.

The foot-high, silvery cone had an integral curl at the

top, like a just-dispensed soft ice cream cone. Through this curl and around the cone's grainy, patterned surface darted a thumb-sized cylinder of light. Bright yellow, two inches long, it was not constrained by glass or any other visible mechanism. Its cone-orbiting path appeared random, sometimes circling the base, sometimes the crest, occasionally passing through the loop of the small curl at the top. The mechanism was absolutely silent, emitting not a whir, not a hum, not an isolated electronic buzz.

Appropriately intrigued, Boyes leaned close and stared at the simple, orbiting light. "You're right. This is very interesting. No, extremely interesting."

Harry tried not to grin. It was a reaction he'd witnessed many times before. "Worth a buck?"

Ignoring Harry's request for a fiduciary evaluation of the object's worth, his visitor inquired sharply, "What is it?"

"Beats the hell out of me. I call it the gadget, because that's what it looks like." He wheeled himself forward. "Watch this."

Extending his right arm, he timed his reach so that his fingers would make contact with the swirling light as it swung around the base of the cone. Upon contact, a second cylinder of orbiting light appeared, bright red this time. Repeating the gesture produced a third orbiter, this one lime green. The lights not only circled the cone, they passed through one another, changing colors whenever they briefly merged. Soon Harry had half a dozen lights darting like overgrown fireflies around the cone and through each other. They gave off no heat and no sound. When Harry made a show of blocking their passage with his hand, they went over or around his outthrust fingers, seemingly of their own volition.

After a while, the newly conjured lights winked away

one by one, leaving only the original yellow cylinder steadily orbiting its silvery cone.

Standing next to the wheelchair, Boyes was staring, his eyes just a little wider than normal. "What powers it?"

Harry shrugged. "Batteries, I guess. Though I'm damned if I can figure out where they go in. I haven't been able to find the compartment lid. Maybe you need a special key to get inside it. Don't really care, so long as it keeps going."

"How long has it been running like this?"

"Ever since I found it. Round the clock, twenty-four hours a day." He grunted softly. "Damn good batteries."

"You found this?" With undisguised reluctance, Boyes tore his gaze away from the cone. "Where?"

This was the best part, Harry knew. His favorite part. He spoke slowly, savoring every word. "It fell out of a flying saucer." He pointed eastward, toward the Saltlick Mountains. "I was camping, out looking for turquoise and jasper, and this big metal disc about the size of a Learjet popped right out of an arroyo not a hundred yards from where I was parked. Wobbled a little, like a fawn taking its first steps, and then pow-bam-goodbye-ma'am it went straight up out of sight. But while it was hanging there, doing that little wobble, the gadget fell out."

He waited, anticipating the usual hoots of derision, the sarcastic comments, the smarmy sideways glances. But Boyes surprised him. The visitor's voice remained calm, his attitude respectful.

"I don't know how it's generating those lights, and I've never seen metal like that. If it is metal. And you say it's been running ever since you found it."

Harry nodded. "That's right. Nonstop. Like I said: good batteries."

"Or something. That trick you did with your hand.

Do the lights always appear in the same order, or can you bring up different colors at different times?"

"Sure can." Harry proceeded to demonstrate. "See? It's all in where you put your fingers."

After the second light display had gone the way of the first, Boyes turned to the man in the chair and announced calmly, "I'd like to purchase the gadget from you."

Harry smiled knowingly. It wasn't the first time someone had tried to buy the gadget from him. "Sorry. It's not for sale. It's the one real out-of-the-ordinary item in my collection. If I sold it, I really wouldn't have anything special to show people. I'd lose my big draw."

"Yeah, I can see how many customers it draws. But I don't want you to think I don't understand," Boyes told him. "I will sign a proper notarized bill of sale and give you five thousand dollars on deposit. I'd like to have some tests run on the gadget. If they come out the way I'm hoping they will, I will then pay you a balance due of one hundred thousand dollars."

Well, Harry mused. This was a new one. "I'll be damned. You believe my story, don't you? You're the first one."

"I don't believe your story. Not yet. That's why I want to have tests run." Boyes nodded in the direction of the gadget. "But I believe in what I can see with my own eyes strongly enough to make the offer, and give you the deposit."

"A check, I suppose." Harry found himself stalling for time. His visitor's offer, coupled with his apparent earnestness, had thrown him off stride.

Boyes nodded toward his car. "I had a good week in Reno. I have twenty-two thousand four hundred dollars and change in a money bag in a hidden compartment in the trunk of my Cadillac. Five down, one hundred thousand on successful completion of tests. I can provide you with telephone numbers, credit card numbers, dozens of personal references. I'm a pretty successful guy, and I can deliver on what I promise." He leaned forward solicitously. "What do you say?"

"If you think the gadget is worth a hundred grand, that says to me maybe it's worth two hundred grand." Harry grinned up at his visitor, showing missing teeth.

Boyes's return smile was forced. "Like someone's going to come along tomorrow and offer you more."

"Might," Harry declared. "Or maybe I'll get a hold of a professor or two at the college over in Reno and have them run a few tests for me."

"That's hardly fair. I'm the one who suggested that course of action."

"Fuck 'fair.' " Harry took a swipe at the place where his legs should have been. "Don't talk to me about 'fair.' "

"All right." His visitor took a deep breath. "Ten thousand now, two hundred thousand if the tests prove out."

This time Harry had to think a little longer, and his reply came harder. "Man, the more you look at it like the way you're looking, the more I think maybe I'd better have this checked out on my own."

"They'll take it away from you," Boyes warned him. "You're a nobody, you have no clout, and if you let others get a hand on it, they'll steal it right out from under you. The government, some big corporation. They'll screw you out of your rights of ownership, and nobody will give a damn."

"Let 'em try. I'll take the story to the media."

Boyes chuckled, and the sarcasm that heretofore had been absent from his voice materialized in his laugh. "And they'll all believe you, right? Even if you can get some tabloid to print your story, and find a lawyer to take your case on contingency, whoever rips you off will tie your claim up in court until you're dead or don't care anymore. Then there's the little matter of taxes. I'll give you cash. Why not accept my honest, straight-up offer now? Two hundred grand would buy you a lot of creature comforts. New handicapped-equipped van, all kinds of amenities for that dump you're living in, trips, live-in help if you wanted it—what do you say?"

"If it's worth ten grand to you on the spot and two hundred thousand later, it might be worth my while to try and find another legitimate buyer. If I could get it auctioned, nobody could steal my claim to ownership."

His visitor stepped back. "You think too much. That's how people lose in the casinos. Doesn't matter whether its craps, or baccarat, or keno. They all start thinking too much. You have to be quick enough to react instinctively." Turning, he started for the door. "Think about my offer, Harry. But don't think about it too much. I'm going to give you some time to think, and then I'll be back."

As soon as he heard the Caddy fire up and spit gravel, Harry wheeled himself out onto the porch of the old gas station. His visitor had left in a hurry, accelerating in the direction of the snowcapped Sierras and the civilization they represented far faster than was necessary.

Who could he call on for help? The nearest sheriff's deputy was based in Palo Verde, thirty-five miles to the south, and the chances of getting him to come out to the place on a supposition and a suspicion were about as good as Harry holding the winning ticket in the next lotto. A natural loner in a lone place, there wasn't really anyone he could call to come keep him company while he waited to see if his visitor made good on his promise to return.

He worried about it, because he hadn't liked the look in Boyes's eyes when he'd departed, hadn't liked the cant of his jaw or the hostility implicit in his posture. None of it boded well. Harry had a couple of guns, but he didn't fool himself about any imagined ability to repel boarders.

He could take the gadget, climb in the old station wagon, and drive into town—and do what? Sit in his car until something happened? Until Boyes found him? He had no doubt that anyone who could make a legitimate offer of two hundred thousand dollars for the gadget could find him. He had no money to run with, and even if he did, where would he run to? Metaphorically, of course, he thought bitterly.

Maybe the smart thing to do was make the best of it. Until his visitor returned, he could at least do what Boyes had suggested. He could think about it.

The glow was very subtle. It would have awakened a dog immediately. Ex-soldiers required only a little more exposure before their field-sensitized senses kicked in and responded. Despite the passage of years, Harry had not lost that.

So it was that he found himself carefully picking up the shotgun from its resting place next to the bed, hauling himself into the wheelchair, and heading cautiously outside the trailer. If the sight of his shaggy, unkempt self clad only in slippers, underwear, and oil-stained sweatshirt wasn't enough to scare off any intruders, maybe the shotgun would suffice.

As he neared the crumbling stuccoed back of the old garage, wheeling his way silently between lovingly tended cacti and poorly labeled rusty mining implements, he saw that there were actually three lights. By far the brightest came from the dry riverbed that wormed its way through rock and dry soil half a mile north of the station.

The others were nearer, and flickered within the garage. That was where he kept those few items of his collection that could be considered valuable. That was where he kept the gadget.

Whoever was inside had not only broken the lock but also disarmed his admittedly simplistic alarm system. His lips tightened. If that slick son of a bitch Boyes had come back early and with help, they weren't going to leave without participating in a twelve-gauge discussion on the merits of breaking and entering.

But there was no car, unless its headlamps were the source of the light illuminating the edges of the distant wash. Why park way out there? he wondered. Even if they had a four-wheel, it seemed unnecessary.

Slowly, he made his way around to the rear of the station and worked his way up the ramp that led to the back door. It, at least, was still closed. Good time to have a power chair, he told himself. Another luxury he couldn't afford. He couldn't have cared less, except that in order to get his chair up the ramp to where he could open the door he had to use both hands, which meant putting the shotgun down on his lap however momentarily.

The door opened silently: not surprising, since the alarm system had been disarmed. Easing himself inside, he closed the door behind him. No doubt Boyes wasn't expecting trouble from a reclusive double amputee. He was in for a serious surprise. You didn't have to pull triggers with your toes.

On silent rubber rims he rolled into the museum and headed for the nearest light switch. He never reached it. Mentally prepared for falling fists or clutching hands, he did not anticipate being halted by a glow—but that was exactly what happened.

There were two of them. The largest stood nearly seven feet high, tall enough to have to maneuver between old hanging lamps and a rotting crystal chandelier. Its companion was considerably smaller, topping out at maybe four feet. Lean and lanky, clad in what looked like fleecy gold, they revealed pale white skin that would not have lasted five minutes in the northern Nevada sun without burning.

Skinny, they were, with long thin legs and arms that terminated in two sucker-tipped fingers apiece. Their faces were comparably elongated, with loose flaps of brownish skin on either side that could as easily have been gills as ears. Jet-black hair trailed from midway down the back of the neck and was gathered together in an incongruous ponytail by more of the woven gold material. Their eyes were vertically oval, black, and fitted with slightly convex dark-blue pupils. The mouths were small, round, lipless, and toothless. The distinctive glow they were emitting came not from them but their attire.

They might be advanced, but they were not omnipotent. They had not detected his entrance, and were clearly surprised when he rolled into view. At least, he chose to interpret their slight retreat as surprise. Captivated by their alienness, he gingerly laid the shotgun down on the floor and rolled slowly toward them.

"Hello." He raised one hand, palm upward, because that seemed to be as appropriate a thing to do as anything else.

In response, the smaller one looked up at the larger and mouthed something that sounded like wind whispering through holes in rock. The larger replied, and then both turned to gaze at him. Emboldened, he resumed his advance.

"You two look like you could use a good feed. But I have the feeling this isn't a social call. Let me guess: You're here for the gadget."

There was no reply. They simply stared, following him

with their unnaturally prominent pupils as he wheeled himself over to the display case. Parting the doors, he lovingly removed the gadget from its pedestal. As always, the intensely bright yellow cylinder continued to circle its silvery cone. He spun the chair.

"Guy came by today wanted to buy this. Two hundred thousand he offered me. I have a feeling I can't do anything to stop you if you insist on taking it back, but I just want you to know that I could sure use that two hundred thousand. Like I told him, if I shopped it around I could probably get more. Especially now that I know it's, well, genuine."

Again the shorter visitant looked up at the taller and spoke. Receiving a reply, it stepped forward. Harry held his ground, a simpler decision to make in the face of conflict when you don't happen to have any legs. But he had the feeling he would have held it anyway.

Two long arms extended in his direction, the sucker-tipped fingers outstretched toward him. The meaning of the gesture was plain enough. So was Harry's response. Tense but with little to lose, he held on to the gadget, and waited, and watched.

After a minute or so the more diminutive of the two aliens stepped back. It had not tried to take the gadget, had made no threatening gestures. What it did next surprised Harry almost as much as the aliens' actual initial appearance. It also explained some things.

The smaller alien put one two-fingered sucker-tipped hand on the larger one's arm and turned its head away from Harry. It did this by rotating its skull almost a full 180 degrees on its neck. The larger creature wind-whispered something to the seated human, then started to turn. It struck Harry then that they did not intend to take the gadget from him by force. Maybe an interstellar version of the old finders-keepers law applied here. Or maybe there was something going on that he did not understand.

Either way, he thought he had it figured out. Their shape might be alien, and their posture, but the relationship between them could only be interpreted in one way. At least, given his limited store of knowledge and imagination, he could only interpret it in one way. For all he knew he could be completely wrong, galactically off-base. But, what the hell . . .

"Hey, wait a minute! If it's that important to you . . ."

They turned back at the sound of his voice, not because they understood the words. Smiling even as he wondered how it would be interpreted, Harry held out the gadget. He was going to miss it; miss the looks on the faces of the astonished travelers who visited his museum, miss playing with the bright little lights, miss the extra dollars it brought him in tips—but what the hell . . .

"Here you go, kid. I lost a toy or two when I was your age, too. Or your size, anyway. Next time, don't be letting it hang out the window when you take off. Or wherever it was hanging when you left without it."

As the smaller alien accepted the gadget, one of its fingers made contact with Harry's. It was amazingly cool to the touch, like tinfoil that had spent an hour sleeping in the refrigerator. Then the hands withdrew, clutching the gadget.

The two aliens never changed expression. They might be incapable of doing so, he realized. But neither did they leave. Instead, both approached and began to examine him more closely, running those strangely flexible fingers over his face, his body, the chair. Up close, he found that their golden suits generated not only soft light but soft heat. Sitting in the chair in his underwear, he could sympathize. The high desert got plenty cold at night.

A sucker-pad touched him in a sensitive place, and he

laughed, causing both his gentle examiners to draw back
sharply. "Hey, watch it! That tickles."

When he reached out to touch the smaller alien, he
was infinitely delighted to see that it did not pull away
from him.

"What do you mean, it's gone?"

Boyes hovered menacingly over the man in the wheelchair. The two unimaginative types flanking him scowled
down. They were hot, and tired. It was evening, the sun
had set, and already they were regretting having left their
regular gigs in Reno to haul all the way out here to the
middle of nowhere. But the guy who had hired them had
promised that there would be little or no trouble, and
thus far he had certainly delivered on that. As much as
anything, they had been brought along to intimidate. It
annoyed them that they did not appear to be having the
desired effect on the clown in the chair.

Harry spread his hands. "I told you, I gave it away.
Back to the original owners. They showed up two days
ago, and I gave it back to them."

"I can't believe this," Boyes muttered. Ever since he
had arrived to find the gadget gone, he had been muttering it a lot. "Wait a minute. You just gave it back?"

"That's right. I gave them back the gadget, and before
they left they gave me an old bike. Looks like a classic,
but I thought the idea was pretty funny. Giving me a
bike, I mean."

"Watch him." Fury bubbling in his eyes, Boyes strode
off toward the sad-looking garage-museum, leaving
Harry waiting under the baleful gaze of the two hirelings.

"You guys get out this way much?" he inquired
conversationally.

"Shut up, jack," the nearest meat ordered him. "We're

not liking this any better than you." He wiped at his fore-head. "Christ, it's hot out here! How do you stand it?"

"I've been in hotter places. Arabia. Bosnia."

The other dog showed a flicker of interest. "You were in Bosnia? That how *it* happened?"

Harry snorted. "Didn't happen crossing Silver Creek Road in Tahoe."

His transitory nemesis nodded. "My dad was in Bosnia. Worthless bastard, except for that. They say he did good there."

"Sorry."

"Hey, don't you be sorry for us. You'd better hope that—"

"He's telling the truth." They all turned in the direc-tion of the gas station as Boyes came stomping out. "It's not there." Approaching the chair, he leaned over its oc-cupant and glowered.

"You don't think I believe a word of this, do you?"

Harry shrugged. "What are you gonna do? Tear the place apart? If I did still have it and wanted to hide it from you, you know you'd never find it. I know this country, and you can't dig it all up." His eyes rose to meet those of his visitor. They did not swerve, or fall.

"As for beating it out of me, I've taken worse than anything your hired donkeys can hand out."

"You think so?" Unexpectedly finding himself pinned by that unwavering stare, Boyes suddenly blinked and straightened. "One thing at a time, I suppose." He eyed his companions. "Search the trailer first. Then we'll start in on the museum and the rest of this junk out here. And if we don't find it pretty quick," he paused meaningfully, "maybe we'll find out whether you're as tough as you think you are."

They did not bother to keep an eye on him. After all, it wasn't as if he was going anywhere. As for the possibility that he might have a gun stashed somewhere, Boyes secretly hoped that he did. It would give them an excuse to shoot him, useful in the event the law became involved. Not kill him, of course. Just shoot him. In that event, it would be a simple matter of their swapping a call for medical assistance in return for the gadget. He was not concerned about Harry's possible prowess as a sharpshooter. The two men he had brought with him were professionals, and he had been assured they were competent.

They were working their way through the tired, slovenly bedroom, ripping out drawers and tearing apart storage boxes, when they heard the boom and the subsequent ascending whine. Rushing out back, they saw the small silvery disc rising into the remnant blue of late evening. It trailed a pale pink streak and a somehow triumphant howl behind it. Very quickly, it was gone.

Gone where, Boyes could not imagine. But he would have given a great deal to know.

"What the fuck?" one of the hired pair mumbled. His partner swallowed hard, his gaze focused on that impossible patch of prevaricating sky.

Boyes found himself nodding knowingly. "He said they gave him an old bike. I should have paid more attention to what he was saying. No—I should have *thought* more about what he was saying. He called the generator a gadget. I wonder what it was he called an 'old bike'?"

Next to him, the meat whose father had been in Bosnia shrugged. "You got me. But whatever it was, it seems to work fine without pedals."

PEIN BEK LONGPELA TELIMPON

Papua New Guinea is one of the most beautiful, most fascinating places left on the planet. The best diving, incredible natural wonders (thirty-eight of the forty-three known species of birds of paradise . . . quick, what's the highest point of land between the Himalayas and the Andes?), and some of the most primitive yet wondrous human cultures left around.

The highland peoples of PNG were the last large group of humans to have contact with the outside world (1932, when some Australian gold prospectors wandered into the hitherto unpenetrated mountains). There are still undiscovered tribes living in the razor-backed, jungle-wracked mountain valleys. Upon contact, some eventually find their way down into the cities, only to find themselves confronted with and bewildered by the trappings of what we like to call modern civilization. Sometimes the resultant confrontations are amusing. Sometimes not.

Pein bek longpela telimpon is a phrase in Melanesian Pidgin, a trade language still in frequent use in New Guinea and throughout portions of the South Pacific. It translates loosely as "Long-distance payback" . . .

Wahgi first heard the muffled screams and angry curses as he was rummaging through the Dumpster. Not that this was unusual. Late at night in Boroko there were frequent fights between men who had blown their weekly paycheck on cheap beer. Wahgi saw them staggering drunkenly out of illegal pubs, stumbling between tired whores and their pseudo-macho customers, arguing with predatory taxi drivers over disgraceful fares—even the chickens that clucked and pecked their way across the central square around which the run-down shops were situated were usually in a rotten mood.

But this encounter was different.

Instead of trade pidgin, the combatants were spewing an inarticulate mush of proper English, Strine, and several foreign tongues Wahgi did not recognize. That was notable. After four P.M., the few tourists who braved the square in search of artifacts, Sepik River wood carvings, and illegal bird-of-paradise plumes were usually gone. After five, when the last European-owned stores padlocked their security screens for the night, only local people were left. To hear European tongues this late at night suggested goings-on that were far from normal.

Like everyone he knew, Wahgi was intensely curious about the wonderful things white people carried around with them. He was among the first of his tribe to come down from the Highlands into the capital in search of work to help support his family. Highland people learned quickly, and it did not take a village Big Man to realize that these wonderful objects could only be obtained in exchange for a pocketful of money. Yams were not accepted currency in the city stores, and only rarely would a sympathetic checkout clerk, perhaps not long down from the Highlands himself, accept a pig. If anyone had told Wahgi a year ago that it was better to possess a fistful of brightly colored paper than a corral full of pigs, he would have scratched at his arse-grass and looked upon them as if they had taken leave of their senses.

But the fact that the Highland people had only made contact with Western civilization in the early 1930s did not mean that they were irredeemably ignorant. Only isolated.

What bad thing could possibly happen to him if he just went to see what was going on? Certainly he wasn't having much luck riffling through the contents of the smelly Dumpster. Stretching himself to his full five foot five, he boosted himself up and out and followed the sounds of dissension. Scattered among the shouts and curses like corn seeds between rows of sweet potatoes was much labored grunting and snorting. It reminded him of rutting pigs crammed into a pen too small for them.

There were four men fighting in the dark covered accessway that ran between the Ha Chin dry goods store and the *niuspepa* shop. Even though he couldn't read, Wahgi liked to go into the *niuspepa* shop to look at the pictures in the glossy magazines, especially the ones that showed women of all colors in skimpy clothing. That is, he did until the bush knife–wielding shop manager chased him out, realizing that the hick Highlander had no money.

Concealing himself in a corner near the back alley that intersected the accessway, he watched the fight in silence. Even though he could see no *longpela naips*, or machetes as they were called in the Steamships stores, he could tell that the fight was serious. Though he couldn't see which of the four men was wounded, fresh blood, black and wet, was running on the cracked concrete, mixing with the betel nut juice stains. He wondered what they were fighting about, here too late at night in an unlit passage in a poor shopping area like Boroko.

Then he saw the suitcase. It was much smaller than the ones the ground crews unloaded from the planes at the airport. Too small to hold much of anything in the way of clothing, which is what he knew white people usually carried in their baggage. The small suitcase lay off to one side, propped against the grille of iron bars that protected the *niuspepa* store. Was it worth four men fighting over? If so, it might be full of something valuable. Maybe, he thought excitedly, money paper.

He gauged his chances. The men were wholly occupied with one another. In the village he had been a good hunter, bringing back tree kangaroos, monitor lizards, rats, hornbills, and crowned pigeons. Like many Highlanders he was small and stocky. If they saw him, would they forget about their own fight and come after him? Though new to Port Moresby, he was confident he knew the hidden places of Boroko better than any European.

Besides, he hadn't eaten since yesterday.

Waiting until he thought the moment just right, he slipped out of the shadows and slid along the wall, keeping low. Providentially, the suitcase had a handle fastened to the top. He was a little surprised to find that the case was made of metal instead of the soft fabrics and leathers he was used to seeing at the airport, but it was astonishingly light. Modest in stature the Huli peoples might be, but every man was muscled as hard as the stump of a mahogany tree.

Gripping the suitcase in a fist of iron, he slipped back the way he had come, keeping the black iron security bars pressed against his spine. Busy with one another, none of the combatants noticed him. As soon as he reached the alley, he turned and ran. That was something else Highlanders were good at.

He did not stop until he was halfway to the suburb of Koki, where he shared a ramshackle hovel of salvaged wood, cardboard, and corrugated iron with two other young men from the village. Like all the buildings in Koki, it was built on stilts out over the water. It was not a bad place for poor people to live. No one could sneak up on you unless they had a good, quiet boat, and the tide provided the services the nonexistent sewage system could not.

Pausing on the Ela Beach road beneath the harsh yellow lights of a British Petroleum station, he settled down beneath a hibiscus bush to inspect his prize. Even to his country eyes the case looked expensive. Though small, the lock proved resistant to his probing. But only momentarily.

One of the night attendants at the station was another Huli who hailed from a village not far from Wahgi's village. He had struck up a casual acquaintance with the man, and their clans were not currently at war. Though suspicious, the attendant lent him the hammer and heavy screwdriver his fellow Highlander requested. He knew Wahgi wouldn't run off with them. That would have put the attendant in deep trouble with the station's owners, which would have turned into a payback situation against Wahgi's village. Every Highlander treated the ancient tradition of payback with extreme respect, and Wahgi was no exception.

Modern as it was, the lock eventually yielded to Wahgi's strength, persistence, and single-minded determination. After returning the tools, he went back under the bush to examine the case's contents. In these he was both disappointed and puzzled.

The case contained a number of small electronic devices that were as alien to Wahgi as if they had fallen from the moon. He knew what a radio was, and a television, and an airplane, because he had seen them up close, but otherwise his knowledge of contemporary twenty-first century technology was lamentably limited. Another section of the case was full of paper, but to his disgust and disappointment none of it was money. Though colorful, the papers were much too big to be currency: PNG, Aussie, or otherwise. He did not know what they were. Perhaps his roommates Gembogl and Kuikui might know, though they had spent little more time in Mosby than had he.

He was philosophical about his theft. The contents might be valueless, but the case itself was certainly worth something, even with a broken lock. Leaving it under the fragrantly flowering bush, he went once more into the station, this time to beg a length of used twine from his fellow Huli. With the lock broken, he needed something to secure the case.

When he returned, something inside was beeping insistently.

Slowly and with commendable caution, he reopened the case. The noise was coming from one of the small electronic devices. Gingerly lifting it out of the case, he turned it over in his hands. It was about the size of two packs of cigarettes. On its front were a large number of illuminated buttons above which a small yellow light was blinking. This he eyed in astonishment, wondering how anyone could manufacture so small a bulb.

Could the device hurt him? He knew he should find a way to stop the beeping, or he might draw unwanted attention to himself. The Mosby police were not gentle with thieves, especially those who stole from visiting Europeans. He had seen how buttons could turn a radio on and off. Perhaps one of the buttons on the device could do the same to the insistent beeping sound.

Experimentally, he began pushing them one after another. Each time he depressed a button, it responded with an electronic chirp, but the continuous beeping never stopped—until he pushed one of the buttons near the bottom. Not only did the nerve-wracking beeping cease, but the yellow light turned to green.

"Stavros, Stavros . . . *was ist mit ihnen los? Sprechen sie*, dammit!"

Wahgi almost dropped the device. Then he realized what it was: some kind of telephone, but unlike any he had ever seen before. For one thing, it was infinitely smaller than the ones that were fixed in the public boxes. For another, it was attached to nothing. From it issued a voice that was as clear as it was unintelligible.

"*Stavros!*" The tone was angry and insistent.

Maybe, he thought, there might be a reward for such a unique and therefore probably expensive telephone. Could he make the irate individual on the other end understand him?

Leaning toward the device without knowing where to direct his voice, he said in his best rudimentary English, "Hello. Good morning. How are you? *Yupela wantok me?*"

This resulted in a long silence from the tiny telephone, and Wahgi wondered if he had somehow broken it by speaking into it. Then the voice returned, no longer irate but obviously confused. Confused, and curious.

"*Ya?* Stavros? So you are now speaking English? *Warum?* Why?"

Stavros, Wahgi decided, must be the name of one of the four men whom he had seen fighting. The owner of the case, or at least its keeper. And like the man on the other end of the line, he had spoken English—as well as other things.

"I no—I am not Stavros," he informed the telephone. "I am Wahgi."

There followed another extended pause that was broken by a stream of furious foreign syllables that the Huli decided he would not have been able to follow even if he could understand the alien tongue. Then another interlude, after which a new voice spoke. It was much more controlled, much calmer than its predecessor, and its English was far better. To Wahgi it sounded like American English, not Aussie or British, but he could not be certain. Sometimes it seemed to him that there were as many varieties of English as there were languages in Papua New Guinea.

"To whom am I speaking, please? You said that your name was Wahgi?"

"Yes." Wahgi was relieved to be talking to someone whom he could understand, and who might be able to understand him in return. But he suspected the person on the other end would have little or no knowledge of Tok Pisin.

"Wahgi," the voice inquired in a sweetly reasonable tone, "where are you?"

"In Mosby—Port Moresby. The capital."

The voice faded, as if its owner was momentarily speaking to someone close to him. In the same room, perhaps. "At least that fits." Louder, and obviously to Wahgi, it added, "Look at the bottom of the phone you are holding. There should be a word, or words, there. What does it say?"

Wahgi found the single word easily. "I see what you are talking about, but I do not know the word." He added apologetically, "I cannot read."

"How many words? Can you count?"

Of course he could count! Did the other man think he was empty-headed? "Just one."

"How many letters in the word?"

Wahgi counted, laboriously but effectively. "Six."

A murmur of voices could be heard over the phone. "Good," the other man said. "Now Wahgi, this is very important. Where did you find this telephone?"

The Huli considered, then decided to plunge ahead. How else was he to find out what the case and phone might be worth, or how big a reward he ought to ask for? "In a small suitcase."

The man's tone changed ever so slightly, but not so slightly that Wahgi failed to pick up on it. "Two men should have been watching this case and its contents. Do you know where they are?"

Wahgi looked up as a pair of fruit bats with four-foot wingspans settled into the tree alongside his resting place. On the busy road, cars and taxis whizzed past without stopping. "Yes. When I left them they were fighting with two other men. In Boroko." He thought rapidly. "I took the suitcase for safekeeping."

"That was very clever of you, Wahgi. Very clever indeed. And I know that the case—it's called a briefcase, by the way—is safe with you. Now, my friends and I would like to have it back. If you will tell us where you are, we will send other men to take it off your hands."

"It is not heavy," the Huli replied with unconscious irony. "Will I get a reward?"

More muttering on the other end, a few violent words in that strange alien tongue that were overridden by still louder words from the English speaker, and then the voice was back on the line.

"We'll be glad to give you a reward, Wahgi. So long as you return the briefcase and its contents in good condition." Anxiety crept unbidden into the man's voice. "They are in good condition, aren't they?"

The Huli decided to be honest. "I broke the lock. To make certain the contents were okay," he lied easily.

Rather than upset him, this seemed to amuse the other man. "That's all right, Wahgi. The lock is not important. There should be some papers in the briefcase. Papers with colored printing on them and brightly colored borders. Are they still there—in good condition?"

"Oh yes," Wahgi assured him readily. "They have not been harmed at all."

Softer mutterings from behind the speaker. "That's just fine, Wahgi. Now, what would you like for a reward?"

Large numbers being foreign to traditional Huli culture, Wahgi stalled for time. What was larger than twenty? What was the briefcase, and more importantly, the pretty papers it held, worth to the man on the strange telephone?

"What is your name, and what is the name of your village?" How much should he ask for? he thought tensely. He had heard many numbers on the televisions in the pubs. Which one would be suitable?

For the second time, the other man sounded amused. "My name is Eric Werner von Maltzan, Wahgi, and I am speaking to you from the village of Zurich."

"Zurich. I do not know that village. Is it in Australia?" Australia was the only country Wahgi knew besides Papua New Guinea.

"A little farther," von Maltzan told him. "About your reward?"

Wahgi had decided. "I want a million kina." *Million* was a term he had heard during sports programs, and it had sounded pretty big to him. Would it be too much? Were the telephone and the papers worth more? Having dealt in pigs, he knew how to bargain. You did not need a big education for that.

His request certainly had an effect on the other man, and those Wahgi believed to be in the room or hut with him. He could hear them arguing in their strange tongues. Crossing his legs under him and watching the flying foxes spit pits from the fruit they were peeling and eating, he waited patiently. With the lateness of the hour, traffic on the nearby main road was becoming infrequent.

Eventually von Maltzan came back on line. "That's about five hundred thousand American dollars, Wahgi. That's a great deal of money."

Wahgi did not know if it was, but decided to take the other man's word for it. After all, he reasoned, if von Maltzan knew about briefcases and telephones and colored papers, he should know something about money.

"That is the reward I want."

Again von Maltzan could be heard arguing with other men. "All right, Wahgi. You'll get your reward. Now, here's what I want you to do. Go to the airport. Not the public terminal. The private one next to it. In the main building you'll find—"

"No."

The other man hesitated. "What's that?"

"No. I do not know what time it is in Zurich village, but it is very late here, and I am very tired. I am going home, to talk with my friends. Can you call me on this telephone later tonight?"

"Yes, but—"

"Then that is what I want you to do." He started to put the phone back in the briefcase.

Entirely composed up to now, von Maltzan's voice began to crack. "No, Wahgi, *nein*! Don't do that! It's vital that you . . . !"

The Huli was pleased to discover that despite its tiny size, lack of a connecting cord, and strange appearance, the telephone still operated very much like the other telephones he had seen in use around the city. When he found the button that turned it off, he was delighted. The beeping that had so startled him at first and had precipitated the conversation resumed immediately. It continued until Wahgi found another button that turned it off for good. Satisfied, he put the device back in the briefcase and tied it up with the length of twine. Then he resumed his hike back to Koki, dashing across the two lanes of highway.

Gembogl and Kuikui were lying on their torn, bedbug-infested, salvaged mattresses when he arrived. Kuikui lit the single kerosene lantern and put his machete down as soon as he saw who was standing in the doorway.

"Where have you been, Wahgi? We were worried about you."

"Wake Gembogl. I have something to show you both."

As the three men sat in a circle on the floor, Wahgi undid the twine and triumphantly showed them the contents of the case. "This is called a briefcase," he explained with the air of a new schoolteacher.

Not to be outdone, Kuikui added, "*Brief* means *small* in English."

"That makes sense. And this—" He held up the satellite phone. "—is a telephone."

A doubtful Gembogl took it and held it closer to the lantern. "It doesn't look like a phone."

"It is. I used it to talk to a man in a village called Zurich. He promised me a reward for returning the briefcase."

That caught his friends' attention. "How big a reward?" Kuikui asked.

"A million kina."

Gembogl burst out laughing. "*Wanem!* A million kina? For a briefcase and a bunch of papers?"

Kuikui was less skeptical. "Wahgi may be telling the truth. You know how peculiar Europeans are about their papers and things. I have seen them in the bank, fussing over them like women over shells."

"A million kina. We could buy a car with that." Gembogl sounded wistful.

"Many cars." Kuikui was more economically learned than either of his friends.

"Then we agree on the amount?" Wahgi's gaze traveled from one man to another. They had shared privation and insults, hunger and spiteful taunts from the more sophisticated townsfolk. Now they would share in his reward.

Gembogl was shaking his head. He was the youngest of the three who had come down from the Highlands to seek work in the city. "I can't believe this. I just can't believe it. It's too good to be true. Of course we agree on the amount," he added as an afterthought.

Kuikui urged his friend, "Call this man back. Tell him we have discussed your proposal and we are all agreed."

"Yes, call him back," Gembogl said excitedly.

"I can't." Wahgi picked up the phone. "I don't know how to use this. But I think he will be calling me." So saying, he pressed the button that had successfully shut off the beeping. It recommenced instantly, as if it had never stopped.

"Now watch." Exaggerating his movements for maximum effect, the Huli pressed the button he had used to activate the device previously.

"This is Eric Werner von Maltzan calling for Wahgi. Eric Werner von Maltzan of Zurich calling for Wahgi of Port Moresby, PNG." Though clear enough, the voice sounded very tired.

"See?" Proud of his newly acquired technical skill,

Wahgi responded. "I am here, *pren* Eric. With two of my friends. How will you get my reward to me?"

"Just leave everything to me, Wahgi. I will take care of—"

"Just a moment." It was Kuikui. He was staring at the open doorway and frowning. "I thought I heard something."

"We should be careful." Gembogl kept his voice down as the older man blew out the lantern. "A million kina is a lot of money."

"Yes. Wait here." Picking up his machete, Kuikui moved purposefully toward the open doorway. His friends waited in the darkness.

"What is it?" The voice on the phone sounded more anxious than ever. "What's going on?"

"Probably nothing, *pren* Eric." Wahgi spoke in a whisper. "Just some noise outside. My friend Kuikui went to check on—"

The staccato burst of sound splintered on the Huli's eardrums. He had heard that sound before, once during a riot and again during a military parade. It was the sound of a gun going off. Not a shotgun, but an automatic gun that could fire many bullets without stopping. Gembogl sprang for his machete while Wahgi grabbed the briefcase and stumbled toward the rear of the shack.

The voice on the phone never stopped. "Wahgi! What was that? It sounded like an Uzi!"

"We are being shot at!" Clutching the phone in one hand and the briefcase in the other, Wahgi pushed up against the back wall of the shanty. Outside were plank walkways, and below, the sewage-saturated part of the harbor that surged back and forth beneath Koki.

"In the briefcase!" the voice on the phone told him. "A plastic egg the size of a man's fist! Put it next to the phone." Fumbling among the devices and papers, Wahgi

found the object described and did as he was told. An
electronic tone sounded from the phone, in response to
which a red light appeared on the side of the egg shape.

"I did what you told me to," he stammered into the
phone. "What do I do now?"

"Run, jump, get away, Wahgi—and throw it at the
people with the guns!"

"Kuikui, Gembogl, run away!" he shouted. There was
no reply as he tossed the red-eyed ovoid onto the floor
and pushed through the flimsy rear wall of the shack.
As he did so three men burst through the doorway.
Two were tall and European while the third was Melanesian, but no Highlander. A slim, fine-featured coastal
man, Wahgi saw in the glow of the lights they carried,
probably from down near Milne Bay.

As he fell toward the outriggers moored below, the
sun seemed to come out behind him. It was a sun full of
thunder, as the shack, the wooden planks on which it sat,
and a portion of the surrounding walkways erupted in a
ball of white-hot flame. Screams filled the air as other
shanty dwellers, explosively roused from their sleep,
staggered out of their thrown-together homes to gape at
the fireball that was rising in their midst.

Wahgi landed hard in an open outrigger, twisting his
ankle and hitting his jaw on the side of the narrow craft.
But there was nothing wrong with the rest of him. Carefully placing the briefcase in the bottom of the boat,
he untied it and began stroking toward shore, toward
Ela Beach. As he paddled, the phone jabbered frantically
at him. He ignored it, occasionally looking back over
his shoulder. Where the shack had been was a flame-
lined hole in the elevated walkway. The supporting stilts
had been blown off right down to the water, like man-
groves that had been logged. There was no sign of his in-
terim home, of the other two men who had lived there,

or of the three heavily armed intruders who had burst in on him.

They had not paused to talk or to ask questions, Wahgi reflected. They had simply shot their way in. He was sorry for Gembogl and Kuikui, and angry at what had happened to them, but he now knew one thing for certain: The briefcase and its contents were unquestionably worth a million kina.

Maybe two million, based on what had just happened.

Safely ashore on the narrow city beach, he abandoned the outrigger to the vagaries of the harbor currents. Exhausted and out of breath, his left ankle throbbing, he threw himself down under a coconut palm and opened the briefcase.

". . . are you there, Wahgi! Can you hear—"

"What happened?" he asked von Maltzan. "What did you do?"

"Those gunmen were after the briefcase," the foreigner explained. He did not need to do that. Of course the gunmen were after the briefcase. Did he still think Wahgi was stupid? "I used the phone to activate the grenade you threw at them. Where are you? Are you all right?"

"Yes, I am all right. But my friends are not."

"I'm sorry. Now will you listen to me and not hang up anymore? If you do, I won't be able to help you."

"Never mind that." Tasting wet saltiness in his mouth, Wahgi felt for his teeth. One was missing, knocked out when he had hit the side of the outrigger, and blood was trickling over his lip and down his chin. To a Huli it was nothing more than an inconvenience. "I want my reward."

"Yes, yes, of course, but—"

"I want it left for me in a paper-wrapped package at

the main airport cargo pickup counter, with my name on
it. By tomorrow morning."

"It'll be there, Wahgi. No problem. But please, do one
thing for me. Leave this phone on in case you run into
trouble again. That way I can help you. Keep it close at
all times. Other people want what is in the briefcase, and
as you have seen this morning—"

"It is night here."

"All right, all right. As you have seen this night, these
others are willing to kill to get it."

"I will not turn the phone off again," Wahgi promised.

"Good! Tomorrow morning, at the Jackson's Airport
cargo counter. Look for your package."

The voice went away, but the green light remained on.
Wahgi surmised that it indicated the line was still open to
him if he needed to use it. Looking around, he sought
and found a picnic bench across the street from the
Ela Beach hotel. In an emergency, he could run in that
direction. Port Moresby hotels always had guards on
duty around the clock. They would not interfere in a
fight to help him, but their presence might well dis-
courage an attacker from using a gun in the presence of
armed witnesses.

Stretching out on the warm sand beneath the table,
he felt he had done all that he could until morning.
Dreaming of a million kina and sorrowing for his dead
kinsmen, he fell into a deep and placid sleep.

Parker put the silencer to the side of the sleeping man's
head and pulled the trigger once. There was a soft *phut*
followed by the sound of bone splintering. Blood spurted
briefly, quickly slowing to a trickle. Unscrewing the silencer, he placed it and the gun back in their respective
jacket holsters.

"Poor dumb blackfella," he murmured emotionlessly to his companion as the other man picked up the briefcase. "Never had a clue what he was dealing with."

McMurray murmured something into the telephone in the briefcase before turning it off and closing the case. "Probably thought he was safe, he did. Wouldn't have understood if you'd taken the time to try explaining it to him." After a quick look around to ensure that they had not been observed at work, they headed for the car parked in the nearby beach lot. "Tracked the phone's location via satellite search from Zurich, and its internal GPS pinpointed it for us. There was never any place for the sorry bugger to hide."

"Not as long as he left the phone on active sending." Parker opened the door on the driver's side and slid behind the wheel, nodding at the briefcase as he did so. "The bonds still in there?"

His colleague nodded. "Doesn't look like they've been touched. A hundred and sixty million Swiss francs' worth of convertible paper." His eyes gleamed. "It's bloody tempting, you know."

"Now mate, none o' that." The engine on the rented car coughed to life. "You know they'd send blokes like us after us if we were to try and disappear with that."

"It was just a thought, Eddie."

"Well, blow it out your arse. Let's get back to the hotel. First Qantas out of this shithole tomorrow, we're on it."

Gembogl watched the men drive away. When he was sure they had left, he ran to the picnic table. He saw instantly that Wahgi was dead. The car had stopped at the petrol station across the street, and he hurried across the road toward it. While one of the men pumped fuel, he slipped inside the station and in a frantic, hushed stream of words began relating what had happened to the silent attendant. The man was a Huli and therefore, however distant, a kinsman.

The knock at the hotel door the following morning prompted McMurray to grab his pistol and station himself flat against the wall to one side of the portal. Nodding to his partner, Parker approached cautiously and without a word put his eye to the peephole set in the door. The tiny Fresnel lens showed a small black woman clad entirely in white standing on the other side. She was holding an empty laundry basket.

"Who is it?" McMurray asked tightly.

Making a disgusted face, Parker whispered to his colleague. "It's a maid." Nodding sourly, McMurray put his automatic pistol back in its shoulder holster.

The woman on the other side spoke matter-of-factly when Parker cracked the door. "You are checking out this morning, sir. We have a big tour group coming in, and I need to take away your dirty linen."

"But we're not ready to—oh, all right!" He slipped the door's security latch. "But be bloody quick about it!" To McMurray he muttered, "We don't need any of the help complaining to management that we're keeping them from doing their job." Curtly, he pulled the door inward.

The maid came in. Calling her diminutive would have flattered her. She was maybe four foot six, but perfectly formed. Cradling her basket, she headed toward the beds as Parker closed the door behind her, enjoying the sight of her compact ass twitching from side to side beneath the tight white maid's uniform.

A dozen very short, very muscular men burst through the half-open door like circus midgets shot from a single cannon. They had wild kinky hair that spread out from

the sides of their heads, skin dark as bittersweet chocolate, and physiques like miniature linebackers. They also
wielded knives and machetes like the exploded com-
ponents of a berserk threshing machine.

Parker was hacked to bits before he could react.
McMurray went down with his hand on the stock of his
machine pistol, but before he could find the trigger a
bamboo arrow caught him in the throat and went completely through his neck. A foot of fire-hardened shaft
emerged from the back. He had time enough to marvel at
the incongruity of it. A bloody great arrow! In this day
and age!

"Who . . . ?" he gasped before the blood welling up in
his throat choked off any further speech.

He did not recognize the young man who came forward to stand over him.

"You killed my friends. Wahgi and Kuikui." He gestured at the watching coterie of small but ferocious men
who filled the room. The maid had left to stand watch
outside. "This is payback for what you did to them. A
friend who worked at the petrol station where you
stopped last night after doing your killing owed my village some old payback. We got on his motorbike and followed you here. Madani who works for the hotel is an
Engan, not Huli, so we now owe her tribe big payback.
For compensation we will give her village ten pigs for her
help this morning in sneaking us into the hotel."

"Ten—pigs . . . ?" McMurray choked. He was fast
bleeding to death.

He did not get the opportunity to do so. The oldest
man in the group—short, white-haired, but straight as
an arrow—approached and with a single swing of his
bloody machete, cut the European's head half off. He
apologized to his companions for not making a better

job of it. He was not as strong in the arms as he used to be, he explained.

As they were making preparations to leave, something began beeping within the briefcase. Opening it, Gembogl removed the strange telephone. Remembering how Wahgi had used it, he pushed the appropriate button.

"Parker?" a voice inquired. "You should be departing with the case in an hour or so. Don't leave any tracks. I know you're not in London or New York, but there's no reason to make things easy for the local police, no matter how primitive they might be, *verstehen*? You never know—one of them might even know how to spell Interpol. I'll be expecting you tomorrow at the airport." The voice paused briefly. "Parker, are you there?"

"It looks valuable." Curious, the wiry elder examined the phone.

"Who said that?" The voice on the other end grew alarmed. "Parker, who's in there with you and McMurray?"

"What should we do with it?" Another man was using a bedsheet to wipe blood from his machete.

"It may be valuable, but it killed Wahgi and Kuikui." Raising his arm and ignoring the sudden stream of frantic babble that spouted from the device, Gembogl brought his own blade down sharply. State-of-the-art it might be, but the satellite phone was no match for a honed machete. It splintered into fragments of metal and plastic.

As they were about to leave, Gembogl picked up the briefcase. "And this, what should we do with this? Destroy it also?"

The old man regarded it narrowly. "It killed Wahgi and Kuikui too—but you said it was worth a million kina?" The young man nodded. "Then we will keep it, and hide it until we can understand how to make it work for us. Just like we are learning to make other things from the outside world work for us." Turning, he shook his woolly white head as he walked toward the door. "These white people make many magical things work for them, but between you and me, man to man, I will still take a good machete over a device that talks through the air any day."

SUZY Q

"Oh Suzy Q. Oh Suzy Q. Oh Suzy Q, yes I love you, oh Suzy Q."

Puccini it's not, but certain song lyrics stick in the mind like gum under the desk in front of you in high school. Transcending lyricism, they become mnemonics. Ask anyone of my generation to sing you the words to "The Mickey Mouse Club Song" and see how many on the verge of senility can spout the entire rhythmic banality—hopefully with a proper modicum of embarrassment.

What does this have to do with Alien Abductions, which was the anthology this story was written for? An alien abduction, like everything else, is often so much a matter of perspective. I hesitate to call it a shaggy dog story . . .

_____

She felt that she understood them fairly well. Under the circumstances, that was as much as could have been expected. Whether they understood her was another matter entirely.

It had been difficult at first. They did not look or sound like anything she had ever encountered before, and they had a unique, utterly distinctive smell: a cross

238

between the pink roses in the garden and old man Charlie Woods, who lived next door and with whom she enjoyed an ongoing relationship that Joe had tacitly assented to for years. Yet in spite of their strangeness, she had found herself oddly drawn to them. But then, she had always suffered from an excess of interest in the new and exotic.

She knew she shouldn't have gone after them. No one had the slightest idea where she was headed at the time, and now it was very likely that no one knew where she was. Her evident interest seemed to puzzle them. Whether they would have ignored her or not she did not know, but at the last minute, just as she had decided that she had seen enough and had better start back home, they had scooped her in as easily as she would have picked up a baby rabbit, and taken her with them.

Doubtless she ought to have resisted. Joe would have—but she wasn't Joe. Deep within herself she knew that it was wrong, that she should have put up a fight, or at least called out. That she did none of those things seemed to surprise them. In their peculiar way they were as taken with her as she was with them.

Others were not so amenable.

She encountered her fellow captives inside the ship. A man was fighting and screaming as they secured him to a bench or table. The process was interesting to observe. One of the creatures held a device from which spewed what appeared to be tightly restrained ropes of light. It reminded her of the way Joe liked to eat Cheez Whiz right from the can. Friends of theirs thought it a disgusting habit, but when the two of them were playing and laughing and Cheez Whiz was flying all over the house, manners didn't seem to matter. It had struck Suzy on more than one occasion that most people not only didn't have much fun, they did not even know how to *have* fun. If one thing could be said to characterize her long relationship with Joe, it was that the two of them always knew how to have a good time.

The unknown man presently being light-strapped to the table-bench certainly wasn't having fun. He was crying. This disturbed Suzy, and she tried to remonstrate with the busy creatures on the man's behalf, but they ignored her. Or perhaps they simply didn't understand. Certainly their language was entirely alien. When they crowded close around the man his blubbering dropped to a nervous whimper. Though she could sympathize with his position, his distress made no sense to Suzy. Sure, these strange beings were odd-looking, with their imposing, bloated heads and multiple arms and leprous skin. They also had very big teeth and exceptionally large, penetrating eyes. Four apiece.

So what? She knew plenty of people who were equally strange-looking, and she didn't break down in their presence. As far as she could see, the visitors were not hurting the man. So why was he so distraught? Still, the urge to try to comfort him was strong. She felt it was up to her to share what reassurance she could from within the serenity of her own self. It was something she was very good at. Many of her and Joe's friends had remarked on it.

When she called out to him, his moaning stopped and he looked sharply in her direction. Seeing her standing there, he looked first startled, then confused. When one of the creatures started toward her, the man began shouting at it. Unafraid, Suzy remained calm at the approach of the lumbering, toothy alien, tracking its progress from behind bright brown eyes. Finally it halted, towering over her, those sharp teeth very close. Dealing as she did with strangers every day (though none quite so strange as these), she met its quadruple gaze without flinching. One of several multiple limbs reached for her.

It urged her, gently but firmly, toward the bench. Relaxing, she allowed herself to be guided, not resisting at all. These beings had done her no harm, and she therefore saw no reason to be afraid of them. Her natural curiosity overrode any sense of fear. The compelling digits pressing against the back of her neck were warm and strong. If necessary, she could try to break free of the firm, clinging grasp—but to what end? Like the man, she was trapped inside the alien craft.

She found herself right up next to the bench. The limb that had been pushing her steadily toward it now relaxed. She was free to step away if she wished, but instead she remained by the side of the bound man. He was watching her intently, pleading with his eyes as if he thought she might somehow be able to come to his aid. She studied his face. He looked to be older than Joe, but not by very much. A taller, slimmer version of Charlie Woods.

Though the illumination in the room was dim, with a distinct bluish tint, she found she could see clearly. In any event, it would have been impossible to miss the large, complex device that was hovering above the table. In the shadowy, accented light, two of the aliens began to make adjustments to mechanisms whose design and purpose were unfamiliar to her. Emitting a soft whine, the hovering machine began to descend. The indirect lighting suffused its surface with a dull silvery patina. His eyes drawn to the movement, the man on the bench started screaming again. Suzy failed to comprehend any reason for his profound agitation.

The device halted about a foot above the heaving,

twisting chest. A bright purplish beam emerged from a small cone to strike him in the face. Almost immediately, his screaming stopped, for which Suzy was grateful. The unceasing shrieks of despair had begun to get on her nerves.

Instruments emerged from the underside of the machine, glistening and delicate. Some were made of metal, some were transparent, and the substance of others she was unable to identify. They reminded her of the tools at the garage where Joe worked. Unsurprisingly, their purpose was as unknown to her as their composition. Their functions were soon demonstrated, however, as they dipped down to swiftly and efficiently crack the recumbent man's chest cavity. As the operation unfolded, the alien next to her, the one that had impelled her to move to the side of the bench, rarely took its multiple eyes off her. When she reacted with nothing more than quiet, polite interest to the procedure that was being performed on the table, it turned and conversed in a low rumble with the alien on its left.

The procedure did not take long. After conducting a rapid yet detailed examination of the man's internal organs, skeletal structure, and nervous system, the creatures smoothly replaced everything they had removed. Colored lights resealed the gaping cavity in the human torso, and the eyes-wide-open yet motionless man was removed to a place where Suzy was not allowed to follow. Concerned, she wanted to check on him, only to find herself firmly restrained. Sensing the strength in those alien digits, she did not put up a fight. Humming methodically, a flat mechanism made several passes over the now unoccupied table until the last of the blood that had pooled up on the slick surface had been evaporated, leaving it once more clean, sterile, and dry.

She became aware that an alien on the opposite side of

the table was eyeing her meaningfully. Once she met its gaze, it tapped the flat, stark plain of the operating bench with the tips of two limbs. Its intent was unmistakable.

Smiling brightly, she hopped up onto the gleaming table. Her ready compliance occasioned another round of rumbling conversation among the nearest of the creatures. The one that had drawn her forward to watch the previous examination leaned over the table and appeared to engage in a brief argument with those on the other side. She felt powerful digits curling around the back of her neck to draw her off the table. Once again, she complied. Not that she could have resisted if she had wanted to. These visitors were much stronger than she was, a good deal stronger even than Joe.

A woman was brought into the room, her flesh wan and sickly looking in the bluish haze. She was quite young, with hazel eyes, dyed blonde hair, and a stocky yet supple shape. Presently, she had a dazed look about her. As Suzy looked on, the operational routine she had just observed was repeated, complete with the preliminary struggling and screaming. As before, the purple beam put a stop to all that.

She was permitted to observe two more dissections and examinations, whereupon the alien that seemed to have taken a personal liking to her escorted her to a chamber fashioned from some kind of metallic black gauze. There was no furniture, and the light seemed to issue from the enclosing material itself. With nowhere to go and nothing to do, she sat down on the floor and waited.

Eventually, a small machine brought food and water. She eyed the food with understandable reluctance, but a quick taste sufficed to suggest that it was harmless and nutritious. The water was as pure and clean as any she had ever sipped. All in all, she was quite content with the situation, except for one thing.

She missed Joe.

He would be missing her, too, she knew, as well as worrying himself sick about her. When he returned from his job at the garage and found her absent from the house he would grumble and make dinner, take a shower, then sit down to watch the ball game on the new television. When she was not back by the time the evening news came on he would start to become really worried. First he would probably check to see if she was visiting any of her friends in the neighborhood. When that proved fruitless he would start making phone calls.

There was nothing she could do about it. There was no way to let these creatures know what she wanted. They didn't understand anything she said, and their method of communication remained impenetrable to her. On the plus side, she was fascinated by them, by their surroundings, and by their activities. For their part, they seemed to enjoy her company. Whether it was her individual appearance, the evident interest she had taken in their work, or her willing compliance with their orders she could not have said, but for whatever reason, after that first day they never again tried to put her up on the examination table.

More people were brought in, to have their bodies opened up like cans of dog food, to see their insides removed for examination and study and alien handling before being replaced and their owners sent on their way. Suzy beheld it all with the same unflagging interest. Strangeness and strangers had always intrigued her, sometimes to her detriment. On more than one occasion Joe had warned her about blindly placing herself in situations that might expose her to serious danger, but she had invariably ignored him. After each of her little adventures he had lectured her severely, sometimes even shouting, but the love he felt for her eventually muted his tirades. It was something she knew she could count on. No matter how mad he became at her, she always knew how to calm him down and win him over.

She missed him more each day.

The sustenance that was being supplied graduated from adequate to excellent. It improved with every meal, as if the aliens were studying her eating habits and adjusting the diet they were providing accordingly. Some of the culinary combinations she was offered proved to be as tasty as they were exotic. After a while, though, the novelty began to pale, and she found herself missing dinner with Joe in front of the TV, him bellowing his irresistible, hearty laugh as he commented on the activities on screen, her listening and except for an occasional excited outburst letting him do all the talking. At such shared moments they were completely comfortable with one another, a sign of a healthy and mutually respectful relationship. They had been together for more than ten years now.

The aliens did their best to keep her occupied. In the company of the being who had initially taken a special interest in her she was allowed to see most of the interior of their strange craft. Nothing was placed off-limits. It was as if they knew that it was all far beyond her comprehension, that she could take nothing in the way of secrets away with her. In this they were quite correct, but Suzy did not feel in any way slighted. She was as confident of her intelligence as she was of her attractiveness.

She found it all fascinating, even if she understood nothing of what she saw. She did not even worry about ending up on the examination table. It probably helped that she had never been one to think very far ahead. Unlike Joe, who spent too much of his time lost in preoccupation and worry, she was quite content to live for the moment. He was fond of remarking how much he envied that ability of hers, and wished he could learn to live like that himself.

There finally came a day when she was escorted to a part of the craft she vaguely remembered. Her memory of the place was confirmed when her alien (she had come to think of it as "hers") manipulated a discoloration on the wall to create an opening to the outside. Familiar world smells rushed in on her: oak trees, cloying humidity, something dead nearby. It was very late on a particularly dark night, and trees blocked her view of anything in the distance. Joe, she thought. It was time to leave—if they would let her.

Perceiving her emotion, the creature placed that by now familiar collection of alien digits against the back of her neck and gave her a gentle push forward. Turning, she looked up at it, seeing the four eyes staring back down at her. It was letting her go, but reluctantly. It had become attached to her. She could sense it; she was good at that. Nor was she surprised. Full of pride, her Joe had commented repeatedly about how she had that effect on people. Where he was gruff and brusque and downright antisocial at times, his Suzy made up for it by being open and friendly to all who came their way. Sweet and kind, she was: Everyone found her irresistible. Not a day went by that he didn't give thanks for having her in his life. From the first time their eyes had met, he had known that she was the one for him. Her best qualities, it seemed, even worked on aliens.

Again the digits pushed. With a last backward glance she turned and exited the craft. The experience had been captivating, even enlightening, but while her interest had never flagged, she was glad they had decided to let her leave. The ache in her chest was the longing she felt for Joe. Behind her, the opening vanished and the craft began to rise silently skyward. She tracked it with her eyes for a long time, until it was out of sight and lost among the stars.

How they had managed to release her so close to her home without their sizable craft causing a general commotion among the townsfolk she could not begin to imagine. She knew only that a few familiar twists and turns would bring her out of the field and back onto the main road. By the time she reached the outskirts of town her legs were beginning to ache. Close to the house, she lengthened her stride and picked up her head. Joe would be frantic over her extended absence, and she would have to hasten to reassure him that nothing untoward had happened to her, that she was all right. There was, of course, no possible way she could convey to him the details of her experience.

He was there, all right, sitting alone in the little living room gazing glumly at the television. When she walked in he gaped at her for a moment before exploding to his feet.

"Suzy! Suzy Q, my God, I thought—I didn't know what to think!" He opened his rough, strong arms to her, and she threw herself joyfully into them. How could she explain what had happened? How could she convey the astonishment and singularity of where she had been and what she had seen? She could not, of course, but it didn't matter. It was a memory she would keep for herself, a wonder she could never share, not even with the one person in the world who was most important to her. All that mattered now was that she was back home, and that

Joe was all right, and that she was all right, and that they were once again all right together. He hugged her so hard the breath went out of her, and she struggled to respond the best way she knew how.

Her tongue darting out from between her jaws, she began to lick his face, over and over.

THE LITTLE BITS THAT COUNT

When I was asked to do a story for an anthology called Moon Shots, to celebrate the anniversary of mankind's first flight to our one big, fat, inescapable satellite, I initially balked. What more was there to say about one of humankind's greatest achievements, and a comparatively recent one, at that? So many words had already been written about the enormous scientific and economic undertaking, about the heroism of everyone from the lowliest engineer to the most noble astronaut. Better writers than I had written moon stories. Heinlein, Clarke, all the giants of the field. What more could I add, and in a short story, no less? The task seemed as insurmountable as a slippery, dangerous crater wall.

One thing I determined from the start: that whatever I wrote, my story would treat this monumental human undertaking with the dignity and respect it deserved. After all, I wouldn't want Buzz Aldrin mad at me the next time we met . . .

"Morning, Hank. Anything to declare?"

Beneath his shiny, chromed helmet the guard looked bored, sounded bored, was bored. And why not, Henry Deavers thought? His was a boring job. Not nearly as exciting as Henry's. Nevertheless, the guard smiled

249

pleasantly, his expression neutral as Deavers replied in the negative. Mechanical in his movements, the immaculately groomed younger man waved the technician through and turned his semisoporific attention to the next worker in line waiting impatiently to exit the facility.

Henry passed through the primary metal detector, the shape-and-form detector, the chemical sniffer, the secondary metal detector, waited while his weight was checked and his retina scanned, and repeated the nothing-to-declare routine at the last guarded checkpoint before emerging into the hallway that led to the parking lot. Waving good-bye to coworkers Ochoa Hernandez and Laura Patrick, he made his way to his four-year-old sedan, thumbed the compact remote on his key chain to unlock it, and slipped in behind the wheel. The guard at the gate let him pass and left the barrier up so Ochoa and Laura could follow, Laura in her Taurus and Ochoa on his presumptuous, growling Fat Boy. Once on the main access road they headed in different directions: Ochoa and Laura north along the coast, Henry inland. Behind them, the stark sentinels of the Cape's launching platforms stood silent and waiting against the tepid, pastel Florida sky.

Maneuvering the steering wheel languidly with the heel of one hand, the pungent smells of sea and space receding rapidly aft, Henry Deavers relaxed. He'd gotten away with it again.

How many times was it now? More than several thousand, at least. He should know exactly, but after the first five years he had grown tired of keeping the count in his head. It was enough to have it at home, buried innocuously on his computer in the midst of a list of household items. A file inoculated with innocuousness, he mused contentedly. No one could imagine that next to the mundane columns that listed books and recordings and insurance numbers was one that kept careful track of pieces of Moon.

Because Henry "Hank" Deavers was a thief. Had been a thief for a little more than ten years now. Had been thieving nearly every week of those ten years, without once getting caught. He chuckled at his foresight, smiled grimly at his patience. It had not been easy. The temptation to steal much more each time was always great. But greed, he knew, could trip up even the cleverest thief. So he had begun modestly and remained so, knowing that time was on his side. Today was yet another confirmation of the efficacy of caution.

It was just as well that he was nearly sated. They were going to begin moving the entire facility next week, shift it to Houston. His opportunities for thievery would transfer with it, but he did not care. Ten years of stealing was enough. His retirement was in the bank, as it were, though safely stored in plain sight at home. No one had ever suspected, even though several friends and neighbors had passed right by his hoard. A few had even gazed directly at it, suspecting nothing.

His most recent pilferage reposed, as it always did, in his shoe, under the conveniently high arch of his left foot. Two fragments of stone smaller than his little fingernail. Dull grayish-white in appearance, they would automatically have been ignored and dismissed by anyone not knowing what they were or where they had come from. Chips of rock rendered immensely valuable because they had not come from the beach, had not been picked up in a supermarket parking lot, had not cracked loose from a friend's decorative garden wall. Their origin was to be found in the sliver of silver that was just now becoming visible above the horizon behind him. They had come from a small, shallow valley called Mare Trigonis that lay two hundred thousand plus miles away.

Tiny pieces of Moon rock.

Working in the lab, slaving long, tedious hours for an unchanging salary, garnering none of the glory or recognition of scientists or astronauts, Henry Deavers had hit upon the idea some twelve years ago of stealing pieces of Moon. With the resumption of the lunar landing program and its regularly scheduled flights from orbit, Moon rock had once again become available, but only for study and exhibition in the world's great museums and scientific laboratories. The public clamored to see it, photograph it, touch it. They had to content themselves with small samples locked away in secured glass cases, because the great bulk of material the astronauts brought back vanished into labs and institutions of higher learning and advanced study around the world. A few billionaires managed to acquire tiny fragments; the ultimate collector's trophy. One Saudi prince had a shard the size of a pencil eraser set in a platinum ring. Among common, everyday millionaires the demand for the material was intense. It was the supply that was lacking, strictly controlled as it was by NASA and its associated agencies. This state of affairs was about to change.

He, Henry Deavers, senior lab technician, was going to change it.

Ten years he had been smuggling tiny chips of Moon rock out of the preparation lab, using a system of hide-and-seek he had laboriously perfected. Involved as he was in the initial stages of preparing specimens for trans-shipment to laboratories and universities around the world, he quickly discovered it was possible to adjust the records ever so slightly without drawing attention to the manipulation. No one missed the tiny slivers he slipped into his shoes, between sock and leather. Only one trip to the bathroom was necessary to make the transfer. The key was to take only minuscule fragments, no more than two at a time, sometimes only one.

His largest prize to date was not big enough to be set in a ring surrounded by diamonds, but sealed in a presentation case of polished Lucite, it would bring a fine price. Multiplied by thousands, even deducting the seller's commission, it would be more than enough to make him rich.

Over the years he had watched everything settle neatly into place: the shadowy network of brokers who would shield his privacy when in a few months the fragments of Moon began to come onto the market, the secret bank accounts in the Cayman and Cook Islands where his share of the profits would be deposited, the falsified identity papers that would attest to the death of the rich cousin in Austria who upon passing had willed his entire fortune to Henry J. Deavers, thereby explaining the lab technician's sudden wealth, and much, much more. He was quite confident. After all, he had been preparing for the culmination of his scheme for more than a decade.

He was whistling happily by the time he pulled into the driveway of the unassuming suburban home. Billie was waiting for him, persevering and unsuspecting as always. Kind, good-natured, unimaginative Billie. They had been married a long time. When the money began to roll in, he had no intention of divorcing her. For one thing, he was used to having her around. For another, it might draw suspicion to him. Easy enough to keep his wife and add a decorative mistress should the desire strike him. Or two.

Reaching down, he paused to stroke Galileo and Copernicus, their two grown tabbies. Billie had recently adopted a third stray, whom she promptly named Aristarchus. Ari for short. Theirs was a lunar household, in

more ways than his wife suspected. She was proud of his
work at the Cape, even if he dismissed it as the repetitive
and deadly dull routine he knew it to be. "My Hank," she
would tell new acquaintances, "he works in the space program!" She was happy in central Florida, happy with their
life together and content in its predictability.

Prepare yourself for a change, Billie my girl. Get ready
for early retirement and an extended vacation. Cousin
Badenhofer is going to die on the twenty-fourth of next
month, right on schedule. Following a quick, prepre-
pared probate, your easygoin', easy-lovin' Hank is going
to take you to Europe and other wondrous points east.

Hurriedly running through the day's requisite catch-
up small talk, he left her to finish making dinner and
headed, as he always did, for his workshop. Only rarely
did she venture into the confusion of tools, lumber, and
accumulated building supplies, just as he spent little time
poking through the incomprehensible depths of the
kitchen cabinets. The cats followed him, rubbing up
against his legs and meowing for attention. Absently, he
would bend to scratch one or the other behind the ears,
or smooth out a fluffy tail.

The heavy-duty paper sack was not hidden. There was
no reason to hide it. He kept it near the back of the workshop, propped up between some salvaged one-by-six
planks and splattered cans of paint. It was almost three-
quarters full, containing between eight and nine pounds
of Moon rock in the form of tiny, inconspicuous, patiently smuggled shards, taken one or two at a time from
the preparation lab at the Cape. Pounds! To this hoard
he would now add the two chips riding uncomfortably in
his shoe.

Like escorting fighters leaving a slow-moving car-
rier, the cats peeled off to inspect a possible mouse hole.
Henry started to reach down to remove his right shoe,

feeling the shards shift against the sole of his foot. His eyes flicked in the direction of the bag—whereupon he paused, still half bent over, and stared. Stared without moving.

The bag was not there.

He did not have to pinch himself. His wakefulness was an unequivocal, crushing, inescapable reality. The bag was gone.

Frantically, he searched the immediate area, then started on the rest of the workshop, making no more noise than was necessary. Curious, newcomer Ari helped him look, without having a cat clue as to what her master was so desperately hunting. Her presence brought him no luck. The sack, the fruit of ten years' careful brigandage, was missing. It was not leaning up against the cans of old paint; it had not risen up on unsuspected pseudopodia and walked to the other side of the workroom; it was not there.

Stunned beyond measure, he sat down heavily in the capacious old easy chair Billie had bought for him six years ago at a garage sale in Daytona Beach. His heart was racing as he strove to calm himself. *Think!* Goddamn it. Who could have known about what he had been doing? Who might have observed him on his regular visits to the laboratory rest room?

That was it! No fools worked in the lab. Someone had seen and taken note of his surreptitious activities, had figured out what he was doing, and had decided to bide their time, letting him do the dangerous work of thievery only to steal from him in their turn. His lips compressed tightly together, and a muscle in his jaw twitched. They wouldn't get away with it. He had friends, he did. Knew people not involved in the space program, unsavory folk who had helped him with his grand design. One of his lab colleagues was going to be receiving a visit from the bearers of serious trouble. All he had to do was figure out who it was.

If he didn't recover the sack, that someone might be him, he knew. His "friends" were expecting a delivery of thousands of tiny fragments of Moon, had been preparing to receive it for some years now. If he did not produce it, they might very likely be inclined to express their disappointment in violently antisocial ways Henry chose not to try to envision.

A bit bewildered by the uncharacteristic intensity he displayed at the dinner table, Billie avowed as how she could not remember anyone from the lab visiting since yesterday. Yes, she had been out shopping for a few hours this morning, but why should that be occasion for comment? What was the matter? His face was so red and—

Wordlessly, he pushed back from the table and fled from her concern. A careful check of the driveway produced no clues. No skid marks left behind by tires in a hurry to leave, no telltale fragments of left-behind evidence. He went across the street, then up and down it, querying neighbors. Had they seen anyone parked at his house this morning? Had any trucks made deliveries to the neighborhood? Most critically, had they seen anyone walking in the vicinity of his home carrying a large, nondescript, reinforced paper sack?

Eyeing him askance, his neighbors replied regularly and depressingly in the negative. Disconsolate but not yet broken, he returned home and somehow forced himself to engage in halfway normal inconsequential chatter with his wife while they ate dessert. That night, the usual evening of television and conversation was pure hell. Despite his exhaustion, he did not sleep at all.

It *had* to be someone at work, someone at the lab. Realizing that he could expose them, his contacts would not have taken the cache. Why should they risk that anyway, when there was plenty of looming profit to be had by all? No neighbor would enter his workshop without him present, even if Billie would have been willing to let them in. Thieving kids would have taken glue or chemicals, while addicts looking to support their habit would have stolen tools. No, it was unarguable: No one would bother to steal a sack of splintered rock who was not cognizant of its true nature.

The next day he confronted one colleague after another, meeting their eyes and searching their faces, trying to single out the individual who had appropriated his birthright. Whoever it was did not crack. Darapa he suspected immediately. The man was too clever by half, too smart for his own good, and a foreigner besides. Noticing his stares, the smaller man turned away uneasily. Yes, it could well be Darapa, Henry thought. Or possibly Glenna, hiding behind her spotlessly clean suit and thick glasses, striving to maintain an air of mousy insignificance. It did not matter who it was. He would find them out, and then he would contact his new friends, and someone would get hurt. He took perverse pleasure in the anticipation.

Nearly a week passed, however, without him arriving at a conviction. He knew time was running out. He would have to do something quickly. Having been assured of and promised delivery of the merchandise by a certain date, his "friends" would be busy trying to deal with a long list of increasingly anxious and very important clients. They would be growing uneasy. So was Henry. They were not the sort of people he wanted to keep waiting.

Just before dinner, it struck him. His own mind-set was the source of the trouble. Having engaged for so long in illegal activity, he had automatically assumed that his loss must be due to the same. All week he had been tearing himself apart and unnerving his fellow workers for no reason.

It was Billie. It had to be. For reasons unknown she had moved the bag. She never bothered anything in his workshop, hardly ever went in there, in fact. But such a scenario was not unprecedented. Once, she had decided to reseal the back deck, and had helped herself to the big can of spar varnish he kept in the back. Another time, he recalled her borrowing a screwdriver when the one she kept in her kitchen work drawer proved too big and bulky for the task at hand.

No reason to panic, he told himself. Even if she had used some of the fine "gravel" to line the bottom of a pot for a new houseplant or something, it would still be available for recovery. And if, for some horrid reason, it was not, surely she would not have used all of it for some such purpose without his permission.

She was standing by the sink scrubbing a skillet when he came out of the workshop, smiling as warmly as badly jangled nerves would allow him.

"Hon, there was a sack of small rocks, really small rocks, in the workroom. Back by where I keep the paint and some of the lumber. By any chance, have you seen it?"

Glancing back at him without stopping work, she looked thoughtful for a moment, then smiled. "Oh, that?" She nodded, and the terrible tension that had gripped his gut for days at last began to subside. "Sure, I found it."

He swallowed hard but kept smiling. "Where did you put it, hon?"

Her expression fell. "Oh, did you need it? I'm sorry, Hank. I didn't think it was anything important. What was it for—making cement or something?"

"No," he told her, more tightly than he intended. "It was not for making cement. What did you do with it?"

"Threw it out. About a week ago." She was openly apologetic. "I'm really sorry. Whatever it was for, I'll buy you a new bag."

His legs started to go, and he just did make it to one of the kitchen chairs. "You . . . threw it out." His tone was hollow, echoing inside his head. It sounded very much like the voice of a dead man. Which he would be when his business partners came looking for their promised merchandise. Unless—he raced to the Cape and confessed everything to Security, and had himself remanded to protective custody.

No, wait! There was still a chance, a possibility. Maybe she had "thrown it out" outside the house, in the yard. Even if the birds had been at it, even after she had watered down the grass and plants, he still might be able to recover the bulk of the priceless, irreplaceable lunar material.

"Where . . . is it now?" He was amazed at how calm he was, how steady his voice and comprehensible his words. "What the he—what on Earth did you use it for?" On "Earth," he thought. How droll. How very amusing. In his mind's eye he saw his disappointed friends removing his appendages, one by one, without anesthetic. Not starting with his fingers. Or maybe just a quick, clean, free flight out over the Atlantic—only watch that first step. His blood chilled.

"I'm really sorry, Hank." Despite his strenuous attempts to hide his feelings, she could sense how upset he was. "I didn't have any choice. I mean, we were all out, that was the day my car was being worked on, and the box was really stinking. I remembered seeing that bag the last time I was in the shop and I thought it would work. I'll replace it, I promise. Please don't be angry with me." Her nose wrinkled up. "Believe me, if you had been stuck in the house with that smell, you would have done the same thing."

"Sure I would," he mumbled, utterly distraught. Blinking, he looked up. "Smell? What smell?"

"You know." Her pleasant, matronly smile returned. "I was right about the stuff in the sack, anyway. It worked just fine." Relieved, she returned to her dirty dishes.

Ohmigod, he thought. Ohmigod, ohmigod. This past week, when he had been searching frantically, had been interrogating his neighbors, had been trying to stare down suspected coworkers, it had been *in the house all the time*. Right under his nose, so to speak. Hysteria built within him, and he fought to keep from being overwhelmed by it. A dozen times, a hundred, he had walked right past his precious stolen lunar hoard without suspecting, without thinking, perhaps even glancing in its direction. Never realizing. Smelling, but never realizing.

Billie put the now gleaming, freshly scoured skillet in the dish drainer and started on the dirty forks and knives. "I can tell you that the cats were crazy for it. Acted like it was the best stuff they'd ever used. Naturally, when they were finished with it, I had to throw it out." Once again, for the last time, her nose wrinkled in disgust. "What would anyone want with used kitty litter?"

SIDESHOW

A Flinx and Pip story

Many years ago, Judy-Lynn del Rey edited a sequence of original novelettes in a series called Stellar. When she asked me for a Flinx & Pip story to include, I was at something of a loss as to what to do, never having utilized the characters in anything shorter than a novel. The result, "Snake Eyes," was a lot of fun.

Time passes, and Chris Schluep at Del Rey Books asks for another F&P short to include in this anthology. Once again I'm caught wondering what might be appropriate, and fun, when it occurs to me that even the heroes of long-running series need a vacation once in a while. Flinx not having been home in a long time (insofar as he has a home), I thought it was time he paid a visit to his old empathizing grounds.

Of course, this being Flinx, even a vacation back home couldn't possibly turn out to be as peaceful and relaxing as he would hope it to be.

You never know what you'll see on a side street in Drallar.

From time to time, Flinx felt the pull of the only home he'd ever known. So, in the course of his wanderings, he would return now and again to the winged planet of Moth, and to the simple dwelling still occupied by the irascible old woman he, and everyone else, called Mother Mastiff.

It was good to roam the backstreets and alleys of the hodgepodge of a city, taking in sights both new and familiar; inhaling the amalgamating aromas of a hundred worlds; observing the free-floating, arguing, laughing, chattering farrago of humans, thranx, and other citizens of the Commonwealth. Here he had no responsibilities. Here his only concern was relaxation. Here he could mix freely without constantly having to look over his shoulder to see if he was being followed. Here he could—

Without warning, Pip, his Alaspinian minidrag, promptly uncoiled herself from his shoulder, launched herself into the fragrant, damp air, and took off down a minor side avenue crammed with vendors and street merchants. Fortunately, he reflected bemusedly as he took off after her, she flew high enough to avoid precipitating a panic. Among those strollers and vendors who did see her, few were knowledgeable enough to identify her and recognize her lethal capabilities.

She landed on a diffusion grating the size of a dinner plate that projected from the crest of a three-story building. As soon as he slowed, staring up at her, she launched herself into the air and glided back down to settle once more on his shoulder, her petite but powerful coils securing herself to him.

"Now, what was that all about?" he murmured soothingly to her. "What set you off? I'll bet it was a smell, wasn't it? Some kind of exotic food full of especially attractive trace minerals?" The only problem with this theory was that the nearest food stall lay two blocks distant. No vendors of unusual victuals were open nearby.

What *was* close at hand was a performance by one of Drallar's innumerable, alien, untaxed, and probably illegal street performers. The human was short, florid of face, glistening of scalp, and thick of arm, leg, and middle. His black sideburns fronted his ears and threatened to overwhelm his jawline. His trained subordinate was decidedly nonhuman, not quite as tall, considerably slimmer, and clad in an elegant coat of soft white fur marked with bright blue stripes and splotches. Its eyes were elongated and yellow, with dark blue vertical pupils. Dressed in short pants and matching vest of garish green and gold silk, with flower-studded beret and oversized necktie for emphasis, the alien was performing a simple yet lively dance routine to the accompaniment of music that poured from its master's quinube player. Almost lost among the fur and silks was the control band, no thicker than a piece of string, that fit tightly around its neck.

Watching the performance, Flinx let his peculiar talent expand to encompass the appreciative crowd, not all of whom were human. The expected emotions were all there: amusement, low-grade wonder, expectation, curiosity. With growing maturity, he had developed the ability to focus his abilities on selected individuals. Probing the musician-master, he sensed approval and contentment, but also an underlying, simmering anger.

Well, the personal emotional problems of the player-owner were no more his concern or responsibility than were those of the hundreds of intelligent beings whose feelings he had sampled since awakening in Mother Mastiff's home early this morning. After watching the performance for another couple of minutes, mildly admiring the owner's skill with the quinube and his creature's agile, three-toed feet, he turned to leave.

Immediately, Pip rose from his shoulder and hovered. Spectators who had ignored the minidrag's colorful presence on Flinx's shoulder now found themselves drawn to the deep-throated whirring of the flying snake's wings.

More instinctively wary than educated about the mini-drag's potential, a few moved aside to give her more air space in which to hover.

"Now what?" An irritated Flinx extended his left arm. When he moved toward her, the obstinate flying snake continued to refuse the proffered perch. "I don't have time for this, Pip!" Actually, he had nothing but time. Not that his assertion mattered, since the minidrag comprehended only his emotions, not his words.

He eventually raised the level of the former to the point where she finally settled, albeit with evident reluctance, onto his forearm. As soon as she had curled herself securely around it, he began stroking her. When she tried to rise again into the air, he held her firmly in place, his right hand keeping her membranous wings collapsed firmly against the sides of her body. Anyone else presuming to physically restrain the minidrag's movements would have have found themselves with maybe a minute to live, a victim of Pip's incredibly toxic and corrosive venom. Despite her obvious desire to spread her pleated wings again, she would no more harm Flinx than she would one of her own offspring. While she continued to twist and wriggle in an attempt to get free of his grasp, she did not bite, or worse.

They were nearly back to Mother Mastiff's place before she finally relaxed enough to where he felt safe in removing his restraining fingers. Instead of attempting to fly off, she slithered up his arm to curl comfortably around his neck, as if nothing unusual had happened. Shaking his head as he tried to figure out what had gotten into her, he entered the humble dwelling.

It was far less humble within. His travels and adventures had allowed Flinx, during a previous visit to Drallar, to cause the home to be furnished far more lavishly than it appeared from outside. Given a choice, he would have moved Mother Mastiff to another, better section of the city entirely. Upon listening to his proposal, the old woman's reaction had been wholly in keeping with her peppery, independent self.

"And what be a 'better' section of the city, boy? Fancier streets—with no character? Bigger houses—that ain't homes? Folks with money—and no soul? No thankee. I'll stay here, and happily so, where I've stayed all these many years." Wizened eyes that could still see clearly had met his own without wavering. "Was once good enough for you, boy, when I bought you. But—" She hesitated. "—I *could* use a new cooker."

He'd bought that for her, and much else. Tucked in between two larger, newer structures, her home now boasted the latest in household conveniences, as well as a self-adjusting, transparent privacy ceiling through which she could admire the stars and the sweep of part of Moth's famous broken rings.

She wasn't at home when he arrived. Though it was growing late, he didn't worry about her. A small smile curved his lips. Old she might be, but he pitied anyone who accosted her on the streets. Expecting an easy mark, they would find themselves confronted with an explosive bundle of experience and harsh words—not to mention a lightweight but lethal assortment of concealed weaponry. Mother Mastiff had not survived the mean streets of Drallar for so long by wandering about unprepared to deal with whatever they might happen to throw her way.

Probably visiting Mockle Wynn, he mused, or the Twegsay twins. She knew half the population of this district, and they her. He'd see her again tomorrow.

After checking in with his ship, the *Teacher*, he prepared supper for himself and Pip. The minidrag had seemingly returned to normal. She ate quietly, evincing no interest in abruptly flying through the door in search

of attractions unknown. Afterward, he relaxed in front
of the tridee he'd bought for Mother Mastiff, finishing off the evening with a reading of a portion of the new
thranx research report on Cantarian hivenoids, before
retiring to the small bedroom that was kept ready for
him whenever he might choose to visit. Lying on his back
on the lightly scented aerogel bed, staring up at the
starfield through the tough but transparent ceiling, he
wondered which of the flickering lights in the night sky
he ought to visit next. Wondered which might be the
more interesting, or possibly hold a clue to the mysteries
that were himself.

He had just fallen asleep when he felt Pip stirring
against his bare shoulder. Almost instantly, his eyes were
open and he was fully alert, having developed the ability
early in his childhood to awaken to full awareness on a
moment's notice. Extending himself, he sensed nothing.
Similarly, Pip remained on the bed. Had either of them
been in any imminent danger, she would have spread
her wings and risen ceilingward, assuming a defensive
posture.

Even so, there was obviously something in the room
with them.

As quietly and slowly as possible, he rose to a sitting
position. His nakedness did not trouble him. Clothes
were for the insecure, shirt and pants hardly weapons in
any case. His manner of fighting did not require that he
be clothed according to community standards.

The figure that crossed from the now open window
toward the door that led to the rest of the house was
bipedal and short of stature. Therein the similarity to
anything human ended. Reaching toward the bed's headboard, Flinx waved his open palm in the direction of a
sensor. Instantly, the bedroom was flooded with soft,

subdued light. The responsive, sensitive ceiling opaqued accordingly.

Startled by the unexpected burst of illumination, the trespasser threw up both arms to shield its eyes. Its small mouth opened, but no sound came out. As the long, vertical pupils contracted against the light, Flinx recognized the intruder.

It was the white-and-blue-furred performing animal he had seen earlier in the day.

As naked human and equally unclad intruder eyed one another uncertainly, Pip rose into the air and flew toward it. The elongated, vaguely sorrowful eyes tracked the minidrag's path. Whether out of ignorance or familiarity, the creature showed no fear as Pip glided in its direction. Nor did it panic when the deadly flying snake landed on its shoulder. Quite the contrary. Reaching up, it began to gently stroke the minidrag with the three long, flexible furred fingers of one hand. Flinx tensed as physical contact was initiated. Highly protective of both her human and her wings, Pip rarely allowed herself to be touched by others.

Yet now, instead of reacting aggressively, she completely relaxed, as if she'd settled into the comforting grasp of an old friend.

And still, Flinx felt nothing. As Flinx sat on the side of the bed, it didn't take long to postulate that *something* about this creature had drawn Pip's uncharacteristically single-minded attention earlier in the day. Was it an empath, an empathetic telepath, like himself and the minidrag? But if that was the case, then why couldn't he feel the slightest emotional emanation from the voiceless nocturnal visitor? By letting his talent range in the direction of nearby apartments and other buildings, he knew that his often erratic ability was functioning. But from the intruder, he sensed nothing. Yet there was palpably something at work here. What was he overlooking?

Certainly not the crash and fracturing that came from the front door, as three figures burst into the house. They headed straight for the bedroom, as if they had a map. A glance in the direction of the alien dancer's now softly phosphorescent control necklace explained why they didn't need one.

Two of the intruders were big, burly, and as sour of expression as the emotions they openly projected. Standing between them and holding a weapon of his own was the alien's owner. His emotions were darker still. While he did not quite transude murder, the potential underlined the rest of his clearly projected feelings.

Taking his time, Flinx slipped on a pair of pants. Pip was airborne. Interestingly, she hovered not close to him, but above the furry alien visitor. The latter, Flinx noted with interest, had pressed itself into a corner of the small room. Though its eyes were alien and unreadable, there was no mistaking the energy and effort it was expending to keep as far away from the three uninvited visitors as possible. For his part, the emotions its owner projected in its direction were utterly devoid of anything resembling affection.

"Pretty clever of you, kid." Though Flinx was now two and twenty years and stood taller than average, he still had the face of a youngster. "I remember you from the afternoon show earlier today. Thought you could get away with this, eh, *blaflek*?"

Focusing his attention on the trio of weapons at hand, Flinx casually slipped into a shirt, careful to make no sudden moves as he did so. "Get away with what?"

"Stealing my Aslet monkey. You're not the first *blaflek* to try. You won't be the first to succeed."

So that's what the creature was called. From his voracious research, Flinx knew what a monkey was: a kind of primitive Terran primate. The creature cowering silently in the corner of his bedroom didn't look much like a monkey to him. He had never heard of Aslet.

He had, however, heard of similar scams. Raised on the streets of Drallar, he had encountered numerous schemes and swindles, and in his youth had even participated in a few.

"I didn't steal him," he replied calmly as he pulled his shirt down over his head. "He showed up here on his own." He nodded in the direction of the open window. "Let himself in pretty quietly. His fingers must be as nimble as his feet, even if he is short a few. Knows his way around basic security systems, too." He eyed the man evenly. "I wonder how and where he learned how to bypass those?"

Smiling grimly, the owner shook his head. "Nice try, kid, but it won't wash. You're a thief, and we're turning you over to the police."

So that was how it worked, Flinx realized. Send the Aslet into somebody's home, preferably someone who had been in the audience for one of the creature's earlier performances. That would establish a connection and provide witnesses. Then claim it had been stolen, and threaten to have the "thief" arrested. Unless, no doubt, some sort of accommodation could be reached that would avoid the need to involve the authorities. Even as they stood there confronting one another, the owner and his goons probably had a bought cop or two awaiting their possible arrival down at the nearest police office. Simple and clean. No doubt most confused, challenged victims paid up rather than risk the possibility of spending time in a correction institute, or the indignity of being exposed in a court trial.

"If you had a legitimate claim about a theft, you

would have brought the police along with you, instead of these two." He indicated the pair who flanked the owner.

The shorter man grinned. "You're a clever little snot, aren't you? So you've figured it out."

Flinx smiled faintly. "I live offplanet now, but I grew up here."

The owner gestured with his weapon. "Doesn't matter. My friends down at the patrol office will listen to me, not you. Of course, such unpleasantness can easily be avoided."

"I wonder how?" Flinx was much more curious about something else. It would have to wait. "Why pick on me?" He indicated his surroundings. "Neither my mother, whose home this is, nor myself are particularly well off. Why make targets out of us?"

"I don't pick 'em," the owner grunted. Turning, he pointed toward the creature huddling in the corner. "He does." The man squinted at his surroundings. "I agree with you, though. This isn't one of his better choices."

Flinx frowned. "The Aslet chooses the mark? How—at random?"

The owner shrugged. "Beats me. When I'm in the mood and have the time to do a little business, I just let him loose. After he's had time to make his way across part of the city, my associates and I track him down." Meaningfully, he ran a finger around his neck. "Transmitter is easy to follow." Reaching into a pocket, he pulled out a tiny device and aimed it in the Anslet's general direction. "He doesn't like me much, but that collar makes him do as he's told."

"I don't like you much, either," Flinx declared quietly.

The owner was not offended. "You'll do as you're told, too. I'm not a greedy person. A thousand credits will get all of us out of here, including the monkey, and you'll never see any of us ever again." His smile returned. "Unless you decide to catch another performance, that is."

"No," Flinx told him.

"No?" The man's smile vanished. "No what?"

"No money," Flinx replied. "No credits. Not a thousand. Not a fraction thereof. Get out of my mother's house."

The two men flanking the owner stirred slightly. The owner sighed. "Look, kid, if there's no available credit, you can pay us in goods. I saw plenty of valuable stuff when we came in." He shrugged indifferently. "Or we can shoot you, take what we want, and if anyone investigates, claim that you attacked us when I tried to reclaim my property."

In response to Flinx's rising level of upset and concern, Pip began to dart back and forth against the roof like a giant moth, the equivalent of pacing nervously in midair. Curious, the player-owner looked up in her direction.

"What is that thing, anyway?"

"That," Flinx murmured, enlightening both the speaker and his two accomplices, "is an Alaspinian minidrag. You don't want to make her any madder than she already is now."

"Why not?" The owner smiled. "Is it going to bite me?" The muzzle of his pistol came up.

"No," Flinx told him. "She doesn't have to."

The owner nodded. Turning to the man on his left, he uttered a single brusque command. "Kill it."

Sensing the man's intent by reading the homicidal emotion that rose suddenly and sharply within him, Pip darted forward and spat. Striking the would-be killer in his right eye, the gob of corrosive poison ate immediately into the soft ocular jelly and entered his bloodstream, the incredibly powerful neurotoxin proceeding to instantly paralyze every muscle it encountered. When it reached his heart and stopped that, the man collapsed.

His single shot went wild, blowing a hole in the roof and showering the room with shards of photosensitive gengineered silicate. Rising above the noise, the now panicked shouts of the owner and his surviving associate echoed through the room.

From a drawer in the bed's headboard, Flinx pulled the small pistol he always carried with him in places like Drallar. Unfortunately for the intruders, he did not have time to reset it to stun. The second henchman got off one blast, destroying a fair chunk of the wall behind Flinx's bed, before Flinx put him down for good. Given time, he would simply have used his nascent ability to persuade all three of them to leave. Regrettably, the attack on Pip had reduced the time available for subtle emotional projection to none.

Bug-eyed, the owner fled. He made it as far as the front door he and his friends had blown in. Before he could dash through the opening, something brightly colored, diamond-patterned, and superfast materialized before his eyes.

Then there was only the brief but intense burning, burning in his eyes before he died.

Emerging from the bedroom, his small pistol still gripped tightly in one hand, Flinx walked over to the body of the owner. Smoke rose from his face, the hall-mark of an angry Pip's attentions. In his other hand, Flinx held the small device the man had withdrawn from his pocket and pointed in the direction of the alien Aslet. He'd dropped it in his haste to flee.

Letting it fall to the floor, he aimed his pistol at it and fired once. Emerging from the bedroom behind him, the Aslet started, then relaxed. Once again, its mouth moved and no sound came out. The alien's attitude, if not its expression, was readily comprehensible even across interspecies boundaries. As Flinx looked on, Pip landed once again on the furry shoulder.

Flinx gazed long and curiously into the elongated alien eyes. The emotions of the three intruding humans had been clear to him as day. But this peculiar creature continued to remain as emotionally blank as a section of insulated wall.

"I think," he murmured aloud, even though there was no one around to hear him, "we need to find out what you are, besides an agile dancer." He started back toward his room. Behind him, Pip continued to rest contentedly on the Aslet's shoulder, allowing it to stroke the lethal coils without interference or objection. Mother Mastiff would be furious at the damage to her home.

Aslet, it turned out when he presented himself and his furry new companion to the relevant local government bureau, was a newly classified world on the fringes of the Commonwealth. In addition to being the abode of the usual extensive panoply of new and intriguing alien life-forms, it was also home to a primitive species of low intelligence and simple culture. Most definitely not related to any known species of monkey, the natives of Aslet lived in caves and utilized the simplest and most basic of primitive tools.

They also, he learned, communicated in high-pitched squeaks and squirps that were above the range of human hearing. The Aslet Flinx had liberated had been trying to talk to him all along. Flinx, along with every other human and thranx, simply did not possess auricular equipment with sufficient range to detect the alien's verbalizations.

Flinx tried to imagine what it would be like to be constantly screaming your pain, daily pleading for help from a world full of diverse sentient beings, all of whom would appear to be suffering from universal and total deafness.

The Aslet, it was reported, were exceedingly emotional creatures, given to a wide range of displays that evidently supplemented their limited ultrasonic vocabulary. Like their vocalizing, these emotional projections were also beyond anyone's ability to perceive, including Flinx.

But not, apparently, Pip.

The flying snake had been drawn to them immediately, during the forced performance he and Flinx had witnessed on the streets of Drallar. No wonder that when temporarily set free by its owner, the intelligent Aslet had homed in on Pip, locating the empathic minidrag snake in the midst of the city's innumerable twists and turnings. The revelation added directly to Flinx's store of knowledge about himself. Evidently, there were sentient emotional projections that were beyond his ability to perceive. But those were not the final thoughts the experience left him pondering as he bid farewell to the now collarless Aslet, soon to be repatriated by the government to its homeworld.

If no human could sense the very real emotions of something like the Aslet, he found himself wondering again and again, nor even hear, much less understand, their language, might there not be, out there, another species more powerful than any yet encountered that would view humankind in the same unintentionally uninformed light?

Was there even now, on some far-distant world, a collared human being made to dance and perform tricks for a species that could neither understand, nor hear, nor sympathize with the unfortunate captive?

Not for the first time, when he gazed up at the stars, he found himself wondering if there were worlds among that scattered multitude he might not be better off avoiding . . .

Jemunu-jah didn't want to have to take the time to rescue the
human. If it was foolish enough to go off into the Viisiiviisii all by
itself, then it deserved whatever happened to it. Kenkeru-jah had
argued that it was their *mula* to try and save the visitor, even if it
was not spawned of the Sakuntala. As ranking chief of the local
clan Nuy, his opinion was listened to and respected.

Jemunu-jah suspected that the much-admired High Chief
Naneci-tok would also have argued vociferously against the decision to send him, but she was still in transit from an important
meeting of fellow Hatas and was not present to countermand the
directive. As for the war chief Aniolo-jat, he did not seem to care
one way or the other where Jemunu-jah was sent. Not that the
cunning Hata-yuiqueru felt anything for the missing human, either. All the war chief wanted, as usual, was to conserve clan en-
ergies for killing Deyzara.

Perhaps it was Jemunu-jah's cheerless expression that caused
the two Deyzara passing him on the walkway to edge as far away
as they could without tumbling right over the flexible railing.
The speaking/breathing trunk that protruded from the top of
their ovoidal hairless skulls recoiled back against the edges of
their flat-brimmed rain hats, and the secondary eating trunks that
hung from the underside, or chin region, of their heads twitched
nervously. Their large, protuberant, close-set eyes nervously tracked
him from behind their visors. Another time, Jemunu-jah might
have found their excessive caution amusing. Not today.

He supposed Kenkeru-jah was right. Chiefs usually were. But
for the life of him, he could not understand how the death of a
missing human, and a self-demonstrably reckless one at that,

could affect the clan's *mula*. But the chief had made a decision. As a result, he now found himself directed to present himself to the female in charge of the human community on Fluva. Since Lauren Matthias's status was equivalent to that of a senior Hata, or High Chief of the Sakuntala, Jemunu-jah would be obliged to put his own feelings aside while showing her proper respect. He smoothed his long stride. Actually, he ought to be proud. He had been selected as a representative of his people, the best that Taulau Town had to offer. But if given a choice, he would gladly have declined the honor.

At slightly under two meters tall and a wiry eighty kilos, he was of average height and weight for a mature male Sakuntala. Though smaller than those of a Deyzara, his eyes provided vision that was substantially more acute. From the sides of his head, the base of his flexible, pointed ears extended out sideways for several centimeters before curving sharply upward to end in tufted points. The outer timpanic membrane that kept rain from entering his right ear was in the process of renewing itself, and was slowly being replaced by a new one growing in behind it. As a result, the hearing on his right side was at present slightly diminished. It would stay that way for another day or two, he knew, until the old membrane had completely disintegrated and the new one had asserted itself.

His short, soft fur was light gray with splotches of black and umber. The pattern identified an individual Sakuntala as sharply and distinctly as any of the artificial identity devices the humans carried around with them. In that respect, he felt sorry for the humans. Despite some slight differences in skin color, it was often very difficult to tell one from another.

His cheek sacs bulged; one with the coiled, whiplike tongue that was almost as long as his body, the other with a gobbet of khopo sap he alternately chewed and sucked. Today's helping was flavored with gesagine and apple, the latter a flavor introduced by the humans that had found much favor among the Sakuntala. He wore old-style strappings around his waist to shield his privates while the bands of dark blue synthetics that crisscrossed his chest were of off-world manufacture. Attached to both sets of straps were a variety of items both traditional and modern, the latter purchased from the town shops with credit he had earned from providing services to various human and Deyzara enterprises.

Now it seemed that despite his reluctance he was about to provide one more such service. Despite the prospect of acquiring *mula* as well as credit, he would just as soon have seen the task given to another. But Kenkeru-jah had been adamant. He was as stuck with the assignment as a kroun that had been crammed into the crook of a drowning sabelbap tree.

Raindrops slid off his transparent eyelids as he glanced upward. Not much precipitation today: barely a digit's worth. Of course, it had rained very heavily yesterday. Clouds, like individuals, needed time to replenish themselves. The fact that it rained every day on most of Fluva seemed to be a source of some amusement to newly arrived humans. Once they had been stuck on Fluva for about a season, however, Jemunu-jah had observed that the weather rapidly ceased to be a source of humor for the bald visitors.

Well, not entirely bald, he corrected himself. A fair number of humans owned at least a little fur. In that respect they were better than the Deyzara, who were truly and completely hairless.

With an easy jump, he crossed from one suspended walkway to another, saving time as he made his way through town. A few humans could duplicate such acrobatic feats but preferred not to. One spill into the water below, arms and legs flailing wildly, was usually enough to prevent them from trying to imitate the inherent agility of the tall, long-armed Sakuntala. No Deyzara would think of attempting the comparatively undemanding jump. Human children could not be prevented from trying it, though. This was allowed, since the waters beneath the town limits were netted to keep out p'forana, m'ainiki, and other predators who would delight in making a meal of any child unlucky enough to tumble into unprotected waters. That went for Sakuntala children as well as human and Deyzara, he knew. But when *they* jumped, Sakuntala youngsters only rarely missed.

The rain intensified, falling steadily if not forcefully. Making his way through the continuous shower, he passed more Deyzara. Like the humans, the two-trunks wore an assortment of specialized outer attire intended to keep the rain from making contact with their skin. To Jemunu-jah this seemed the height of folly. For a Sakuntala, it was as natural to be wet as dry. As visitors who came and went from Fluva, the humans could be excused for their reticence to move about naked beneath the rain. But the Deyzara, who had been living and working on the world of The Big Wet for hundreds of years, should have adapted better by now. For all the many generations that had passed, they still displayed a marked aversion to the unrelenting precipitation, though they had otherwise adapted well to the climate. The one month out of the year that it did not rain was their period of celebration and joy. In contrast, it was during such times that the Sakuntala tended to stay inside their houses, showering daily and striving to keep moist.

It all seemed very backward to Jemunu-jah, even though he had viewed numerous vits that showed many worlds where it rained only intermittently, and some where water fell from the sky not at all. If forced to live on such a world, he knew he would shrivel up and die like a gulou nut in the cooking fire, or in one of those marvelous portable cooking devices that could be bought from the humans or the Deyzara. Rain was life. There would be no flooded forest, no varzea (as the humans called it), without the rain that fell continuously for ninety percent of the year.

With the water from the many merged rivers of the varzea swirling ten meters below the suspended walkway and the surface of the land itself drowned twenty to thirty meters below that, he lifted himself up onto another crossway. This strilk-braced major avenue was strong enough to support multiple paths, and was hectic with pedestrians. Humans mixed freely with Sakuntala and Deyzara, everyone intent on the business of the day. Nearby, a spinner team was busy repairing a damaged walkway, extruding the strilk that kept the town's buildings and paths suspended safely above the water. The silvery artificial fiber was attached to huge gray composite pylons that had been driven deep into the bedrock that lay far below the turbid waters and saturated soil. On the outskirts of the sprawling community, a carnival of lesser structures whose owners were unable to afford pylons hung from the largest, strongest trees.

The single-story building in front of him was the administrative headquarters of the Commonwealth presence on Fluva. Jemunu-jah had been there a few times before, on official business for the greater A'Jah clan. That particular business being of lesser importance, it had not given him the opportunity to meet Lauren Matthias. He had heard that she was very good at her work, not unlike Naneci-tok, and could speak fluent S'aku. She would not have to strain her larynx in his presence. His command of terranglo, he had been told, was excellent.

A single human stood guard outside the building. He looked

bored, tired, and despite his protective military attire, very, very wet. Visible beneath a flipped-up visor, his face was frozen in that faraway expression many humans acquired after they had spent a year or more on Fluva. He was nearly as tall as a Sakuntala. Drawing himself up to his full height, Jemunu-jah announced himself.

The guard seemed to respond to his presence only with great difficulty. Water ran down his face. It was not rainwater, because both of them were standing under the wide lip of the roof overhang that ran completely around the front and sides of the administration building. Jemunu-jah recognized the facial moisture as a phenomenon humans called "perspiration." It was a condition unknown to the Sakuntala, although the Deyzara suffered from it as well.

"Limalu di," the guard mumbled apathetically. Jemunu-jah was not so far removed from the culture of his kind, nor so educated, that he did not gaze covetously at the long gun that dangled loosely from the human's left hand. A single swift snatch and he could have it, he knew. Then, a quick leap over the side of the deck into the water below, and he would be gone before the sluggish human barely knew it was missing.

With a sigh, he shifted his gaze away from the highly desirable weapon, away from the ancient calling of his ancestors. He was here on clan business. He was civilized now. "I am called Jemunu-jah. I have an appointment with Administrator Matthias," he responded in terranglo.

Reaching up to wipe away sweat and grime, the guard blinked uncertainly. "Appointment?"

"Appointment," the lanky, gray-furred visitor repeated.

Eyeing the Sakuntala with slightly more interest, the guard tilted his head to his left and spoke toward the pickup suspended there. "There's a Saki here to see Matthias. Says he has an appointment." Jemunu-jah waited patiently while the human listened to the voice that whispered from the tiny pickup clipped to his left ear.

A moment later the guard bobbed his head, a gesture Jemunu-jah knew signified acceptance among humans. Parting his lips and showing sharp teeth, he stepped past and through the momentarily deactivated electronic barrier that was designed to keep out intruders both large and small. Another door, Jemunu-jah reflected as he entered the building. Humans and Deyzara alike were very fond of doors. The Sakuntala had no use for them.